THE
CONFUSION
OF LAUREL
GRAHAM

THE CONFUSION OF LAUREL GRAHAM

ADRIENNE KISNER

FEIWEL AND FRIENDS

NEW YORK

A FEIWEL AND FRIENDS BOOK

An imprint of Macmillan Publishing Group, LLC
175 Fifth Avenue, New York, NY 10010

Our books may be purchased in bulk for promotional, educational,
or business use. Please contact your local bookseller or the
Macmillan Corporate and Premium Sales Department at (800) 221-7945
ext. 5442 or by email at MacmillanSpecialMarkets@macmillan.com.

Library of Congress Control Number: 2018955486

ISBN 9781250146045 (hardcover) / ISBN 9781250146038 (ebook)

Book design by April Ward

Feiwel and Friends logo designed by Filomena Tuosto

First edition, 2019

1   3   5   7   9   10   8   6   4   2

fiercereads.com

To Mom & Jeanne:

At least there is less swearing in this one?

THE CONFUSION OF LAUREL GRAHAM

I heard a bird sing
In the dark of December.
A magical thing
And sweet to remember.

"We are nearer to Spring
Than we were in September,"
I heard a bird sing
In the dark of December.

—OLIVER HERFORD

Never let them see you sweat.

That's not the Birdscout motto. But it fucking well should be.

"Who can tell me three of the feathered friends we might find on our walk today?" I said.

Sixteen pairs of eyes stared back at me, wide and unblinking.

Homeschoolers. Unschoolers. Some kind of schoolers that meant they weren't in the overcrowded gray-and-red brick elementary building seven blocks away and were instead standing at the entrance of the Sarig Pond and Jenkins Wood Nature Sanctuary with me. I thought home-non-unschooling would make them wild, free nature lovers . . . but no. Most of them were looking at their smartwatches, secretly texting one another.

"Okay, who can tell me *one* creature we might find today?" I tried again.

"Um," a tiny girl with cat-eye glasses said. "A squirrel?"

I sighed. Unfortunately she was right. Squirrels were the bane of birders everywhere. (Well. Except maybe in places where there were no squirrels, which were sadly limited.)

"Good guess!" I said.

She grinned. It's best to encourage the little ones. They were prone to unpredictable sudden movements that could veer off the path and ruin your day. Best to keep them on your side. "Can anyone guess a creature *with wings?*"

"Robins?" another boy tried in a bored voice.

"Yes!" My fist shot into the air. "Sweetest of songbirds! Harbingers of spring! Portents of luck and fortune!" Those last two were debatable at best, but sometimes you needed to finesse bird symbolism in order to win a tough audience. A few heads swiveled my way at that, so I felt I'd made the right choice for the greater good.

"Really?" the bored boy asked.

"You bet. Birds bring messages of all sorts to humans. But there are way more interesting things about them than *that*. They have their own language to communicate. They can fly hundreds of miles and never get lost. They fight for what's theirs. They are warriors."

"Cool," the boy said. "Do you think we'll see some of those smart ones?"

I smiled to myself. It only takes one to turn a crowd. "Why, yes," I said, peering at the nametag slapped on his fuzzy lapel, "Isaac. I do. Follow me."

Six cardinals (two female, four males), two nuthatches, sixteen (give or take) common grackles, three red-bellied woodpeckers, and one red-tailed hawk later, I delivered the kids back to their adults.

"Feel free to take some pamphlets on your way out," I called. "Nature story time starts on May 30!"

I retreated into the tiny, cramped office of the Birdscout Nature Center and sunk into a chair. Birding with the unenthusiastic could fucking wipe a girl out.

"Oh. Hey," said a voice. I looked up to see a familiar shock of dyed hair shaved into a crest peeking through the door. "If it isn't the Birdscout-in-chief. Is Jerry in?"

"Out sick today," I said. "Risa. Your hair . . . ," I started.

"What about it?" she said. I could hear a warning in her voice.

"It reminds me of a wire-crested thorntail."

Risa's face broke into a grin. "You got it! *Of course* you are the only one who noticed. I love them."

"They *are* exquisite," I agreed.

Risa and I looked at each other for a moment. It was odd that we were having this conversation, since it wouldn't be precisely accurate to call us friends. We were more . . . what?

Enemies.

Ah. Yes.

We were one hundred percent enemies.

But sometimes, even enemies had great hair.

I watched Risa's expression change as she seemingly remembered our actual affiliation at the same time I did. "Okay, well, if you see him sometime soon, tell him I need him to sign my co-op hours sheet."

"Okay. Will do."

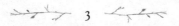

She paused, like she almost wasn't going to speak but then changed her mind. "Have you finalized your entry yet? For the photo contest?"

"No. You?" I said.

"No. I tried to get a picture of the heron but then I tripped on a root," she said.

"That sucks."

"Right? Such a rookie mistake. But I bet everyone around here is going to turn in a fucking heron anyway. Or, god help us all, warblers."

Heat crept up my back. I had no fewer than twenty-three shots of our four resident herons (male and female) that I was considering entering into *Fauna* magazine's annual Junior Nature Photographer competition. Not to mention several dozen shots of a Cape May and one of a male Swainson. That last one turned out blurry, fuck me, because of course the Swainson flitted out of the frame. This was my last shot to win the *Fauna* competition (since I'd be too old next year), and I wanted to conquer first place so badly I could practically taste it. The money would be nice, and my grandma (a former winner herself) would love the free lifetime subscription (added to the prize since her time).

But because *Fauna* was the biggest and best birding magazine in the US (possibly the world, save maybe *Le Bec* in France), the bragging rights alone were worth it.

Particularly if it meant I'd beaten Risa, who I was pretty certain sabotaged my entry last year.

"Yeah. Probably. But the summer birds will be here before you know it. And there are some impressive blooms in Jenkins Wood. There is already a patch of *Monotropa uniflora* at the base of Elder Oak. It looks like a proper fungus graveyard. Bet it'd be epic in moonlight at the right angle."

"Are you going for that shot?"

"I tried. It just looks stupid. The flash washes it out and using moonlight through branches isn't exactly my forte."

Risa snorted. "I hear you. Okay. Well. Good luck."

She almost sounded like she meant it. I stared at her absolutely rockin' hair as she left.

I tidied the desk and took a bunch of Ranger Jerry's old newspapers to the upcycling bin. The weekend craft people would have a field day Mod Podging on Saturday. I surveyed my work with satisfaction. I was once again reminded how grateful I was for my co-op assignment (even if Risa was there, too). I had always envied the juniors, who were allowed to avoid going to school for all but a few hours on Thursdays during spring term because of their work/volunteer co-ops in years past, but now it was my turn. It had been the best development of my life thus far. Most of my friends were out at the local newspaper or lawyer's or doctor's offices and made more money than me. Because my life goal was to be the world's best nature photographer and take my place aside my hero, master birder Brian Michael Warbley, spending April till August leading nature walks and birding tours was way more my speed. Even if the pay was technically shit.

Like, literally. Jerry gave me a bag of fertilizer for Gran's garden to compensate me. But it was the best stuff we'd seen and we needed it for her bird-attracting flowers, so I wasn't too salty about it.

I rounded the pond on trash removal detail, but my phone buzzed in my pocket. *Elder Oak. Sixty paces due east! Now!*

the text from Gran read. I was still technically on the clock, but Jenkins Wood was part of my work space and I could always pick up garbage along the trail to make seeing Gran official business if needed.

Be right there. Don't leave! I texted back.

You know I'll always wait for you, Laurel.

I grabbed my camera, locked the Birdscout Center door, and jogged as lightly as I could around the wooden decks surrounding the pond to the woodland paths. I nodded to Elder Oak, the oldest tree and guardian of the entrance to Jenkins Wood, and tried to make my way as quietly as possible sixty paces east through a rough path covered in dew-wet leaves. I picked up a few discarded wrappers along the way, darkly noting that they probably came from the awful Birdie Bros (a group of dude birders who had terrible nature manners matched only by their preternatural ability to get rare warbler shots).

I finally found Gran half-hidden in fern fronds about halfway up a hill. I crouched in the grass, rocks crackling underneath my boots.

"Shhh," whispered Gran.

"I didn't even say anything," I whispered back.

Gran glared at me as something rustled in a shrub a few feet away. A beak poked out of glistening leaves, then a head, then downy feathers on spindly legs. Gran gave a tiny yawp, and pointed her high-powered binoculars in the bird's direction. I pulled out my camera and my shutter clicked like an automatic weapon.

"Did you get it?" said Gran without looking at me. She

stared at the bird, and the bird stared back at her. I stared at both of them, wondering at how quickly the feeling had left my crouching legs.

Note: Do more crunches. Strengthen core and calves. A girl does not become Brian Michael Warbley, the King of Birders, with numb appendages.

Then something even worse happened.

I sneezed.

This spooked Gran's avian friend and he took flight into the trees.

"Seriously, Laurel?" Gran said.

"I'm sorry! I'm so sorry. Fucking pollen. You know that. I couldn't help it."

"Language," Gran said. "Do you know what that was? That was a white-winged tern. A new addition to our life list. I never expected to see one out here, on a random day of all things. But there it was. You'd think I'd have learned by now—birds always surprise you." She leaned back and looked at her camera. "I heard a rumor there was one around here yesterday, but to actually see it . . ." She trailed off as she pulled out her phone to alert her other bird people.

"His black-and-white head." I marveled at it. "It was gorgeous." I tipped toward Gran and stretched out my legs. I held my tiny digital screen out to her. "See him—I got a pretty clear shot. Most of them are blurry from him getting spooked by my seasonal curse. But a few are good."

None were really good enough to help me be crowned *Fauna*'s Junior Nature Photographer national champion, fuck it all. But, even so. A new bird for the life list was something.

As Brian Michael Warbley says, "A bird that you've seen is worth ten in a book."

"He is stunning." She slipped her phone back into the pocket of her vest and reached over and gave me a shove. "I'm glad I got to see him with you. I gotta say, he is in the top ten on my life list with the snowy owl and king eider I saw in Greenland. Sisimiut also had the northern lights! Superb. One day, kid. Just you wait. We'll go and the aurora will knock your socks off. No winter allergies in Greenland." She grinned. "Want to go to Eat N' Park?" she said.

"I'm at work."

"But Jerry isn't here." Gran grinned.

"How do you know that?" I said.

"I have my ways. Come on. You know you do way more hours here than you are required anyway. What's thirty mere minutes with your old grandma?"

"I guess I could go for a cinnamon bun."

"That's my girl," Gran said.

Gran's house sat conveniently at the edge of Jenkins Wood. We slipped into Gran's tiny hybrid and she drove us to the diner. Since we'd spotted a new life list bird, Gran talked me into fancy chocolate waffles with fruit and let me have *bacon* to celebrate. Gran was a vegetarian verging on vegan, but she was weak in the face of breakfast.

"How goes school?" she asked.

"Fine," I said. "I'm hardly there this semester. Academic classes were stacked in the fall and winter, so these last few weeks I'm mostly Birdscouting for co-op."

"Get any good shots for the contest?" she said.

"Yeah, I guess." I shifted in my seat. "I had some herons, but . . ." I trailed off.

"Herons are good luck. Messenger birds. They bring good omens."

"You say that about all birds."

"Not cormorants. They work for the devil."

"Stop it." I laughed.

Gran shrugged. "Tradition. What can I say?"

"Everyone is going to submit herons or warblers," I said, thinking of Risa. "I need something *different*. Something *extraordinary*."

"All birds are extraordinary. Like people. You know that. You know what a group of warblers is called? A confusion. A confusion of warblers. Isn't that remarkable?"

I grunted. I had several memory cards and two extra hard drives full of photographic evidence that some confusions were pretty fucking boring. At least when *I* tried to capture their image.

Gran paid our bill and drove me back to co-op. She dropped me off with barely a goodbye, because her birder friends had caught wind of her find, and they were meeting up again to try to see the elusive white-winged tern.

"Good luck," I said. "Remember what Warbley says. 'Birds come not just to those who watch, but those who wait.'"

"Yes, yes. I think I've heard you quote him a time or forty. Make great art. You have a *Fauna* family legacy to protect," Gran said, holding my camera out of the window of her car. "And text me if you see the tern again." She sped off, practically leaving me in the dust. I grinned to myself, looking at my pictures. None were entry-worthy, but the appearance of something rare made me feel that the perfect shot was just around the corner.

"You know, Brian Michael Warbley won first place in the *Fauna* contest when he was a high school junior," I said to Sophie, who hadn't cared about Brian Michael Warbley since we'd become best friends in second grade.

"Uh-huh," she said, rinsing her brushes in the basement sink.

I swung my legs against the counter where I sat waiting for her. I watched the glitter in her halter dress glisten in the slanting sunlight through the small window.

"His new book, *Warbley's Birding Bests*, highlights some of his early work. It's terrible. Allegedly this is a picture of a Kirtland's warbler"—I held up the book to the back of her head—"but it's so grainy you can't tell."

"Yup," she said, banging the bottom of a can.

"Here is the only shot of a phoenix rising from its own ashes, naked and without its flaming feathers. This really started his career," I said, closing the book.

"I would imagine. One could say it elevated him to mythic status." She turned around and grinned.

"So you were listening."

"I always listen, bird nerd. Come outside."

I followed Soph up her basements steps and out into the yard. She needed to draw me for her portfolio. There were a lot of sketches of me throughout the years. I still had one that won third prize in the fourth-grade art show. That was back in the day when she could still convince me to match her signature look, involving dresses and braids.

"Why can't we do this indoors?" I said. I swatted at a mosquito. It was early for them, and this concerned me for my summer in the woods.

"Better light out here," she said. "Early light is best."

"Truth," I said.

Sophie sketched me in silence for a few minutes. I fiddled with my camera settings. I was allowed to move when being sketched, but not much.

"Does Ms. Rizzo ever wonder why you draw the same person over and over?" I asked.

"No, a lot of people have go-to models for their assignments. I change your hair occasionally to make it seem more legit."

"Oh, you should sketch Risa from co-op," I said. "Her hair is always amazing."

Sophie looked up at me. "Risa? You mean Risa Risa? Person who allegedly ruined your setup last year and caused a ruinous *Fauna* debacle that made you cry?"

I looked back down at the camera. "Well, yes, technically. But she has this great new look."

"Hmm," she said. "Well, if you want to ask her for me, I would consider it."

"That's probably not going to happen."

"Yeah, I figured." She held up her sketch. "This is super rough."

"I'm usually sitting here for an hour or more. This is what

you can do in fifteen minutes?" It really looked like me. Better, actually. Less rumpled. "It's like I can actually see your progress. The last time you did this, my legs were strangely elongated."

"It's the same with your pictures, you know. They used to be all blurred Kirtland's warblers, and now they are more 'fledgling first flights' and all. With real live baby birds and everything."

"You are just saying that," I said.

"I am incapable of lying," she said.

That was true. Sophie was honest to a fault. It helped her portraiture. Maybe my cargo pants and recently laundered "Mother Flockers" shirt were more prim than I imagined.

"You at the art center today?" I asked.

"Nope. Elder care. It's art therapy day. I think we are going to make flowers out of recycled water bottles."

"Awesome," I said.

"And you are going to admire the hair of your nemesis," she said.

I shrugged. "I'm only human," I said. I put my camera in its case and shoved it next to Warbley's newest book. "You know, in the last chapter of *Birding Bests*, Warbley reminds us—"

"Oh, do save it for later. I like to spread out my Warbley wisdom so that my heart doesn't just overload."

I gave her my "to love me is to love Warbley, deal with it" face. She threw her "I seriously don't give a shit about the bird guy" back.

"Have fun at co-op," she said.

"It's for the birds. HA! Get it, because I said . . ."

"Seriously, shut up," she said.

I clapped her on the back and hopped onto my bike that waited for me on the side of her house. It was going to be a great day. I'd show Ranger Jerry the new Warbley book. At least he'd care.

Or pretend to, anyway.

FIELD JOURNAL ENTRY
MAY 1

Mom was crying in the kitchen.

Must be Thursday, I thought.

"Want some toast? It's crunchy and delicious!" I said out loud. Sometimes I could lift Mom out of a funk by the sheer force of relentless optimism.

Mom shook her head, two tears skiing down the hills of her cheeks until they collided on her chin.

Aaaaand sometimes I couldn't.

I pulled out the bread drawer from our ancient kitchen counter. I slid back the metal top and grabbed two pieces of wheat. With enough melted butter, Mom would eat the toast if I put it in front of her. Not even the Drama Queen could resist salted dairy products.

"Chad and I broke up last night," she said.

Further confirmation that it was, in fact, Wednesday. The breakups always seemed to come midweek.

"Sorry," I said. I patted her shoulder sympathetically. I could hardly keep Mom's boyfriends straight. Chad was a

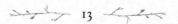

tool, that much I knew. He was skinny, bald, and obsessed with hunting. He wasn't mean to Mom or me. But even after months of seeing Mom, he had still called me Lauren instead of Laurel.

"I just thought he was the one," she said.

"Why?" I asked. Toast popped out of fiery little slots. I stabbed a knife through the charred tops and flicked breakfast onto a plate.

Mom sniffed. "He just made me feel good."

I stifled the urge to laugh or roll my eyes. She said that about all of the guys who trolled through the house.

Chet. Mark. Ethan? No—Edgar. Chad. Brad.

Dad.

That last one had walked me to my first day of kindergarten and kept on walking. He sends me cards on Christmas and my birthday and invites me to stay every summer. I've thought about going, but I knew it would be like a punch to Mom's throat.

Many things were like that, though, on a long-enough timeline.

A punch to Mom's throat.

Sometimes changing the subject worked to cheer her up.

"I know you worked late last night, so I didn't get a chance to tell you! Gran and I saw a white-winged tern! It's pretty rare around here! I haven't had a new one on my life list in months! He was black and white and perfect all over!" *Feel the magic, Mom*, I thought at her. *Breathe in my exclamations of pure bird-induced joy.*

Mom blew her nose into a napkin. She inhaled sharply, a sure sign that clouds gathered and tears would soon rain again.

I sighed inwardly. There was no winning back her mood today.

I debated my options. Stay here, or use an acceptable excuse to break free of the kitchen soap opera.

I decided on option two. It was an extraordinary spring day, and I should live the fuck out of it. Maybe some of my positivity might filter through the air to Mom somehow.

"I want to check in with Gran before co-op. Hang in there. You are beautiful and I love you," I said to Mom. I backed out of the kitchen as fast as possible and grabbed my backpack. I biked to Gran's cottage on the edge of the woods. I found her in the little garden behind her house. Most of the fruits and vegetables were starting to sprout and bloom and peek out from their winter sleep.

"Laurel," said Gran. "To what do I owe the early morning visit?"

"Mom broke up with Chad."

"I thought his name was Brad."

"No, that was the last guy. I think. This one was definitely Chad."

"Ah, I see. Did we like this one?" she asked.

"Nope, not even a little," I said. "But she wasn't going to be cheered up, so I thought I'd come over here. Just to. Um. You know."

Just to go to the one place where I felt really at home. Gran smiled, as if she knew what I was thinking.

"See the tern again yesterday?" I asked.

"Nope. He left. Louise was so mad. She says it doesn't really count if I didn't see him where he lives, but whatever.

I'm now fourteen birds ahead of her. Bitter birders are the worst." Gran chuckled. "Get any new shots?"

"Nope. The art left, too," I said.

"Hang in there, sweetheart. It'll come."

"Maybe I should branch out," I said. "I only ever do around here."

Gran considered this. "Maybe. There are a lot of state parks around here. But don't underestimate what's right under your nose. Your pictures of the pond at dusk and dawn are some of the best I've ever seen," Gran said.

I believed she felt that way. Twelve of my pond pictures hung around her small cabin. She said she paid less in heating bills because all my framed pictures served as insulation.

"But I've done it all! The trees! The water! The flowers! Your garden, even."

"Try more animals. Or the birds, then."

"Birds stay in one place for a second. All I get is a blurry mess," I said. "The movement of their wings is so freaking fast."

"True. But keep trying. These kinds of things are much about patience. And maybe a little luck or magic." Gran winked at me. She got up and dusted off her dirty jeans. "Help me bring my stuff to the storage bench."

"Maybe I could . . . ," I started, but was interrupted by a shrill call from one of Gran's trees. I looked up but couldn't see anything. "What was that?" I asked. The blank look on Gran's face seemed to show that she didn't know, either.

The call erupted again. Two short, high-pitched bursts and a longer, more melancholy song.

"I've never head that one before," I said, excitement blossoming in the tips of my toes. It spread like wildfire through my body. Two new birds in one week! I fucking love spring.

"Me either," Gran said. She looked like a kid on Christmas. "Laurel, we have to find him. Maybe it's a pet that got out. Or maybe it's a second rare find! Louise is going to *hate* me. Let me get my binos!"

Gran ran into the house to find her high-power binoculars. I dug my camera out of my bag and aimed it toward the tree, hoping to snap an image I could enlarge. I didn't have my best lenses, as they made my camera harder to transport, but I did what I could. Gran emerged from the house and shoved a pair of binoculars into my hands. "You are going to be late for co-op, so hurry. Go to the other side of the trees." I did as instructed and saw a few sparrows and a dove. The call echoed above my head, until it moved farther into the forest. Gran came up beside me and we stood for minutes in the silence.

"The one that got away," I said. The wildfire of excitement slid down my legs and slunk back into my feat, barely more than a spark now.

"Today." Gran nodded. "But there's always tomorrow."

"Yes!" I said. "And you need to text me if you hear it again. I'll play hooky for this one."

"You'll do no such thing." But she shot me a mischievous grin. "Of course I'll text you," she whispered.

Good ol' Gran. She knew my heart like no one else. Even if Dad had left and Mom seemed to barely remember she had a kid half the time, Gran was my constant in this world.

"Promise you won't try too hard to see it without me," I said. "I know how you feel about Louise's competition."

"Pfft. Please. Louise barely knows her binos from her butt. And you know I'll always wait for you, Laurel. Now go to co-op before Jerry tells the truancy office to cart me off to the pokey," she said.

"That's not even a thing."

She shooed me out of her yard toward my bike. "Don't argue with your elders," she said.

Hours later, the sky darkened and the rumble of an approaching storm kept distracting me from the unschoolers identifying different specifies of fungi. Soon the weather caught up with us, and within minutes, increasingly dramatic gray sheets of rain filtered through my shoes and socks until I decided enough was enough. I hustled my restless group of ponchoed children back to their parents.

Any word from the mystery bird? I texted Gran from inside the Nature Center.

Do you work, she replied.

That had to mean no.

I dropped into the Nature Center office after lunch.

"Don't drip on the new posters," said Jerry.

"Glad to see you are feeling better, boss," I said.

"I mean it. Dry off before you laminate them."

"Yes, sir. Oh, Risa asked you to sign her hours sheet. It's on your desk."

"Saw it. Go dry off." Jerry was all business, all of the time.

No one came for a bird walk and talk, or tree tour, or our afternoon Fungi with a Fun Guy program because of the weather. I sometimes wondered if that last one was because everyone knew Jerry was a grumpy mushroom expert at best, and that our advertising threw off spores of lies. But the weather made the most sense.

"Maybe next week," I tried to console him.

Jerry grunted.

I stood on the small porch of the Nature Center watching the angry clouds. I glanced at my ride chained to the covered bike rack. But then my phone buzzed.

Car is in your lot. Dropped it off for you. Got a ride with neighbor Stella. You're welcome.

Okay, maybe Mom could be pretty cool.

I'm going out with Chad tonight for closure. Leftovers in fridge.

Never mind.

I almost wished I had taken the bike path home anyway. The road back to my house from the pond snaked around the mountainside. I crept along at about twenty miles an hour, noting how there was really only a narrow silver guardrail between a precipitous drop and me. Or at least I was pretty sure the guardrail was still there. It was hard to see through the near-horizontal waves of drops assaulting Mom's vehicle.

Halfway home the dreary canopy parted a little, and sunlight peeked through. It was still raining and slick, though. I rounded the bend where the hillside hiking trail followed the highway a bit. I saw a familiar bright orange poncho on the gravel berm. I slowed down even further and rolled up to Gran. I beeped. She looked over and waved at me. I rolled down my window.

"Don't stop here, Laurel. Cars come around mighty fast."

"Yeah, no kidding. Maybe get off the road, then?"

"I am off the road," she said. "Well, mostly." She moved over a few inches.

"Get in the car. I'll drive you home," I said.

"Nah." Gran pointed to something over the guardrail. "I have stuff to see."

"Mystery bird?"

"No. But I'm pretty sure a black-backed oriole was at one of my feeders until a squirrel scared it. I heard him call a few times and figured I might as well get my weekly hike in."

"It's awful out!" I said.

Gran shrugged. "Go on, now," she said. "Go home."

"Promise me if you hear—"

"Yes, yes. Of course. I'll always wait for you. Go away."

I shook my head at her, but I rolled up my window and shifted into gear again. Gran often walked up the hill just to get some exercise, or to get a better view. There was a trail that led back to her house that joined the main path not far from here. She was in her bird zen mode, where she preferred to be alone. But it seemed like a bad idea for her to be out in this weather. I had barely spotted her by the side of the road, and I was practically walking the car around the bend.

Though. Gran was seventy-four. Obviously the woman could take care of herself.

FIELD JOURNAL ENTRY
MAY 2
NOTABLE LOCATION: THE END OF THE WORLD

Even though I went to school for two hours every Thursday so they could make sure I was being a responsible co-op student, I didn't mind because both of those hours were spent with Sophie in the Art and Media lab. The rain had stopped, so I joyfully locked my dry bike in the rack and nodded at a few of my classmates milling around on the sidewalk in front of Greater Shunksville High School. The "Greater" part of the school always struck me to have been a joke on the part of the builders, since only a few thousand people and mostly migrating birds called Shunksville home. Blink and you'd miss most of downtown entirely. I'd gone to school with the same kids for the better part of my life, until a few years ago, when a new manufacturing plant opened and new families started moving in. Since Mom was a teacher's aide at the dinky elementary school, she complained daily about the overfull classrooms and lack of space for the kids to play.

The familiar scent of turpentine and canvas greeted me as I swung the door open to the art room. Ms. Rizzo, the Art and Media lab teacher, smiled over at me.

"Thwatchingsirds?" a voice asked from under a table.

"What?" I said.

"How's the bird watching?" Sophie said more clearly.

"Superb," I said.

"See anything good?"

"No. Heard a new call, though."

"That's good?" She got up and straightened her headband.

"Indeedy. What are you doing on the floor?"

"Finding my artistic muse. Also, my damn brush rolled into a crack and I had to bust it out. This one cost me three hours cleaning the garage."

"Understood," I said. I pulled my portfolio from the rack and spread out my (fucking unoriginal) heron pictures. Ms.

Rizzo basically let the advanced juniors do what we wanted during our extended "A Block" days, so we could work on our co-op portfolios. I was living my best nature photographer life.

Still life was my forte, even though I wished it were birds. Trees. Rocks. The occasional wildflower. I'd tried to mix it up because Sophie was also a sculptor and had convinced me to try to branch out artistically freshman year. I tried 3-D stuff like clay (doves) and (raven) jewelry making to mix it up. After burning myself and setting fire to Soph's second-best sketchbook with my soldering iron, I'd decided (well, Ms. Rizzo vehemently suggested) that the camera was my true calling. I'd gotten a lot better at birds this year.

"These are all just herons," I said to my portfolio.

"I told you. Go shoot the steel mill or a mine or something. Post-industrial Gothic. Find weeds growing out of pipes and things. People will love that stuff," Sophie said. "Didn't your ex-girlfriend photograph that kind of stuff?"

"The lines of those places haunted me. You start noticing how everything is a square or a triangle and how many right angles add up to your life. Can't do it. Also you will recall that I was together with the ex you mentioned for about a week, probably not unrelated to her art." I shook my head for emphasis. "As the master Brian Michael Warbley says, 'Nature is my canvas.'"

"Yeah, 'cause that's normal for a photographer, to get stressed out by the fact that the world is made of shapes. I thought you moved past that after they stopped trying to get you to watch *Sesame Street* with us in Ms. LaPlaca's class."

"Squares are everywhere. Lurking. Squares are brutal. Literally. Brutalist buildings . . ."

"Nature is shapes, Laurel. Mountains. Animals. *Birds*," she said.

"Soft shapes. These are all circles and curves. Jagged rock faces freak me out. When have you seen a rectangular crow?" I said. "As Brian—"

"Yeah, yeah, yeah. I get it. Loser," she said, but the bell drowned her out.

I smiled at my digitally manipulated herons. When I was in a bad mood or upset about the state of the world, I liked drawing little stick arms on them.

Sophie *was* right—I needed to do something new. Something exciting. Something that would move the judges to accept *me* over all the other Brian Michael Warbley wannabes in the world. But what was that?

I got out my laptop and scrolled through pictures of the rust belt, a dirty line that sliced up the eastern part of the United States, in which Shunksville sat firmly in the middle. It wasn't as rusty as it could have been, maybe. New jobs had brought a bunch of stores and stuff nearby, but to me, we still seemed like a place nature was taking back. The cracked seams of earth on a mountain once erased of green by mines had grass peeking out in many places again. Wildflowers (which purists might call "weeds") were persistent little shits and found ways to grow in soil where they had no earthly business surviving. Even the rocks that sat next to abandoned railroad tracks grew moss in shades of sage and juniper and parakeet.

Nature. Gotta hand it to her.

An hour passed and all I had managed to do was decide I hated both buildings and boulders.

"This is pointless," I said to Sophie.

Sophie looked up and turned her sketchbook toward me. "Would it help to know that I've been very productive?"

I cocked my head at Sophie's drawing of me. Paper me smiled at my computer, hunched over in thought. Lines fell in dark waves from my scalp to my shoulders.

"You made my hair look really good," I said.

"I made your hair look like it looks."

"No, you made it look better."

"Did not."

"Did, too."

"Making good use of undirected study, girls?" said Ms. Rizzo from her desk.

"One of us is," I said. "The other one would like to but can't."

Ms. Rizzo got up and glanced at Sophie's drawing. She threw her a thumbs-up.

"Why don't you try landscapes again? Go to that pond you like to shoot when the light is best. A starry, starry night. A time when you aren't usually there so that the world can be new." Ms. Rizzo squeezed my shoulder. "Take heart. You still have plenty of time. Entries aren't due until, what, end of July? You're in good shape." She wandered over to other tables.

"Easy for her to say," I mumbled. Ms. Rizzo specialized in graphic design. Photographing nature at night was not easy. Lighting was one thing, but the reemergence of mosquitos was also soon to be another.

"I think you are putting too much pressure on yourself. You always have a hard time thinking of things in competition season."

"Freaking Risa," I said. "She asked me about it, you know?"

"Ohhh," said Sophie. "What is she doing?"

"I don't know. Something inspired, probably."

Sophie shrugged. "You'll figure out what to submit. Photograph what inspires you. What brings you joy?"

"You." I grinned. "And Gran. And summer birds."

"Yeah, your gran brings me joy, too. Birds? Not so much."

I whacked her with her sketchbook. She'd spent a lot of time at Gran's house when we were little. I don't know how the birding hadn't rubbed off on her, even a little.

At the end of lab, I had produced nothing except herons with mustaches.

"Remember me fondly," I said to Sophie. "Remember the art of my youth, for that is all I will ever have to show."

"No," she said. "I've forgotten it already. See you later."

Once I got outside, I fished around in my backpack to find my phone. I had turned it off for Art and Media, but I needed my internet fix before committing back to nature. There were six voice mails from Mom and more than fifteen texts.

I dialed Mom's cell.

"Hello?" said a frantic voice. "Laurel, is that you?"

"Yeah, Mom, of course it's me. Are you okay?"

"I'm fine, honey. Where were you? I called and called."

"I'm was at school, Mom."

"Yes but your phone!" Her voice rose an octave. "I called the office, but no one there answered, either."

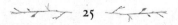

"Maybe they were in a meeting. I'm not supposed to have my phone on at school." I thought guiltily of all the times I'd kept it on for bird alerts.

"Honey. I have some bad news. There's been an accident."

"What? Who? I thought you took the car in for an oil change today," I said, confused.

"Grandma, baby. Grandma has been in an accident. She's downtown at Mercy Hospital. I had to take the bus here . . . but I'm with her. She's in surgery. I think you need to come down here. Just . . . in case."

"In case what, Mom?" Something wasn't sinking in. What Grandma? That's what I called Dad's mom. Wait, she couldn't mean *Gran*? I'd just seen *Gran* yesterday evening.

Actually. Gran usually called with a bird update by now. I'd been so distracted by lab and contest woes that it slipped my mind.

"Things don't look so good. Just—just get down here, okay?"

"Wait, something happened to Gran? Are you sure?" None of this was making any sense. Gran was unstoppable. Gran was a force of nature. *Gran was fine and looking for birds on the stupid mountain path yesterday.*

"Of course I'm sure! Listen—Laurel. Mercy emergency room. Okay?" Mom's voice just got more and more frantic. Emergencies weren't exactly her wheelhouse.

"Okay," I said. "Let me just text my co-op."

It wasn't until I sent Jerry a brief note about a family emergency that it started to sink in. Something had happened to Gran. Gran, my rock, had been unearthed and thrown who knows where. My hands shook as I gripped my handlebars, making my way the few miles to the hospital.

As the sliding doors let me into the emergency department, reality buzzed in my ears. A dad sat with a screaming little boy whose arm stuck out at a funny angle. A girl a little older than me rested her head against a pillar, her eyes half-moons under drooping lids. Nurses, doctors, light, and sound swirled like fog over this antiseptic place. I wobbled over to a desk where a harried-looking woman answered calls with a gruff voice.

"Excuse me?" I said. I hated to interrupt her.

"Just a second, honey," she said. She barked into the phone, punched numbers, sighed at the ringing.

"Busy for a Thursday afternoon," she said, finally looking up at me. "Are you here for yourself?"

"No, ma'am," I said. I recognized her. I'd seen her at school plays and bake sales. She was the mom of a girl in my history class. "My gran was brought in . . ."

She shook her head, as if she, too, were stuck in the emergency room fog. "Fowler. Aurora Fowler. And you are Laurel, right?"

"Yes, ma'am."

"Just a second, sweetheart."

Mrs. Glenn. That was her name. Mrs. Glenn, mother of Tabitha, another Art and Media lab girl. Tabby, everyone called her. Mrs. Glenn, mom to Tabby, nice to people in front of her and hard as steel to the people demanding things on the phone. Good qualities to have in an emergency room receptionist, or nurse, or whatever she was. She wore scrubs, so it could go either way.

None of this mattered, these details. I should be thinking about Gran. Finding Gran. Not remembering a girl I didn't really talk to or knowing her mom's name or memorizing the patterns in the chipped paint in the wall behind her. But right now those normal things felt like a lifeline.

Maybe I should text Sophie. She was good in a crisis. I just slipped the phone out of my hoodie and unlocked it when Mom burst out of another set of double doors past the desk with Mrs. Glenn.

"Laurel," she said. Her bloodshot eyes and puffy red face flashed a warning light that she'd been crying. Gran would always roll her eyes at Mom's constant waterworks, but still alarm bells accompanied her appearance in my head.

"Mom?" I said.

She threw her arms around me. "It's not good, baby. Not good. Come with me." Mom released her grip around my shoulders and grabbed my hand. She waved at Mrs. Glenn, who pushed a button at her desk. The doors swung open for us. I followed Mom down a white corridor. White walls, white tile, white machines. The only color came in a yellow line of the floor, and angry red and green and blue bursts from monitors. People lay in little rooms, some with their doors open, some not. It was silent except when it wasn't—cries or worried conversation or beeps broke the stillness. Mom rushed to a pod where Gran lay.

I gasped when I saw her—like an actual, audible gasp a cartoon character might make. She was Gran but she wasn't. Her eyes closed, her skin pale, wires and bags and those terrible machines attached to her.

"What . . . ," I started, but I closed my mouth. What

would Mom say? Could her words fill Gran up and make her whole and well, so we could leave this place? Would they wake Gran up from her dream so we could leave? We'd drop Mom off at home so that Gran and I could go back to trying to beat Louise and Risa, respectively

"What happened?" I whispered.

"I don't know." Mom shook her head. "She got hit by a car. It was raining all day and night and the oil on the roads . . . for some reason Grandma was out on the highway or something. Up on the mountainside, you know, that hiking trail. You can get onto the road in a break there. She was standing by the bend. A car took the turn too fast and hit her. She landed yards and yards away, down the hill. The driver stopped and was pretty torn up about it. But why was she even *out there*?" Mom looked at Gran. "Why, Mom? What could you possibly have been doing? How could you possibly think it was a good idea to be out there?"

Mom started howling. This wasn't her usual, OMG-BradChad-broke-up-with-me cry. This was soul-deep wailing. I had half a mind to shush Mom. There were other people, sick people, here after all. But then I looked at Gran. If anything was going to wake her up, surely this would.

Gran didn't move. None of the monitor thingies hooked up to her changed at all.

Just then, a woman in a long white coat came in with a man wearing scrubs. They looked at Mom; then they looked at me. Since I was not currently impersonating a wounded animal, the woman addressed me.

"What is your name?" she asked, loudly businesslike over the sound of Mom.

"Laurel," I said. "This is my gran. Um. And my mom."
I pointed to them both, as if there could be some confusion.

The lady nodded. "Is she okay?" She gestured to Mom.

"Oh. Well. My gran, you know?"

"Mommmmmm," my own mother wailed.

She looked at me again. "Do you know what happened?"

I nodded. "I kinda heard."

"We are going to keep her here in the intensive care unit.
Your grandmother will need to have tests. We discussed this
with . . ." She looked at Mom. ". . . your mother. But you
might want to talk it out with her a little later. Is your dad
around? Or another adult in the family?"

I shook my head, and Mom wailed.

Guy-in-scrubs gently shuffled Mom into a chair. He
knelt and spoke softly to her. Eventually she calmed down.

"We can only give medicine if you are a patient here, too,"
he explained. "Since you are in distress, though, maybe . . ."

I sighed. "She'll be okay. Give her a few minutes. Right,
Mom?"

Mom folded up into herself, like an origami swan creased
with grief and pain. "Yes," she whispered.

The guy kept talking to her and she listened. Dude was
like the Mom whisperer or something. God, I hoped it was
unethical for him to date her.

The doctor leaned toward me. "Laurel," she said. "The
first twenty-four or forty-eight hours are important. Hopefully
we'll see signs of improvement. For now, it's a situation of wait
and see. Given the circumstances"—she looked at Mom
again—"maybe you want to go home. Get some rest. We have

your contact info; we will call you if anything changes or if we move her. Okay?"

"Shouldn't we stay here?" I said. "Gran shouldn't be alone."

The woman smiled. "I know this is difficult. But we will take good care of her. I bet she would want you and your mom to take care of yourselves, wouldn't she?"

"Yeah," I said. That was true. When Gran woke up, she'd have a duck fit if Mom was freaking out. That's what she called it when anyone yelled—"a duck fit."

All birds, all the time with Gran.

"I've been here for hours," Mom sniffed. "We could come back in a little bit, Laurel."

"But . . . ," I said.

"A little bit," Mom said. I could hear her voice rise like it did before another duck fit.

"Okay," I said, defeated. "Okay."

We left through the double doors, past Mrs. Glenn, past the sleeping girl and the crying boy, still sitting there. Still sleeping. Still crying.

When we got home, Mom drank the tea that made her sleepy. She hadn't asked me if I needed anything or if I was okay. Maybe she assumed that I didn't. Or that I was. Or maybe she just didn't have anything to give regardless of what I'd say.

It was probably that last one.

I sat down on my bed, cradling the phone to my chest. A sneaky thought from earlier floated back into my consciousness, growing heavier and heavier until it sunk to into the base of my skull—I had seen Gran up there yesterday. I knew then it was dangerous but didn't make her come with me. *I could have prevented this*. I should have kept her from going up there in bad weather. That was *my* fault. If I had just stayed a little longer to talk her into coming with me, or turned around and dragged her, I would have pissed her off, but she would have been *fine*.

But she wasn't fine. She was awful. She was alone in the white room with only wires and tubes for company.

And

    it

        was

my

    fault.

The phone buzzed me out of my spiral. I nearly dropped it, thinking it was the hospital. But it wasn't the ER or the ICU or wherever Gran was at the moment.

"Sophie," I answered.

She started talking before I could get any coherent thought together. "Oh my god, Laurel. Brett's dad heard on the CB that there was an accident and he called his buddy and is your gran okay? What happened?"

"I don't know too much right now. She was hit by a car. Um. In an accident. She was outside, and it was raining, and she was by that fucking trail by the road and you know how slippy it stays all the time . . ."

And if Gran died, it was all my fault, Sophie. Completely, and utterly my fault. Because I saw her there and left.

But I couldn't tell her that. I couldn't tell *anyone* that. Because if no one else knew, then it wasn't really true. Well, okay, I knew. So it was fact.

But no one could hate me for it, at least.

"Laurel, are you still there?" Soph said. She'd been talking that whole time.

"I don't know, Soph," I said. "I don't know where I am without Gran."

"Yeah," she said. She stayed on the other end of the phone, silent. "Do you want me to come over?"

"I don't deserve that," I said softly.

"What?" she said.

"I might have to go back to the hospital," I said. "They are going to call. If she needs us. If they move her. Gran. To another room. Because they said they might do that."

"Okay," she said. "Laurel?"

"Yeah?"

"Um. I'm here if you need me. Okay?"

"I know," I said.

"No, really. I am."

"Thanks, Soph. This just sucks, you know?"

"Yes. Yes, it does."

I didn't know what else to say and neither did she, so we hung up. I watched her face fade from the phone screen. I held my thumb down and tapped into the picture icon. I opened shots of herons and watched them fade over and over.

Bills, feathers, darkness. Feathers, wings, darkness.

It made me feel better.

I rolled over and hugged my knees to my chest. I tried to lie still like a log and take deep, even breaths, like a family therapist once taught Mom and me.

There, completely alone, the night closed in around me. It was too dark and too quiet, even if the hall light glowed in on my lime-green rug and my daisy clock ticked cheerfully on my wall. Gran's heartbeat should be booming from her house, out and over the mile-and-a-half stretch to our driveway, and into the downstairs and the upstairs and through our attic and the rest of Shunksville right now. She was so alive; all of Pennsylvania couldn't contain her. The fact that right now she had shrunken into a damaged body in a tiny pod, left a silence so violent it attacked the ears. The clock ticked out of sync without her steady pulse to guide it.

I picked up my phone again. I willed it to ring. I willed the doctor or even the dude nurse who probably had a thing for Mom to call us. To tell us that Gran had woken up, that she'd be good as new in a few days.

Ring. Buzz. *Something.*

I made a resolution to myself, right then in the too-quiet, too-dark house. Gran was going to be okay. I would *will* her to be okay. If it took talking to her and learning physical therapy or whatever, I would do it. I would think of something that would be the miracle we needed.

FIELD JOURNAL ENTRY
MAY 4

The day dawned bright and beautiful, not that I got to see much of it. Jerry said that I could miss co-op, and had to make up hours only if I wanted to. I was there enough just for fun with Gran that I had amassed way more than I probably needed anyway.

Gran. Lying there in the hospital bed, still as a river stone, as the chaos of the hospital washed over her.

Gran. Her syllable stung. What always seemed a soft,

kind, feathered word now squeezed into the brain with tiny, crushing claws.

I'd seen her. I'd *seen* her. I knew it was unsafe. *Obviously* it was unsafe. But I'd just kept going. If Mom ever found out, she was going to disown me. Kick me out. And I'd have nowhere to go because I'd killed the one thing keeping Mom and I going.

No. Not killed, Laurel. She was only asleep. A coma wasn't forever. Her brain could be there.

Right?

Back at home after another day next to Gran, Mom went straight to her room, only stopping long enough to tell me to wake her if the hospital called with any news.

I went to my own room and collapsed onto my bed. I looked over at my *Fauna* issues from the last decade, neatly arranged on a tall shelf with my Warbley collection. *Warbley's Beginning Birding*, the first of my collection, given to me by Gran on my fourth birthday. *Warbley's Definitive Guide to North American Birds*, Warbley's memoirs, *One for the Life List*, and *Another One for the Life List*. A dozen more.

None of the magazines or books I'd always used as life guides really covered what to do when you accidentally caused one of the world's best birders to nearly die.

Nearly, Laurel. Gran wasn't dead.

Still the tiny claws dug deeper. I could feel this sting in my head. In my chest.

"This can be okay," I said to the *Fauna*s and Warbleys. "Nature persists. Life triumphs. Always."

Their prim rows stood sympathetically. If nature taught anything, it was that death came for us all.

"Not helpful," I said. "I choose to believe that Gran is the exception that goes against the rule." I nodded at them. Sometimes you just had to fake confidence until it became real. Guilt tried to worm its way back, but I'd just have to keep shoving it down.

"Like Warbley says . . . ," I said to myself, but couldn't come up with anything in the moment.

Maybe tomorrow. That was one thing. The birds would fly and sing again tomorrow.

I could depend on that. Even if the feelings I'd shoved to the back recesses of my brain pushed forward, making my temples hurt. Knowing I could hear a bird sing tomorrow, I would make that enough for now.

FIELD JOURNAL ENTRY
MAY 5
NOTABLE LOCATION: THE NEW NORMAL?

The hospital never called overnight. Mom woke up pissed.

"Are you sure you didn't miss a call?" she said.

"Mom, it's a cell phone. If I did, you'd be able to see it," I said. "Would you like some oatmeal? A full stomach might help!" My plan of Everything Will Be All Right if We Will It to Be was in full effect.

"But you could have erased it. To cover up your mistake?" She ignored my offer of breakfast.

"Why would I do that?" I said. If Mom only knew my *real* mistake with Gran, what would she do?

"How would *I* know, Laurel?" Mom said.

"Should I stay home from the Nature Center today? I don't have to go in on the weekend," I said.

"Just tell me now if they called."

"Mom, of course they didn't call. I would have told you." I tried to hand her the phone. "Call them and see what's going on."

She looked like she wanted to throw the cell at something. Or someone. I slowly backed out of the kitchen before I said something to annoy her.

I texted Sophie.

I'm living in peak Mom meltdown mode over here.

Laurel! OMG I was so worried! How is your grandma?

Don't know. No word, I typed.

Well, that's probably good, right?

I don't know. I think they would have let us know if she woke up? Maybe?

Sophie sent back a frowning face.

I texted, *But they also would have called if she got worse. You know Gran. She's tough. She's going to make it.*

Truth, she wrote back.

As Brian Michael Warbley once wrote, "Birds aren't born knowing how to fly, but the ability is still there within them. Make manifest what's inside you." That's what I could do for Gran. Make manifest her ability to wake up, and make Mom feel like everything was going to be okay.

On the other hand, I was the one responsible for Gran's condition in the first place. That might negate all the good energy I put out. That thought pecked on the thin veneer of my cheerful outlook. I shoved it as far from my mind as I could.

But I felt it there, guilt's sharp little beak.

"Laurel," Mom yelled from the kitchen. "Be ready to go in five."

Her words ricocheted against the exposed wooden beams, sending splinters flying in all directions that landed straight into my skin. I sighed. There was nothing else to do when she was like this but to listen.

Mom drove to the hospital, sometimes casting little glares over at me.

"What?" I finally said.

"They didn't call because they hadn't moved her. But she has a bed now. We can see doctors while they are on rounds. Or something."

"Are you mad at me?" I asked.

"No," she said.

"You seem like it."

"I'm just under a lot of stress. My mother and all."

"My grandmother," I thought sadly. But I realized I had accidentally said it out loud.

Mom wilted a little. "I know, baby. I know. I'm sorry. I just . . . I don't understand how she ended up like this. I don't know what we'd do without . . ." She trailed off.

"It's okay, Mom," I said. "I know Gran. This is a setback, but if anyone can come back from something like this, it's her. She needs us to be in her corner!" I almost meant the confidence in my voice.

"Okay, sweetheart," she said.

When we got to the hospital, we were shuffled off to another floor. They had just moved Gran to another pod, with her own nurse. Her wires and monitors were all still present and accounted for, but now she had these fancy socks that expanded and contracted, massaging her every few minutes. Her bed moved like ocean waves underneath her.

"Fancy," I said to her. "It's like a spa, but with drugs."

Gran's face didn't change.

Beep. Click. Whir.

Doctors came and went. They took Gran; they brought her back. Hours passed like this. There was no news to report, doctors said. Gran's brain was damaged, but it was too early to tell. She'd survived, and seemed to be fighting. That was good. But her response to stimuli was not.

It was dark when we left. Mom had fallen into a deep place of silence.

"Should we get takeout?" I said.

Nothing.

"I could make chicken. We should probably do Crock-Pot stuff for a while. I'll find the recipe file."

Silence.

"Did I tell you about the red-tailed hawk's nest we found? They usually like to be downtown, but they've moved to the burbs!" My chatter reached out again and again over the mile to our house, but it couldn't cross to where Mom was.

In a fortunate turn of events, however, I didn't end up needing to worry about food. Casserole dishes had shown up on our stoop like they did after Grandpa had died when I was ten. Gran was well known and word traveled fast around my town. The birders and the leaf peepers and the sewing circle represented in full fucking force.

I should probably stop making fun of Gran's terrible

needlepoint. Those people made the best tuna noodle a girl could ever hope for.

I feel guilty eating chicken, I texted to Sophie later. *Gran would have ten thousand duck fits.*

Wouldn't they be chicken fits? she said.

Fair point.

Try to get out tomorrow. To the pond or woods. Take some pictures. I think it'd be good for your mental state.

Yeah, I said. I had brought my portfolio to the hospital, thinking that I could go through it again next to her. That that might wake her up, somehow. Or that I could borrow some of her winning *Fauna* photography powers. I had a bunch of rock and icicle ones from the past winter that might count as still life.

It struck me that Gran was now a still life.

The doctors had declared there had been swelling in her brain. Or bleeding. Or both, maybe. But she was breathing on her own, though. She was hanging on.

As Brian Michael Warbley said, "Even in the silence of still life, there is life, still."

Mom stayed in her silent weirdness. It was starting to freak me out. This had happened once before, after Dad left. Dishes went unwashed, bills unpaid, groceries unbought. Mom didn't have that much sick time. She could take off of work unpaid, but the whole *unpaid* situation would be pretty bad. Intervention had to come early this time.

"Mom, we can't live like this," I said that night.

"Mmm-hmm," she said.

"We have to make a plan," I said.

"Mmm-hmm," she repeated.

"Are you even listening?"

She stared at me. She blinked. "Yes. Yes, I am."

"What are we going to do?"

Mom sighed. "What we always do, Laurel. I'll go to work. You go to that bird place. We'll take turns visiting Mom. We'll figure it out somehow."

"Okay," I said.

"I'm going to bed. Night," she said abruptly.

"Night," I said. I slumped onto the couch. The whole system Mom and I had only worked if Gran was involved. She was the glue. Without her . . . what? I didn't even know. So there was only one possible solution. We needed Gran.

Something crashed from upstairs.

I jumped. I bolted up the steps.

In Mom's room I found her on the floor next to a shattered glass vase.

"What happened?" I asked.

"I got it out. To look at it. It was a wedding gift. From Grandma. I wondered . . ." Mom sat down on the floor, in the middle of all the shards.

"Don't do that!" I said. "I'll get a broom! Get on the bed, Mom!"

But she wouldn't budge. I swept as best as I could around her. I convinced her to go into the bathroom, where I watched her wash off her hands. I brushed her jeans off into the garbage can. I still wasn't sure I'd gotten it all.

"Don't walk in bare feet, Mom."

She nodded. But then she walked into her room and closed the door.

The whole "breaking" and "falling apart" nature of Mom's act was a little too on the nose. I went downstairs and cleaned up the last few days of cleaning neglect.

I was older this time than when Dad left. I could fill in as glue for Gran's temporary absence.

At least. I hoped I could.

FIELD JOURNAL ENTRY
MAY 6

I decided I had to try to go back to the Nature Center. Being at the hospital so much was beginning to get to me. Birding with toddlers served as a solid distraction. They were a lot like squirrels, but they were *also* enchanted with every blade of grass and snail and slug nature had to show off. So they weren't that bad.

When the Center quieted down, I went out onto the small back porch and sat on the ancient wooden swing. The leaves on the oak and spruce glowed vibrant in the afternoon light. Green peeked out of the forest floor corners and rows, curling the sunlight into warm brown rock. A robin flew up and landed on the banister. He twitched his head at me suspiciously.

"Feeding you would be terrible birder behavior," I said.

He chirped.

"Yeah, I know. This hurts me more than you."

He hopped along the gray chipped paint. He called out and another robin answered him.

"Honestly, worms are a lot better for you."

His beady eyes gleamed a solid "piss off, apex predator" at me, and then he took flight to meet his robin buddy off in another tree. Birds kind of had middle fingers in their wings. Or middle toes, at least. They were definitely experts in communicating their disgust with you.

I grinned. Maybe that's where we got "flipping someone the bird." I'd have to ask Gran.

Gran.

I thought about her garden and her plants and her mail. Was anyone bringing in her mail? No. Who would? Mom had barely been taking care of herself, let alone that kind of thing. I should do that. Get the mail, at least.

After co-op, I got on my bike and rode over to Gran's house. Sure enough, a packet of letters and catalogs for outdoor gear sat in the metal curls jutting from a packed mailbox. I pried it out and piled it neatly on her table inside the door. I checked her fridge and bagged a bunch of rotting fruit and vegetables. She would be so, so ticked off that all that food went to waste. I checked the basement. It only ever flooded in the early spring, but this gave me a sense of purpose. No windows had been left open, no faucets running, no burners heating. The house was fine, aside from the fridge and mail, which had been quickly addressed.

I took the garbage down the stone path through to the edge of the yard. They'd pick it up Wednesday or Thursday. I looked down the abandoned alley. Shards of broken glass sparkled like diamonds, mixing with the stones blacked by passing tires and oil-slick rainbows until the alley dead-ended into the Jenkins Wood's path. It was serene and sad and made me wish desperately that Gran were there with me, yelling at me to hurry up with the damn chores, already.

I turned back toward the house. Mom would soon show

up at the hospital and wonder why I wasn't there. I wondered if I should come over and mow the lawn on Saturday. It was getting frowsy, as Gran would say. I walked to the side of the porch to check if the weed whacker still lived under there. As I peered into the dusty shadows, I heard it.

Two short, high-pitched bursts. One long melancholy song.

The mystery bird.

I backed out of the porch hole and looked around wildly. It sounded again from Gran's spruce tree.

"Where are you?" I asked the sound. "Just hop down, would you? So I can get a look at you. Wait for me!" I grabbed my phone. Maybe if I could get a picture of it, I could get Gran to . . .

Maybe I could look it up in a field guide.

Again and again he called. He moved to a tree by the garbage. I followed. He moved three trees down, high on the uppermost branches, hidden from sight. Over and over he moved until the call was lost amid the woods.

I went back to my bike. My phone buzzed with a dozen texts at once.

Where are you? Are you okay? Why aren't you with Gran? Where are you, where are you, where are you?

I hit Mom's name in my favorites.

"You scared me to death, Laurel, not being where I thought you'd be," Mom started before even saying hello.

"I'm over at Gran's house. Thought I should get the mail," I mumbled.

Silence.

"Oh," Mom said. "Oh. That's a good idea."

"I cleaned the fridge, too," I said.

"Oh," she said,

"I'll come over now."

"Okay."

I looked up at the sky, thanking the birds that Mom accepted this excuse as legit. I bumped down Gran's path on my bike, following the mystery bird's route on my way to the hospital.

But I didn't hear him again.

FIELD JOURNAL ENTRY
MAY 8

It didn't take long for the sameness of the hospital to settle on you like the ache of sitting too long in one position trying to photograph foxes.

Gran had been moved to a step-down unit. She wasn't any better, but everyone seemed to agree she wasn't dying. Her brain didn't register the activity of a person who was walking around yelling at the nightly news and following grand-daughters out into the chill spring morning to add birds to a life list. But it hadn't given up yet, either.

"Heard the bird again, Gran," I said during my afternoon with her. "Still couldn't get a look at him. It was getting dark, though. I'll go back. I think he likes your yard. Probably because you are so close to the pond and woods and stuff. But he's clearly a canopy bird, which helps with behavior identifi-cation if not so much with visuals."

Gran's eyelids fluttered.

I leaned in until my nose was almost touching her face.

"Did you hear that?" I asked her. "Did you understand

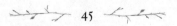

what I said? You're surviving because of that bird, aren't you? You *must* want to know what it is, right? It's still out here, Gran. We could figure it out. You just have to wake *up*. Louise could know, Gran, and you wouldn't. *Louise*."

Her arm twitched.

I sat back excitedly. Mom came in then, looking a kind of tired that no amount of Red Bull could touch.

"Mom. Mom! Look!" I leaned toward Gran again. "Maybe we'll be able to identify a whole new species! Maybe it's not a pet at all, but some weird lost kakapo! Or, well, something else rare because I think kakapos are flightless."

Twitch. Flutter.

"See!" I said to Mom. "I think she can hear us!"

Mom sighed.

"Laurel. The doctors talked to us about this. Bodies move, sometimes. It doesn't mean . . ."

"But she moved when I said things that would be interesting her."

"Responses are often involuntary and don't . . ."

"But it could mean something, Mom. It could, right?"

Mom looked at me for a second. "Sure, baby. I guess. I just don't want you to—you know—get your hopes up."

"Why not?" I said.

"Just in case."

"Mom!" I said, aghast. "We can't think like that!"

"We might have to." Mom sat down on the opposite side of Gran. "I don't want to lose her, either. She's . . . she's my world. Always has been. But. The doctors . . ." She trailed off, staring at all of Gran's beep-and-click machines. She rubbed the soft, thin skin of Gran's cheek. "Listen, I wanted to talk to you about Gran's house."

"What about it?" I demanded. I checked Gran for signs of similar indignation. She didn't move.

"Well. Even if she wakes up, I don't think she's going to be able to go back there. She'd go to rehab, and maybe a long-term care facility. And then . . ."

"You are going to put her in a *home*?" I said. "Like, for old people? She's barely even seventy! Or seventy-ish, any-way. Those places aren't for her. She'd *hate* it there."

"Laurel, I'm sorry I brought this up, now. Maybe we should talk about this later," she said.

"NO. You brought it up now; we talk about it now. I'll go over there. I'll do everything. You don't have to worry about it." I did so much of it at home, what's another house? Maybe I could move in there, actually. It's right next to co-op; it might be better.

"There will be bills to pay, honey. You have to heat a house so pipes don't freeze in the winter. And property taxes. Houses need to be lived in."

"Then get rid of ours," I said. "Winter is ages away. We'll live at Gran's, and when she comes home, we can make a bed-room for her in the dining room. No one eats in dining rooms anyway." *I would make this work.*

"She is probably going to need 'round-the-clock care."

The squawk in my head reminded me that this was my fault. "You did it, you did it, you did it," it called.

"You don't know that. It hasn't been that long! She looks way better than she did last week."

She didn't. But the lie needed to be told in that moment. Gran's eyelids fluttered.

"See!" I said, pointing. "She totally agrees with me."

"Members of Shunksville city council have been approaching her for months now. They want to develop that area and would give us a great price for the land. It would be enough to make sure she has excellent care. You are just a kid, honey. I know I've always put a lot on you because . . . well, I just have. It's how it is. This would be too much. You have the bird place and friends and your photography. Those should be your job right now."

"Since when do you care about my photography?" My voice rose involuntarily.

A nurse peeked her head in. "Um. Everything okay in here?" she said.

"No," Mom said. "But we're trying. I'm sorry."

The nurse looked at Mom, to me, to Gran, and back to Mom again. She smiled at me. "Understood." She left.

"Let's go home," Mom said. "Honey. Again. I'm sorry. I'm not thinking straight these days."

I sighed. "I know. I'm sorry, too. This all sucks." The world had flipped over even though I was clinging to the branch of life as I had known it; gravity itself was shaking me hard to let go. I figured I had a better chance of talking Mom out of her stupid "sell Gran's house" plan if I didn't yell in the not-quite-intensive care unit.

Mom put her arm around me. We walked out of the building and she helped attach my bike to the rack on the top of the car. She used to take Gran and me out to ride the trails in the Poconos when I was a little girl. She'd stopped sometime after Brad left. Or Chad.

Well. Okay. After Dad.

Mom had brought home stuff to do from work. I downed some pity casserole and then went up to my room. I flopped onto my bed and texted Sophie all of the mama drama.

I need guidance, wise one, I texted.

Wait, how is your grandma?

No change. Except that part where Mom wants to put her in a home.

Wow, that sucks. But that's because there is no change?

Yes. Will try to talk her out of it tomorrow.

I'm afraid I have no wisdom. But I believe in you, Laurel. You single-handedly convinced Shunksville Elementary to recycle plastics and to donate unused cafeteria food. You can talk your mom out of putting gran in a home, she said.

They still do that, you know. That program is alive and well. I argued that should count toward my senior project next year, but the project committee was all, "That was nearly a decade ago, blah, blah."

Losers.

Don't I know it, I texted.

We sent each other some hearts. Sophie was usually my go-to for ideas. I put the action into activist, generally. Sophie was the thinker. It concerned me that she couldn't come up with any concrete proposals yet.

Later I wandered back downstairs to steal some of the potato salad that had showed up on the porch this morning.

Mom sat at the kitchen table. She looked up at me. "What

you said earlier—you know I've always cared about your photography. Who bought you your camera?"

"You did. But, *Mom*," I said. "You told me to prepare to be a barista to support myself. You made me pay for half of everything. I had IOUs on my allowance and meager Nature Center salary for months last year."

"The life of an artist is hard. I just wanted you to be able to eat."

"Uh-huh."

Mom smiled at me, in spite of everything. If my brain kind of squinted and looked at life sideways, it almost seemed normal.

Almost.

FIELD JOURNAL ENTRY
MAY 10

Some days at the Nature Center stretched slowly from one hour to the next. When the unschoolers had their Science Museum day or sports day or macramé and cooking cohorts, there wasn't too much to do. Jerry sent Risa to rearrange the deciduous trees library, and let me go out to take pictures. He'd been giving me a lot of leeway since Gran. I'm pretty sure he'd once had a thing for her, after she'd photographed several migrating black-legged kittiwakes and two purple sandpipers. Once those hit the internet, we had birders here for weeks. The donation box had been overflowing. He'd replaced the Nature Center roof with that money.

I meandered onto the woodland path, idly snapping pictures of shadow patterns. Sophie liked to use those as inspiration for her abstract phases. I walked the circuit, ending up at the pond loop. The water and its inhabitants lazed quietly, perhaps also bored without their young visitors. *Fauna* had a "Moment of Peace" feature at the end of each magazine. "Beauty sits still," it always captioned pictures of boulders or sleeping goslings or placid lakes reflecting unmoving mountains. But everything I shot looked dull. Lifeless.

Comatose.

I tried to physically shake the thought out of my head. But the fact was, Gran should be here. The woods knew it. The pond knew it. Even the birds knew, a few glancing at me as they hopped from canopy to line of sight back to the heights I couldn't reach. Gran's realm missed her and I could feel its call brush past me like a breeze.

"Why?" I asked the universe. "Why her?"

No answer came. Try as I might, I couldn't find any reason or rhyme to why this had to happen, not even here, where I'd always found everything I'd needed before.

"I'm sorry," I whispered to Sarig Pond. To Jenkins Wood. To the universe. "I'm so, so sorry."

The trees only watched, their green hanging tendrils swaying gently in the breeze. They couldn't forgive me.

Nothing could.

FIELD JOURNAL ENTRY
MAY 11

The next morning, Sophie was babysitting, so I biked to Gran's house before going to the Center to make up some hours. Even if I didn't have to, it gave me somewhere to be other than alone with my thoughts. Work helped keep a girl positive, and that's what I needed to be.

I searched around in the upstairs closet and found one of the thick, crookedly stitched afghans that I had created during my knitting phase a few years ago. It was ugly as fuck but softer than anything the hospital had. I folded it and put it on the chair in the living room. I could come back and get it on my way to the hospital. I locked the door and hopped on my bike, but then, almost like it had been waiting, a bird called.

Chirp, chirp, trill? No. Chirp, chirp—sing. Sing, little bird. How to even describe it? Maybe it was missing some part of itself, too. That was the best way to characterize the call. Chirp. Chirp. Longing.

I raised my head to the sky and searched.

"Give a girl a break, freaking feathered jerkface," I said.

But it didn't. It sang again from the woods. I began to pedal toward it. I took a moment to silently thank my uncle Dennis, who gave me his old mountain bike. This sucker could do Jenkins Wood trails without so much as creaking. I soared onto the path, sticks and rocks be damned. I stopped near the last tree I imagined the bird stopped at. I waited.

Chirp. Chirp. Loneliness.

"*Yes.*" I fist-pumped the trees. "Don't you want some worms?" I asked it. "Eat on the forest floor, winged adversary!"

It answered farther down the path.

I followed it like that for ten minutes. Eventually the woodland path ends at Sarig Pond and a wooden boardwalk takes you out and around. I rolled to a stop at one of the outstretching docks. A plump gray bird fluttered down next to me.

"Nice brown markings," I said to it. "Light beak. Awesome. Listen, you'd be doing me a solid if you could call right now. I'll wait." It stood there, regarding me with the mixture of curiosity and apathy that most birds did. I tried to imitate the birdcall I'd been following.

The bird laughed at me. With a human laugh.

"How did you do that?" I asked, astonished.

The bird chirped, back in its first language.

"Didn't you know dark-eyed junco have vocal cords? They can talk if they want, but generally people don't listen carefully enough," the voice said.

I turned around to see Risa behind me.

"What?" I said to her

"That was a dark-eyed junco," she said.

"It wasn't the one I was looking for. And now that you say that, I got a junco for the life list years ago. But it didn't have the brown."

"You are coming to work at the Center on a weekend?" she said.

"Doesn't everyone?" I said.

She chuckled. "Not that I know of."

"You hang out with the wrong kind of people, then," I said.

"Apparently."

I scanned the tree line. I could make out the business of other sparrows, and some angry crows were arguing nearby. But no sounds that really mattered.

"Were you looking for something?" she asked. "You can borrow my binos if you want."

Gran called her binoculars "binos," too. It was a birder

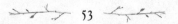

signal. How you knew the real birders from the people who got lost looking for the tennis courts on the other side of the pond and woods.

"I was. I don't know what, though. Not the junco. It's kind of a long story."

"You are looking for a bird you couldn't identify?" Her eyes lit up. "Cool! That *never* happens with you. What did it look like? Have you gotten a picture yet?"

Risa seemed a little too pleased that I couldn't identify a bird.

"I have never seen it. Only heard it. I've lived here my whole life and have never heard it. We think it might be a pet. My grandmother and me."

"Can you imitate it?" Risa said.

"Uh. No," I said.

"Try! Maybe I could help."

What was she even doing? Did she want to get a picture of it first? But desperate times call for desperate measures. I chirped and called for a second.

It sounded more like a dying swan than anything.

"Did . . . uh . . . that sound like it?" she said.

"Um. No." I cleared my throat and tried to make the sounds again.

Risa cocked her head at me, obviously trying to choke back a laugh.

I narrowed my eyes at her. "I told you I hadn't heard it before."

She shrugged, unable to hide her smirk.

"Are *you* working today?" I asked.

Risa looked at the ground. "Yeah. Figured it was better

than being at home. It's a nice day. Extra hours equals extra credit and whatnot."

"Yeah, I had to make up some." I scanned around for the mystery bird but he'd gone again.

"How's your grandma?" she asked.

"Oh," I said, surprised. I hadn't thought Risa would care. "Hanging in there."

Risa frowned. "Tell her I asked about her. I miss seeing her when I take the ElderBirds around."

"Okay," I said. We stood there in awkward silence for a second. I didn't really feel like explaining the coma to her, but maybe the fact that she cared meant a lot in the moment.

"Hey, Risa—" I started.

"Oh, Jerry is here. Gotta go. Good luck with your bird-calls." She turned and walked away quickly.

And the moment with Risa passed, like the movement of wings.

Freaking birds. Fucking people.

FIELD JOURNAL ENTRY
MAY 12

After my extra Sunday shift at the Nature Center, I mowed the lawn at Gran's house. I filled her feeder, thinking maybe it'd attract the mystery bird. But in my heart I knew the best I was doing was helping the stealing asshole squirrels. I listlessly photographed the garden and the trees with uninspired clicks of the lens because I couldn't think of anything else to do.

I heard a jostling inside Gran's house. I went inside,

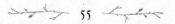

figuring I'd find Mom. Instead there was a strange man. I must have looked totally freaked, because he spoke first.

"You must be Laurel," he said.

"Yes?" I said like I wasn't sure of the answer.

"Oh, hi, honey," said Mom. She came down the stairs. "I didn't realize you were here."

"Taking care of the lawn," I said. "Didn't weed the garden, though."

"They'll bug your allergies," Mom said. "This is Mr. Hughes. He's here to look at Gran's house."

"Why?" I asked.

"Seeing if it needs to be freshened up a bit," he said brightly. "It's in great shape, Ms. Graham. Could use some paint, and maybe some new carpet. And you could consider updating the appliances, but that might not be necessary. It depends on the direction the neighborhood is going to take, after all."

"What does that mean?" I asked.

"Depends on the city council, the school board, you know," he said.

I looked at Mom.

Mr. Hughes chattered on about wainscoting and hardwood floors into the next room, but neither Mom nor I followed him.

"Mom!" I whispered to her. "You aren't still seriously considering selling this place, are you? You can't, you can't, you can't."

"I'm just exploring my options." She paused. "Hanging on to the house won't bring her back to us, Laurel."

"Neither will getting rid of it. We can figure out the money stuff, Mom."

"We really can't."

"But . . ."

"I have to talk to this Realtor. He's doing me a favor, coming out on a Sunday."

I wanted to scream. I wanted to fly into a horrible frenzy. Mom walked away from me back toward Mr. Hughes.

"Fuck!" I said out loud to the empty room.

Short burst, one syllable. A call to indicate danger.

I went outside to her yard. I scared a squirrel off the feeder. "Is this what you want?" I asked the trees. "The house to be sold? Where are you, you freaking bird? Gran!"

Nothing.

My heart raced. I tried to breathe through the reminder that this was all my fault.

The fact was that *I* wanted to be a nature photograph, pristine and unmovable and lovely just the way I was. But things kept changing fast and furious and there was no lens speed quick enough to capture a pretty shot of this, if there was any beauty to be had.

I hopped on my bike then and rode hard. Away from Mom, away from Realtors and away from other uncooperative species. I spun my feet up hills and over the bridge and down the sidewalk until I found myself at the hospital. I didn't remember the trip and looked up, surprised, when I saw the squat red brick building with the large glass windows and intimidating emergency room sliding doors I knew so well by now.

I locked my bike and went up to Gran's room. By now I didn't even have to see the nurse. I sat down at her bedside. If I were honest with myself, I knew in my heart that she wasn't getting better. She was thinner, paler, and something else. Gaunt? Frail? Both, maybe. Nothing like herself.

"Gran," I said. "Mom wants to sell your house. To the city, or something. I *know* that you would be totally pissed by this. That you are. But you have to wake up. You *have* to. You have to tell her because she won't listen to me."

Silence.

"I heard the bird again. I followed it. It likes the woods and pond. Of course. Risa was there. Do you remember her? The one I think messed up my chance at winning *Fauna* glory?"

Nothing.

"Though she has great hair. And, actually, cheekbones. I'm not going to lie."

Not a single number on her monitors flicked up even a notch.

"Listen to this, Gran," I said. I took a drink from my water bottle. I chirped two short notes, and whistled a long, low tune. That was better. It wasn't exactly right, but it was close.

Gran's thumb twitched. Her foot moved.

"Yes! See! This is what interests you. Maybe you don't care about your house. You can come live with us, or buy it back or whatever. But the bird, am I right?"

Eyelids.

"Yes! It's a mystery, and I know you love a good avian whodunit."

More eyelids.

"Great! Awesome. I have an idea. I think you keep sending the bird to me. Maybe it has a message? Maybe it can tell me how to get you out of this? I will find out what the bird is for you. I find it out for you, and you wake up, okay? We will take care of you and then you'll have this one for your life list. You can't die. It's not called a death list."

I swear Gran's head turned a little toward me.

I squealed a little. She *was* there. I *knew* it. No one believed me, which sucked. But I knew how important it was to find out the source of the call and tell her. I *owed* her that much. And then Mom would have to see her reaction. But I'd have to do it before they sold the house. Or . . . something worse.

"I'm so sorry you're here, Gran. I know it's all my fault. You're here. I'll do it," I whispered. "I'll find it for us. For you. Because you always wait for me, right?" I squeezed her hand and kissed her forehead. It was cool, with thin blue veins a lot closer to the surface than I remembered.

Gran twitched.

If I thought about it, Gran believed in a lot of things that some people might find irrational. Reiki. Haunted woods. Blessed ponds. Astral projection. Sometimes I made fun of it, because if I couldn't take a picture of something, I tended not to believe in it. But what if Gran's spirit had somehow gotten detached from her body in the accident? What if it really was a thing that a person's soul could go somewhere else—like, say, a bird, until her body was well enough to have it back? That was *exactly* the type of thing she would always hound me about.

Well, right after telling me to eat vegan and fight Shunksville High to get LEED certified.

She should be dead right now. The doctors all said so. But she wasn't. And the mystery bird that appeared once was now all over the place (even if I couldn't see it). Maybe that bird had a message from Gran. Maybe it *was* Gran.

It made sense as much as anything, didn't it? I mean, why the hell not? The world is vast and weird as fuck.

As Brian Michael Warbley said, "We owe it to the universe to believe in the impossible." And I think that was from last year's issue with the *Fauna* contest winners.

It was a sign.

I had to find the bird. Photograph it. Bring it back to Gran.

And I had to do it before Mom sold the house.

This would be a challenge. But that didn't matter. I had a mission. It would help her. I knew it would.

It had to.

FIELD JOURNAL ENTRY
MAY 13

The quest to find Gran's messenger got off to a slow start. We were having a bit of a mouse problem at the Nature Center.

"They are a part of nature," I argued. "We can't kill them."

"They are chewing through these here damn cords," said Jerry, pointing to the computer. "I can't afford to keep replacing them unless one of you finds me some San Clemente loggerhead shrikes and they go viral."

"Listen," said Risa. "I thought about this all weekend. I brought this." She held up a bottle. "It is technically poison."

I opened my mouth to protest.

"But it is eco-friendly. It more disorients them, shall we say."

"Is that cruel?"

"They'll want water. They'll go outside to find it and get

eaten by the owls or whoever, as was their likely fate anyway. But it won't kill whoever uses them as dinner, like all that shit people use in their homes."

I considered this. We'd lost two barn owls and one red-tailed hawk in the last year. We weren't sure why they died. Risa found one of their bodies and I the other two on our regular trash pickup routes last fall. The unschoolers threw them a lovely celebration of life after the hawk, but all of us had felt the loss. Often no one can pinpoint why a bird dies, but poisoned rats and mice were up there with the likely causes.

"Yeah. I get it." I still wasn't happy. "I'm going to do a sweep and plug up any holes to try to keep the little guys from getting in in the first place."

"Good plan," Risa said. I found at least seven nooks where any small woodland friend might enter the Nature Center. We weren't exactly a world-class eco-establishment. But I stuffed steel wool every place I could until I ran out.

Fauna's annual conservation issue would be coming out soon. I should write them a letter about owl-friendly rodent poison. I bet a lot of people didn't even know that was a thing, even among *Fauna* readers. I could make Gran . . .

Oh. I guess I couldn't make Gran do anything. Except be trapped in a coma. I'd made her do that.

No. Laurel. Stop. Guilt was not positive. Guilt was not productive. Roll it into the tight little knot in your chest and push it down until it rests like a pebble in the shoe. Annoying, nagging, but motivating enough to get you to a place you can rest.

"You okay?" Risa asked from behind me.

I realized that I'd been close to hyperventilating. Sometimes the "Gran is gone and it's your fault" feeling fought back harder.

"Yeah. Sorry," I muttered.

Her face softened. "I did the deed. Laced some of the spots near the chew sites. Hopefully you'll just keep them out."

"Yeah," I said.

"As Brian Michael Warbley said in *Fauna* issue two hundred and three, 'We are stewards of all creatures, not masters. But sometimes stewards must also keep their own houses in order.' I think that's fitting, don't you think?"

"I—I . . ." I stammered. "I do, actually."

"Warbley knows all," she said. Risa quoted Warbley to me.

"Okay, time to make twig wreaths," she said, and walked away. All I could do was stare.

Since Risa had the wreathers, I straightened the back issues of the Center's *Fauna* collection. Issue 203 did in fact have Risa's Warbley quote in an article about jays and crows. Girl knew her *Fauna*, too. That was almost . . . alluring.

I quickly shoved the feeling down to where I kept the guilt, even though that space stayed stuffed nearly full. But I couldn't worry about that now, because I had trails to monitor.

To quote a later article in *Fauna* issue 203, "No matter where the sun is in the sky, there is still time to make it a great day."

FIELD JOURNAL ENTRY
MAY 15

I raised my camera to my eye. You could try to capture a scene using the digital screen, but sometimes framing a shot required a more old-school technique. Skin on cool die-cast metal made me *feel* the shot as more participant, less observer.

"There you are," I said to the pristine red-winged blackbird who sat with his mate on Grandma Maple. I snapped and snapped their picture. Male red-winged blackbirds were just that—ebony bodies with wings of fire and gold. The females had chocolate bodies with taupe stripes. Warbley had said on more than one occasion, "Why don't we call it a male brown stripy bird instead?"

Indeed, Warbley, you sexy birder feminist, you.

I wandered around, shooting our various avian residents, occasionally picking up a stray wrapper or beer bottle. I'd planned to go show the pictures to Gran, even if she couldn't see them. I'd decided that maybe the light from my tiny camera screen could activate her brain. Allegedly computers and phones could mess up your sleep cycle. Who was to say a convergence of natural art and unnatural light might not do the same for coma patients I'd caused to nearly die?

My stash of Gran angst gurgled from its pit in the depths of my body. As was becoming my habit, I slammed a lid back on it.

I slung my camera over my shoulder. My best bird lenses stretched far from the camera body and got to be a bit of a pain to carry around. I used my garbage claw to grab a moldy baseball hat, a few cigarette butts, and chip bags. My second bag held water bottles to give to Sophie for art at the senior center.

When I had nearly reached the end of the woodland trail, bags and lenses caused my appendages to droop from the weight. We cleaned these trails regularly. How could people possibly lose this much shit on the daily? Though, some of it probably got there overnight. I suspected the Birdie Bros came back after hours for adventure night bird seeking, but had never gotten any solid proof. I ambled over to a tree to lean against as I redistributed the trash.

"Stupid bottled water," I mumbled. These would be upcycled, but for every plastic flower made, there were probably hundreds of bottles making their way to garbage oceans in the Pacific. I heard voices coming up the path behind me. I hid on the other side of the tree, technically off path (sorry, Jerry), in no mood to talk to people.

"This is really the most viable tract here," said a voice.

"The elevation makes it less likely to flood, unlike the wetlands," said another.

I peeked around the spruce, curious.

"The elevation brings the most birds here," said a third person. "But they won't put up much of a fuss." The group laughed and kept walking.

I waited a few minutes until their voices faded to silence. What was that about? They were right about the elevation. This end of the woods stood on a hill, which attracted the most migrating birds. The place crawled with bird tourists in warbler season. It'd pick up again for the birds' trips south.

Weird.

I made a mental note to mention this to Jerry another time, since I had about a minute to stash my bottles before my next Birdscout Eagle Eye activity. I decided we'd make male brown stripy bird masks.

It seemed fitting for the day.

"Gran," I said. "Listen." I played her my most recent recording of our bird.

Twitch. Twitch. Leg tremor.

I beamed. "Yes! Great!" My stomach twanged with every one of Gran's ~~involuntary~~ purposeful movements. The usual pricks had faded into a background ache that I soothed with deep breaths of goodwill.

"I am up to about seven hundred pictures in a month," I told her.

Twitch.

"All of them suck. I'm sorry, Gran. I'm not really doing right by the family legacy."

No movement from Gran, but my stomach churned.

"It's barely summer. I have months," I told her. "Like Warbley said, 'Seasons matter, but what is time, anyway?'"

Monitors beeped in reply.

I sighed. "I'm going back to my co-op. I'm converting little birders in your name. The catbirds are particularly popular with the unschoolers. Like you say, they are among the chattiest. They make friends easily."

Gran's foot moved a fraction of an inch.

"See you tomorrow," I said. I kissed her goodbye. Outside on the bike ride to the Nature Center, I noted that the dogwoods had finally decided to bloom. Pink fluttered down onto the pale pavement below, the whir of my tires stirring the petals. As rubber hit concrete, tiny ballet slippers danced and twirled around me. Spring's version of snow burst with vibrant life, in contrast to the world in which I'd let Gran become trapped. Sterile. Empty. Blank.

I hoisted my bike onto the Nature Center rack. I directed my breath out toward the path to the hospital. *Feel the flowers*, I thought at Gran. *They are blooming for you. I'll bring some live color for your room, nurses' orders be damned.*

A few rogue petals in Gran's hand, at least. Her roommate suffered from allergies. I didn't want to cause her to suffer as well. But a few soft, gentle reminders of her wood and pond couldn't hurt.

Even if gathering them for her poked at the most raw places inside of me.

FIELD JOURNAL ENTRY
MAY 20

On Monday morning, Sophie and I sat in her backyard staring at a rock slab. She lived on the opposite side of the "mountain" as everyone called it (it was more like a hill). Since the leaves were still filling in (Pennsylvania winter had hung on like a mofo this year), you could still see the edge of Grandview Cemetery from her porch. Stone angels peeked from between white birch trees, ghosts on top of ghosts. Morning glinted from budding ivory branches, casting a glow year-round, until spring fully birthed green again. All species loved to perch on those jutting twigs and chiseled faces. I always wondered if the graves felt the indignity of being pooped on regularly. Or maybe it just served as a reminder that no matter what, life goes on.

"You can tell a lot about a bird by its wings," I said, clicking shots as I waited for Sophie to take out the trash.

"Oh?" Sophie said.

"Yeah. Long wings indicate bodies built to endure long migrations. Shorter wings aren't bad or anything, though. You couldn't expect a goshawk to chase prey through tight squeezes with the wingspan of a wandering albatross, you know?"

Sophie smiled. "No. I guess not."

"They have this metal sculpture at the Nature Center where you can trace the movement of wings. It's an incredible amount of effort. They don't just flap. It's like this crazy, curvy motion." I inelegantly tried to imitate it for her. "Risa brought it in a couple of months ago. It had been abandoned by the Science Museum."

She stopped midstride to stare at me.

"Okay, so I suck as a bird. I'll never fly," I said.

"You can't get mad that you make a terrible bird. You are a great human. It'd be unfair to the rest of us if you could be both. And funny how the person bringing this sculpture is also the same who disconnected the complicated timer thing to your setup last year, no? Knocked down the camera? So you didn't shoot the diamond-backed parakeet getting it on or whatever."

"It was a ruby-throated hummingbird breeding. You were close." I rolled my eyes. "It was a long shot. And *someone* screwed it up, that's for sure. And I don't know who else would do it. But she's being nice-ish now."

"I will have to readjust my feelings of hate on your behalf," she said.

"Eh. Maybe later," I said.

"Fair enough."

"Come on. We gotta go or we are going to be late. I need to see the Monday birders."

"Wouldn't want to miss them," said Sophie.

I got to co-op and found Risa standing with the Monday birderwalkers huddled in a clump on the boardwalk, binoculars pondward. I tentatively moved toward them, gazing out in the direction they faced. Sitting on half-submerged logs were two black birds, regal necks stretched, wings unfurled to the rising glow in the east. I lifted my binoculars to my eyes to get a better look. The cormorants were back.

"Why do they do that, Mom?" asked Karen (who I thought was only a Tuesday regular).

"To dry their wings, honey. Their bodies don't wick away moisture, so they have to stand in the sun."

"You have to wonder why nature would make a bird with less oil on their feathers. Shedding water is a dead useful adaptation. These guys have to take time out of their day so they don't freeze or something. Better to be a duck," said Louise.

"Cormorants were once thought to be the messengers of the devil," I said.

Thanks to Gran for that knowledge, though Warbley had included it in his latest deluxe field guild.

"No!" said Karen and her mom together.

"Some people said the devil himself took the form of a cormorant to spy on Adam and Eve in the Garden of Eden."

"I thought a snake did that," said Richard.

"Maybe they worked together," I said.

"Cool!" said Karen.

"What are you doing here?" I said to Karen and her mom. A kid named Owen was there, too. "I thought you were my Tuesday birders." I threw an accusing look at Risa.

"Risa emailed all of us to help find your bird. We—" started Karen's mom, but she was interrupted by a hollow echo from the woods. The birders turned in unison toward the trees.

"I think—" I started.

"Shhhh," all of them breathed as one.

We stood, listening. Two tones, then the song.

"Mockingbird," whispered Richard.

"What is it mocking? That's something else," said Louise.

From the far edge of the pond, something answered with the same strange call. We pivoted on the wood toward the other bird, binoculars up. I caught feathers rising.

"*Merde*," Richard said. Gran said that sometimes. I'm pretty sure it was a bad word in another language.

"Did anyone get a look at it?"

"It was too fast."

"Nope," said Owen.

The first bird called again.

"To the woods, people," said Richard.

We followed him on the well-worn path and on the overgrown side trails. My bird trilled and called and sang from the ground layer hedgerows and from a midstory feeder obscured by a fence and most often from the canopy layer *just* out of sight. That avian asshole knew how to avoid detection. It was as if he and his buddies were hanging out in a ninjutsu dojo somewhere among the highest branches.

"This is a new one," said Louise. "It only took a day to get a picture of the Spix's macaws in Brazil. You'd think this thing were hiding for its life."

"To be fair, the guide told us where their nest was," said Richard.

"True," said Louise.

"Are Spix's macaws really that blue in person?" said Karen.

"That they are! And let me tell you about the black stilt we saw . . ."

"On a nature preserve," said Richard. "So it doesn't count . . ."

"We are in a nature preserve right now, Rich," said Louise. "If the bird shows up, it counts on the life list."

Mystery bird cried quietly this time, signaling that it had tired of us all. The usual talk of sparrows resumed.

"Dang it," I said.

"So close," said Owen.

"Let's go over by the gate. They sounded like they were last over there," said Karen.

The gate revealed no birds, mystery or otherwise.

What it did have, though, were four men in business suits simultaneously typing into their phones. It was the oddest species I'd seen in a while there in the habitat.

"Do you think they are texting each other?" I said to Risa.

She studied them. "Birding is more of a flannel-and-denim situation, in my opinion. These guys are wearing Armani with wool overcoats. And is that one wearing a silk scarf? How is he not dying of heatstroke?"

"Does Armani make flannel?" I said.

"I'll be sure to look that up for you when I get home," she said.

The men separated and took pictures of the pond, the woods, the fields past the fence, and gate. One disappeared into the garden off the boardwalk entrance. The birders watched them curiously. Karen took out her binoculars and focused them on one man's phone.

"I'm investigating his call, Mama! Get it?" She giggled.

"I'm glad you are instructing her in the way of bird puns," I said to her mom.

"I believe they are in the curriculum for the Shunksville chapter of the Audubon Society," she said.

"Hi there," Richard said to one of the men when they passed us. "What brings you out today?"

"Hello! Oh, just out here doing some surveying work for the city."

Richard eyed him. "Without equipment?" he said.

The man laughed. "This is an informal visit. We just want to get a sense of this place. It's on the docket for development."

Louise stood blinking at wool-coat guy, as if he'd just suggested she eat a cormorant. "What is on what docket, now?"

"Shunksville and Martintown. You know, the school district? It's been in the news?"

We all stared at him.

He stared back. "They are building new schools. We're here checking out the possible sites for the new campus. I'm sure there are notices up."

There weren't. Notices. I knew every inch of the pond and wood area. Risa frowned at me.

"And they are putting it . . . what?" Louise asked again.

"This is the site for the new campus. A lower and upper elementary school, and a junior and senior high. Four buildings, and a separate recreation/performance space. It'll be glorious."

"What is?" said Karen's mom.

"This place," he said.

The man began to look uncomfortable. I didn't know if it was the conversation or his ridiculous wool coat in the blazing sun.

"The fields here, part of the woods. The wetlands. The last of the houses in the zone will probably be sold to the city soon. So, hello, new school! You'll probably get to go there, little lady," the man said to Karen.

"I'm homeschooled," she said.

"This is conservation land," said Richard.

"Yes," the man said slowly, looking Richard up and down, like he was just figuring out this plan was news to all of us. "Only because the family who owned it wanted it to be. They donated it to the city, but the will didn't specify the use of the land in perpetuity. It's been rezoned. The preserve is now just a suggestion."

"Half a dozen species use this as a migratory stop," said Owen. "Isn't it famous for it?"

"There's a festival every year," said Risa.

The man looked at his phone, clearly over the conversation.

"Well, there's a nice park downtown. I'm sure everyone

can have it there until the new school is built." He turned his back to us and practically ran to join his friend in the garden.

"Wow," said Owen. "This is . . . bad?"

"It doesn't seem like it can be true," said Louise. "Wouldn't we have heard about it?"

"There were town meetings about the new school. This site wasn't mentioned," said Karen's mom.

"Gran's house!" I realized suddenly. "The houses the city wanted to buy. One of those was Gran's house!"

"I didn't know that was on the market," said Louise.

"It wasn't! It isn't." At least, I didn't think it was . . . yet. "People came to Mom. People came to Gran first, I remember. But she wouldn't . . . Mom had to . . . Gran's care is super expensive . . . but as far as I know, it's not sold yet."

Richard nodded. "It would make sense," he said gently. "I wouldn't blame her. But I'm going to do some digging. I feel like conservation land can't be used for development. Plus, building on wetlands is a terrible idea. I remember when Sarig Pond and Jenkins Wood were developed. I was in high school and one of the steel families wanted to give back to the city. You can't just destroy something that has been part of the community for sixty years. And so important to the birds, too." Richard shook his head in disgust. "Louise, let's take a trip into town today."

The two of them walked toward the small parking lot deep in conversation.

"Never piss off birders," Risa said. "They'll end you."

"Let's spy on those guys," I said to her. Thoughts of winding myself around Mom's legs and begging her to keep

Gran's house floated through my brain as my likely evening activity.

Of course, the thought that I could have saved Gran and kept any of this from happening also floated through my brain. That we could lose her, her home, *and* her woods . . . and that it would be all my fault . . . was almost too much.

"Okay," Risa said.

We followed Team Armani around the boardwalk. Nuthatches (male and female) and cardinals (female) hopped above us, and I couldn't help but watch flashes of dull yellow and red and gray skitter the leaves. Watching the men proved a whole lot less interesting. They mostly just texted. I lifted my camera from around my neck and took some pictures of the men.

"Guess Monday bird walking turned into a bust," I said to Risa.

She frowned. "Yeah."

We walked back to the Nature Center, where Jerry had just arrived. We filled him in on the details of the Armani Men.

"Oh, those guys," he said. "Yeah, they came here before. Said the land was for sale, or belonged to somebody who was gonna build on it. Something. Fancy guys like that come around sometimes. It's all talk."

"Are you sure about that?" said Risa.

"Pond's still here, isn't it?" He shrugged and left to check the public bathrooms.

Risa watched him uneasily.

"I get a weird vibe from those guys," she said. "Like they know something. That this isn't something that *might* happen. They look all business."

"Yeah," I said.

I texted Sophie and she said she was doing sudoku because her co-op boss was out sick. I biked to Gran's after lunch, since there wasn't a lot of point in going back to school.

There was a car in her driveway. My stomach dropped. I went up onto the front porch. The chair and little table that normally stood there were gone, as was Gran's mailbox. The mailbox was particularly alarming because the extra key was usually hidden behind it.

I opened the screen to try the doorknob, but it swung open.

"Oh! Hello!" The man who'd been at Gran's house with Mom before stood in front of me. "Lori, right?"

"Laurel," I murmured, straining my neck to look behind him. "I'm just here to get some books."

"Oh, everything's been moved. Thought it wasn't going to be till this evening, but the company had an opening. Your mom knows where it ended up."

"Wait, what?"

"I think she specifically said the books were going to your place. Some of it went to your grandmother's new place." His voice caught at the word "place," as if he knew it were a lie. Gran hadn't moved to a cool new apartment across town. She was trapped inside her body fed by tubes, inside a room that reeked of loneliness.

"What about her furniture?" I said. "Why are you here?"

"Oh. Didn't your mother tell you? You should probably talk to her."

"Talk to her about what? What is going on?"

"House is just about ready to sell. I'm just doing the final walk-through."

I stared at him. "So it hasn't sold yet?" I asked.

"No," he said.

My heart lifted. There was still time.

I went out back to check on Gran's garden. It looked pretty decent, though I would need to weed it this weekend. The fucking asshole squirrels had knocked down the hummingbird feeder again. I made a note to fix that as well.

I made dinner and thankfully Mom didn't have a date. I'd have to play it cool if I was going to convince her not to sell.

I spooned chili into a bowl for her after she'd changed out of her work clothes.

"Hey, Mom. So. Funny thing. There was this man at Gran's house today. And not much else, actually. Everything was gone. He seemed to indicate you hadn't decided to sell it yet. And so, I was thinking . . ."

"I'm going to sell, baby."

I stared at her. Her lip quivered a tiny bit.

"No. See. Here's the thing. The city has this crazy idea about putting some kind of new school there and we can't let that happen. So we can't sell. It's a matter of life and death and birds, Mom. Oh my god, the birds . . ."

"Laurel," Mom said quietly. "I have to do it. The sale of that house will take care of Gran for years. Even if she needs . . . whatever."

"No! Listen! Migration season is in a few months! And . . ."

"Laurel, you can find another job next summer. Or you'll be getting ready for college anyway." Mom sighed. Dark rings bagged under her eyes and a few more silver strands shone in the florescent lights than I remembered. "I don't want you to have to worry about this."

My optimism at talking her out of this plan faded slightly.

"Does Gran know?"

"I told her."

I smiled hopefully.

"No. She didn't react, Laurel."

I smiled harder. "Mom, maybe we can rent the house out like an Airbnb. Make money from it! People come here for the birds in the summer, and the leaf peepers in the fall. It's an investment! And I will have a ton of free time with no school, so I. Could. Make. This. Work." I balled up my fist and punched it into my hand with every word.

"This is my fault, Laurel. I should have looked out for her, not have her look out for me. I'm a grown woman. I should have been there for her. I should be there for you. This is what has to happen."

I said nothing but felt a pang in my side. Mom blamed herself, but it wasn't her fault at all.

"We have each other, sweetie. Okay? We'll get through this."

The pang grew to an angry stab.

"I have to find Gran's bird," I said.

I had hit the right thing to say in that moment by accident. Mom patted my leg. "That's my girl. You worry about your birds, and your pictures. I'll worry about everything else."

"Listen . . . ," I started. But Mom's phone rang and she answered using her ChadBradChetBret voice, so I knew I wouldn't be getting her attention back any time soon.

"The bird is trying to tell me something," I said weakly. "Maybe it is actually Gran." My words hopped up splintered

bark and hid in the wide, leafy branches that grew in the distance between Mom and me. "It's my fault she's in the coma, and she's trying to tell me how to get her to wake up. This might be the only way."

The sound of the truth was lost in the breeze from the open window.

FIELD JOURNAL ENTRY
MAY 21
NOTABLE LOCATION: SARIG POND
LIFE LIST ENTRY 3,285: BLACK-BACKED ORIOLE

The unschoolers were on their spring unbreak, so I should have been happy. But Jerry knew how to end joy pretty effectively.

"The boys are coming today," he said.

"What boys?" I said, hoping that maybe a new toddler group had formed and I hadn't heard.

"Them kids from Fogton. The other co-ops. You know."

I forced my face to emote joy. "Sure, Jerry, no problem." Inwardly I groaned. The nature dude bros from Fogton Prep were the worst. They could be the lifeguards of the River Styx—bronzed, beautiful, but ultimately awful. They were the anti–Eagle Scouts.

What would that be? Piranha Scouts? A troop of bottom-dwellers? No. That sullied several perfectly honorable carnivorous fish.

Damn Birdie Bros. Birders who hated sitting. Hated waiting. They abandoned nature after warbler migration season and I was surprised to see them back for the summer birds they'd grown tired of years past.

I stood, waiting for the Mercedes SUV to pull up (because it was always a Mercedes SUV that carried them), and sure enough it did, fifteen minutes late. Four statues of boys emerged, their hair wavy and golden as fuck in the spring sunshine.

Goddamn, did it annoy me.

"Good morning, gentlemen," I said. "Are you looking for anything in particular today?"

One of them looked me up and down. "What are you offering?" He smirked.

Oh, that I had talons to deal with these morons. I smiled stiffly, hoping that if I ignored the flawed courtship ritual he would give up.

"There were several nests on the last count. Lots of rare-ish sightings."

Their leader, Greg, grinned at me. ~~Bottom-dweller~~ Asshole that he was, he had a camera that was worth at least five thousand dollars and had placed in the *Fauna* shoot more than once. He knew his shit.

"Got a text that a noob spotted a black-backed oriole here today," Greg said.

"What?" I said. There was no way. "On the rare bird alerts?"

"Nope, I have special sources," he said.

"Where?" I asked, mystified.

"I was hoping you could tell me. First sighting was on Sunday. Heard there might even be a nest."

"A nest?" All I could do was repeat what this kid was

saying to me. A fucking black-backed oriole right here in my (well, Gran's at least) backyard and I hadn't even heard about it? And to have a Birdie Bro be the one to tell me served as the ultimate insult. "Wait, did you hear the call? What does it sound like?" So help me if Greg uncovered Gran's bird. Still, discovery often comes from unexpected sources, and I needed the help.

Plus a black-backed oriole would be one for the life list and a total Gran bird to inhabit.

"Nope," he said.

"Well, boys, let's go find it," I said. "I know six places to start looking." The other three groaned. I think at least one of them was also named Greg. Maybe they all were; I couldn't tell the other Birdie Bros apart. They didn't like bird watching if it wasn't some sort of adventure vacation.

We all crept around the pond and checked the nests I knew of. Robin, robin, goldfinch, red-breasted nuthatch, unknown. We stopped at the last one and stared up at a dim outline of tiny forked sticks just reaching over a branch.

Gran? I thought at it. *You there?*

Something made a tiny, strangled sound high above.

Nope. Not Gran.

An onyx shape hopped onto the branch and Greg and I gasped. A white patch splashed over wings like a paintbrush drawn over canvas. A bright yellow-yellow-orange breast practically gleamed. Its deft, beady eye twitched over us down below. It seemed to know we weren't a threat, with our binoculars and overly showy camera equipment. Tiny sounds demanded attention behind the oriole. Mama bird turned her attention to the crew apparently inhabiting the nest.

"Holy fuckballs," I said.

"Right?" said Greg. "Where is that thing from? Mexico? What is it doing up here?"

"No clue," I said. I stared through the binos watching an occasional tail feather poke out of the nest. Not only was there one bird; there was a fucking nest. This was up there with the hummingbird that I tried to photograph last year. The Nature Center had a feeder and I rigged up this whole time-lapse thing to capture it. Hummingbirds move so fast that my pictures were, of course, blurred. But someone (Risa) messed with my timer and knocked down my setup. Asshole Greg ended up getting the best picture of it over at Stackhouse Park (our rival nature sanctuary) and got second place with *Fauna*. Risa got the only shot of it at Jenkins Wood, but didn't place.

Now Greg the tool was doing it again, coming to *my* house and finding a rare bird.

Fucking Birdie Bros.

I texted Risa.

You are not going to believe this, I texted. *There's a black-backed oriole!*

Oh, yeah, she said.

You knew?

Yeah, they've been there for a week or so.

OMG, I texted. I narrowed my eyes at my phone. Risa knew this whole time. Of course.

I'm sorry, I thought you knew, she wrote back.

Sure she did.

After my shift ended, I went to visit Gran. Mom and I had set up some stuff from her cabin on her side of the room. Her roommate also had new pictures up all around her. It made me feel better that whoever this woman was, she was loved. Maybe all that love would rub off on both her and Gran and they'd wake up.

"Hope no one is selling your house, either," I said to her. No reaction.

"Gran, you are not going to believe this . . ." I launched into my oriole tale. I noticed distinct finger twitching.

"I know, right!" I said to Gran, grinning. This had to be real. "Still working on the mystery call. Oriole's have a distinct, brash sound. Not like our bird. So weird," I said.

Nothing.

"But you'll always wait for me, Gran, right? I swear I'm working on it," I said.

Finger twitch.

I marked that as a success.

FIELD JOURNAL ENTRY
MAY 22

"Don't move," I said to the snow goose who sat looking skeptically at Risa and me.

"One of these guys haven't been here in at least two years," she said.

"Probably three," I said.

Both of us pointed our cameras. The snow goose waddled around and took flight out across the pond.

"You get him? You get him?" one of our Classic Friendly Birders called from across the pond.

"Don't think so, you?" called Risa.

"Maybe one good shot."

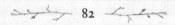

82

"Mother flocker," I said. Three years ago, I'd been there for the snow goose, too. Gran had gotten a shot, of course.

"*Fauna* had a snow goose in issues fifteen, one hundred nine, and two hundred seventy," said Risa. "It wouldn't have won anyway."

"Sour grapes," I said.

"Tasty, tasty sour grapes," she agreed.

The sounds of the Classic Friendly Birders (noted by their desire to share birding with everyone, their lack of competitiveness, and their frequent use of portable birding chairs) were replaced by the deep barking of boys.

"Heron help me," I said. "Birdie Bros."

"Heron help us all," said Risa. "I'd rather clean toilets than deal with them." Risa jogged off down the path, her camera cradled against her snug turquoise shirt that pulled just above her waistband as she ran.

I had to agree with her. Unfortunately, watching Risa run had strangely caused my own faculties to briefly leave. This gave the barkers enough time to cross my path when I'd recovered enough to head back toward the Nature Center.

"Heeeeey," said one of the Bros. "You get the snow goose?"

"Yes. Totally. Several amazing pictures," I lied.

"Seriously? Let me see."

"No. Top secret, I'm afraid. Sorry, boys." I hurried away from them. If they tried to touch my camera without my consent, I would need to open up a can of whooping crane on them.

"Bet she didn't," one of them said. "Whatever. At least Greg got it. Maybe Connor."

Of course Greg got it.

Back at the Center, Risa hid herself among the toilets, and I busied myself with Karen and her crew so that I didn't have to deal with anyone else, but the Bros never came back to the Center. I thought they might, just to gloat, but they were probably already editing their finds to keep in their *Fauna* entry files.

I wished for the hundredth time that Gran were around. She was my go-to artistic reassurance. I could call Sophie, too. But she needed well-spaced *Fauna* angst.

I watched Risa emerge from bathroom duty. She knelt by the cabinets to put away the cleaning supplies. Her shirt did the thing again, exposing the smooth tan skin of her back.

Mother flocker, what was getting into me? I shrugged to myself. Chalk it up to the missed snow goose and *Fauna* pressure from the bros. Damn snow geese, letting the Birdie Bros get a picture. And damned sort-of-enemy Risa and her occasional Warbley quotations and toned back causing inexplicable distraction.

Nature could be so unjust.

FIELD JOURNAL ENTRY
MAY 24
NOTABLE LOCATION: ST. BASIL'S EPISCOPAL
CHURCH, EARLY MORNING.
WHY ARE MORNINGS SO EARLY?

Louise wielded her dry erase marker like an expert swordswoman, deftly marking up an aged whiteboard. She'd called us all last night and instructed us to assemble at the break of day. Richard had new info about the threats to the nature reserve.

"And as you recall, those vigilante folks who tried to mess with the land in Oregon were taken down by birders. This is the same thing," Richard said to the group assembled, his face growing redder with each word Louise recorded.

"A militia in Oregon occupied the national wildlife refuge and birders vowed to work to protect that amazing resource," said Louise. "Here we have local government wanting land with no exact owner. It's not quite identical."

"Fine. Whatever. Local government, local militia, it's all the same to the birds and the land. The birds need it, and someone wants to take it."

"True," said Louise.

"I thought someone donated the land," said Karen's mom (who I just now learned was named Lynn. Probably could have asked her that about two years ago).

"Left it in his will," said Bob (another bird-watcher).

"To the city, just to use as a park and nothing else," said Jane (also another bird-watcher, who was around my age).

"I looked into that," said Richard. "And those suits we met there a couple of days ago were right. The land was bequeathed to the city, and the family said it'd be great if it were a park or something. But it wasn't *explicit*. It's all public record. So the city can basically do what it wants."

"That's just wrong!" said Karen. She looked up from her Audubon Society coloring book.

"Indeed." Richard sighed. "The new school isn't a given. If you ask me, there's something hinky going on here."

"Hinky?" said Owen.

"Underhanded. Low-down. No good. Dirty."

"Got it," said Owen.

"Can we chain ourselves to trees or something?" said Risa. In spite of myself, I eyed her long, long legs and her hair that she'd altered to become more crested partridge. Damn it all, brunette worked for her. And why was she so *tall*?

Laurel. Dude. *Chill*, I told myself. Birds mate in spring, not Laurels. I mean, not that I'd mated at all, ever. Do teenage birds commit? Are there technically teenage birds?

I made a mental note to ask Louise about bird puberty later.

I made another mental note to do no such thing, ever.

Risa was still talking. "Or we could gather signatures or attend the meetings. This place is special to so many people. They can put a new school any old place."

"I think the school board is the place to start," said Richard. "They are the primary source of the hinky, from what I can understand. People with connections wanting to give contracts to their friends. Cheap land keeps costs down."

"These are wetlands they're talking about," said Louise. "Building on them is a bad idea. There would be flooding and structural concerns and who knows what else. Bad, bad, bad."

"Cheap, cheap, cheap," said Richard. He grunted and dropped into a folding chair.

"Like a baby bird says," said Karen.

Richard smiled at her.

"We can get Shunksville Community College in on this," said Risa. "There is a professor there who studies the bats who used to live in the abandoned carriage house until they moved over here. I don't think they are endangered, exactly, but something is up with them. There was an article in the *Shunksville Democrat* a while back. And the bio students study the foxes and voles and groundhogs."

"And the squirrels," said Karen. "They all have little earrings on. That's how you know they have been studied," she said.

Risa nodded. "Exactly. And the dragonflies that live on the pond eat mosquitos and keep us all from dying from equine encephalitis or some other horrible crap."

The birders all enthusiastically agreed, even the quiet knitters in the back, who never spoke and I kept forgetting were there. Gran had introduced these ladies to me years ago, but I always thought of them as "Cast On, Cast Off, and Knit," and I'm pretty sure the fourth woman in their group actually was named Purl (probably spelled Pearl, but I liked it better the other way in my head).

The meeting broke up after that. Owen, Karen, and her mom (Lynn!) moved over to see Richard, so I casually tripped over a garbage can toward Risa.

"How's your grandma doing? She'd be all over this," she said.

"Same," I said.

"Sucks," said Risa. She and I looked into each other's eyes for a second. "Well, I should go. Garbage duty today," she said.

It'd be two hours before the Nature Center would open, but okay. Guess the girl loved her some clean pond and woods. Or maybe she knew about other rare nests she wanted to photograph before I could get a chance.

Since there was so much time before my last day of school,

I stopped at Gran's empty house on the way there. I let myself into the warm, empty rooms. I stared into the fireplace, willing flames to spring up from the dust. But only the clanging baseboards emitted occasional heat. Gran used to chop her own firewood, even though Mom was always on her to just buy it from the grocery store. When the temperature dropped too far into winter to use the fire pit, we'd shove long-handled metal sandwich makers into the coals right here and toast jam-filled mountain pies. Occasionally I could even score a pizza version. My mouth watered at the memory. It tasted suspiciously salty—like tears.

Something struck me, standing there with only memories for furniture. This house was like Gran. Both stood empty and in danger of being lost right now, but both still existed and thus could be saved. I had to try harder because Gran would always wait for me. The *whole world* should stop on its axis and freaking wait. The tides should cooperate and not obliterate coastal towns, the sun would wait patiently to set or rise or whatever depending on where you were. Then fucking towns wouldn't try to bogart wildlife reserves or homes while personal tragedies unfolded in people's lives.

Although if that were the case, the world might never spin. The tide might never come in. And the sun might never rise or set again.

Stupid life.

How did I stop it? I couldn't. So, if the going was going to get tough, the tough was going to have to fucking find something to save everything. I mean, there was a black-backed oriole in a tree in Jenkins Wood. That at least sounded promising. If Gran had become a rare species who lived in

Jenkins Wood, she could be protected by the government or something. Her house, her woods, her pond—saved.

Well played, Gran.

All I needed to do was figure out where she was and then convince everyone of these essential truths.

It'd be a piece of cake!

Or at least a pile of birdseed. Same thing, really.

FIELD JOURNAL ENTRY
MAY 27

School had officially let out, and even though I hadn't had to really go to class for months, it was still awesome. Though everything else was kind of going wrong.

"So you get paid more now?" Sophie asked.

"Yes. There is a summer work grant that kicks in with a small stipend. So it will keep me in digital prints and ice cream. But we will have to strategically plan what movies we want to see because my budget might afford about one a month."

"You could babysit with me."

"No thanks. I almost let the Williams kid throw himself into the wetlands when I filled in for you last time," I said.

"Almost. Babysitting by its very nature is 'almost' letting the kid hurt himself. You got him to eat lunch, too! You are a natural," said Sophie.

"No. Bring the kids to the Nature Center and I'll read to them for story hour. Besides, there are other perks. I can scout shots for the *Fauna* competition. And Jerry gives me his high-end birdseed and stuff. I have word that next month there is fancy woodpecker suet coming my way."

"Wow. Yeah. That sounds like a total bonus." Sophie smirked.

"Whatever." I threw her stuffed rainbow pillow at her head.

She dodged left. "What's going on with the place anyway? Are they really going to develop it?"

I sighed. "I don't know. Sarig Pond and Jenkins Wood have been set aside for birds and wildlife and nature education for as long as anyone can remember. And Richard said the developers he talked to weren't jerks or anything. They were hired to assess the land and told the city it isn't even a great site. Wetlands are terrible for building. But the woods are okay. Their report suggested looking at other sites, but Louise did *even* more digging and found out that some of the city council members are pushing to use the woods because the other sites for the new, merged school district are outside of Shunksville. They want that school *here*."

"Adults," said Sophie, "are dumb."

"Seriously," I said. "*And* it's not like the pond and woods are just expendable. Threatened species of bats live in the abandoned carriage house. Dozens of types of birds use the pond and woods as a migratory stop. We are famous for it! The birds and insects who live here most of the time keep down the mosquito population. Risa also pointed out how many of the college kids from Shunk U study the marmots, and there are like a million Eagle Scouts who do their projects at that place. And then there's Gran's house. Oh my god, fuck me if they rip out the woods." I rolled over and buried my head in a pile of fluff. Sophie had a thing for unicorns.

Sophie lay down next to me and nudged me with her head until I started to laugh and shoved her back.

"Is Risa there this summer?" Sophie asked.

"Oh yes. She's in it for the sweet, sweet cash dollars like me. And the photography, of course," I said.

"And do we hate her currently?"

"No. Not hate. She's been okay. But then she's not. She wears a lot of tank tops these days."

Sophie blinked. "You are noticing her tank tops?"

Heat rose to my face. "I mean. They are clingy."

Sophie looked at me for a moment. "So we like Risa, then? We are not bent on the destruction of her nature photography? And we are happy when she is not wearing much on her chest?"

I shook my head. "We are, at best, neutral about Risa. And her chest." Although, that last bit was less true than the first.

"This could be the beginning of a beautiful, birding love affair," she said. "You and Risa. Or it could be a complete disaster."

"That generally describes most people I meet." I nodded. "But no love affair. Just birding."

"Sure. Whatever you say. I gotta go babysit at the Williams Memorial Day party. Are you sure you don't want to come?"

"I'm sure," I said.

I left Sophie's house and biked over to see Gran. The hospital was slower because of the holiday. Every time I visited her, she looked stretched a little thinner. Like she was being pulled in some sort of tug-of-war between . . . what?

Dreaming and waking, maybe? As Brian Michael Warbley says, "There is little difference between the dreaming and waking soul, if owls screech in both." But Gran lay silent, regardless of where her soul currently hung out.

Maybe it just wore her out, being alive, but not really.

After the hospital, I went to her house. Nothing like a little housework to invigorate the spirit. If Gran wouldn't (or couldn't) move, then I would double up on the business of daily living on her behalf. Maybe a person can't be forced out of a coma by the sheer will of another, but there was no harm in trying.

I found a broom in the corner and idly swept the dust that had gathered out onto the porch. I checked her garden, which, despite being almost entirely neglected, was bursting with color. I watched a female jay and a male titmouse flutter around from fence to grass to spruce to grass again. I envied their purpose. I felt like I just hopped from one place to another. I looked for the bird but couldn't find it. I wanted to save Gran's house and the woods and the pond, but what could I really do there? I wanted to win *Fauna*'s contest, but I had barely taken any pictures recently. I had a hard time focusing without Gran.

I heard the mystery bird in the woods, just outside of Gran's backyard. I didn't even bother to go after it. I went home to my empty house instead.

"At pool with a couple of people from work!" read a note from Mom hanging from the fridge by a magnet. "Come join me!" A couple of people from work undoubtedly included a man. Maybe two; Mom was nothing if not efficient. I just didn't have it in me.

I went to bed instead. I smelled hamburgers from grills

and sweet mowed grass. Summer was here, and with it some of the best birding weather. Gran should be bugging me right this second to be out with her. Instead, I had only the warm breeze that blew in to tousle my hair.

I rolled over and drifted off into a flightless sleep.

FIELD JOURNAL ENTRY
MAY 30

"Read the spider book again," called Karen. She was one of my most loyal Birdscouts, so I did not want to hate her. But a person can only read Eric Carle so many times.

"How about the Charley Harper book, buddy?" I suggested.

"Or the caterpillar book. Or the one about the grouchy ladybug. I love that guy," she said.

"Oooh, do that one!" said Karen's friend Fred.

Damn it, Karen. I sighed.

"Okay, grouchy ladybug it is," I said.

Fortunately, a disheveled-looking Richard burst into the Nature Center. "Laurel, there you are. We need you."

I glanced over at Jerry, who was glaring at a display of feathers that would not stay up on the wall.

"Story time ended fifteen minutes ago," he said. "Birdscout Laurel has to help other nature enthusiasts, my young friends!" he said. He was always kind to kids.

The kids groaned.

"Next story time, I'll do this first. And last. And maybe once in the middle, okay?" Karen pouted but didn't argue. I went outside, where Richard was standing with Risa.

"What's up?" I asked him.

Richard pointed to men in suits walking down the path toward the pond. "The interlopers," he said gravely.

I shoved down a grin at his tone.

"Follow them," he hissed at Risa and me.

Neither one of us thought it wise to argue with him when he was like this.

"Onward," I said to Risa, chucking my thumb toward the retreating suits. We crept behind them, trying to keep our distance. They stopped at one of the outlooks, seemingly gazing at a few black-crowned night herons. Risa gestured for me to follow her off the path.

"What are you doing?" I whispered at her.

"There's no poison ivy here. Just don't step on anything. This is for the greater good," she whispered back.

I waved my arms wildly in protest, but she just kept going without me. Fuck me if Risa was going to single-handedly gather valuable intel *and* probably see a barrow's goldeneye or something. I gingerly ran after her. We ended up in a clump of reeds below the outlook. I nearly fell into the pond as I tried to adjust my footing while stooped low. Risa grabbed my arm to steady me. Her fingers lingered there for a few moments longer than necessary. In spite of the absurd situation, heat crept up from her grasp and spread up my neck. I pushed it to the back of my brain. I had to focus.

"Those are the developer guys," I whispered.

"There's someone else coming," she said.

We crouched lower. A wood duck quacked at us as we accidentally disturbed his hiding place.

"Sorry, sorry," said Risa.

The duck threw us a pissed-off look and took flight.

Voices floated down from overhead.

"Hello there, gentlemen," said one. "Thanks for meeting us here."

"No trouble," another one said. "Good to get out of the office in this weather."

"It's a good spot for a private conversation," a third voice said with a laugh.

"So, what's the word on this place?"

"We are moving forward with the proposal. These woods are actually gorgeous. We are going to suggest using lumber from the trees in the building of the school. That might appease some of the nature freaks." The group laughed.

I shuddered.

"And the surrounding land? There were some zoning concerns."

"Yeah, not a problem. There's three houses along the perimeter. But two are rental properties, and the owners are no longer local. Those can be ours by summer's end. The last house is presenting a small issue, but I'm pretty sure they will sell, too. We have one of our guys ready to press them when we need to move forward."

"Good, good," said the first voice. "And what about the wetlands situation?"

"Well . . ." The voice sounded uncertain. "We have to tell you. Our surveying is clear. If you really want to build on them . . . basically you just shouldn't. It will be prone to flooding. Your foundations could be compromised. Mold could be a problem. There's any number of things . . ."

"And your report reflects that?"

"No," said yet another voice. There had to be at least six men in the group. "The report doesn't say anything right now. I know there are some politics to all of this." The voice paused. "We want you to know that building here is probably a bad idea. It is also an important ecological habitat. And the woods alone aren't big enough for the campus you are proposing, if you really want the merged elementary and junior high here. You will need the pond *and* wetlands. And even if you shouldn't build there, you probably *could*. You could try to plan for these contingencies."

Hawks called above everyone's head, as the men ceased talking. My quads burned. Risa's face looked flushed, like she might take off and peck a few eyes out herself.

"There would be more consulting in the future," someone said slowly. "You gentlemen and your firm would be a great asset to the project. We could probably guarantee you'd have work for at least three years, with generous compensation."

"That's a great offer, Mike. But . . ."

"You should know that there is a lot at stake here for Shunksville. Having the new schools here would create a lot of jobs and bring a lot of attention to a neglected city once known for its coal and steel. You'd be doing a lot of people a lot of good if you could make your report highlight the possibilities here."

"We aren't asking you to lie," said another man. "We'd never ask that. Just make it evident that this is possible, you know?"

"I think we can do that," said the voice.

"Definitely. And it's really only a preliminary study. The

vote on the land isn't until July. Anyone will be able to see it as soon as we file it and bring their concerns to the June or July meetings."

Everyone laughed. Why was that funny? I didn't have much time to think about it because the wood duck returned with two lady friends and all three quacked at us. I tried to shoo them away without giving away our position.

"You have your camera." Risa turned to me and poked at my neck.

"Of course."

"Try to get a picture of these guys."

"The reeds are too thick. And they'll see me if I go up there."

Risa nodded back toward the path. "Don't worry. I have a plan."

I didn't bother to ask what she had thought up because staying hidden sucked more than moving. I (appropriately) waddled up the bank and rolled onto the wooden boardwalk. I shook out my legs until some feeling returned to them and then tried to casually sidle up to the assembled group.

Just then, a furious chorus erupted from the edge of the pond.

"Quackquackquackquack QUACK quackquackquack." A furious fit of green and black and beige burst out of the reeds and veered dangerously close to the assembled suits. The men scattered as I rounded the corner of the boardwalk so my lens was unobscured by trees. I hit the shutter release again and again without paying attention to what I was actually doing. One of the men ran into me.

"Sorry, sir," I said brightly. "I was trying to get a shot of the wood duck. Junior nature photographer competition. *Fauna*, you know? Serious stuff! Be well!" I said.

He looked at me like I had three beaks. He turned back to his friends. I snapped another couple of shots of their faces for good measure. None of the other guys there seemed to register that I had appeared at all. They all muttered to themselves about pointless birds. I was going to argue, when Risa grabbed me by my shoulder and hauled me off, back toward the Nature Center.

"Hey!" I said when we were out of earshot.

"If you or I told them off, we'd blow our cover. We were supposed to get info for Richard. We don't want to tip these guys off to think we heard something."

I rubbed my shoulder. "Okay, okay."

"Sorry about the grabbing," she said more gently. "I was super annoyed at them and super nervous."

"It's okay. I get it. I can't believe you freaked out a bird. Off the path, even! Who are you, Risa Morgan?" I said.

"It was a real duck fit," she agreed.

I grinned. "Oh my god, it was! They *are* pretty bad," I said.

"Did you get their picture?"

I lifted my camera and we stopped to look at the screen.

"I think I have at least one of all of their faces. Those two guys were the same ones from before. I don't know those dude bros, though."

"That one! In the navy suit. Recognize that guy from the news. City council, maybe? The mayor's office? Yes!" She looked at me. "He's the deputy mayor! He's running for mayor in November because the other guy is retiring. Remember he was here last fall when we opened the water fowl exhibit?"

"Yes!" I said. "Well, fuck that asshole. Pretending to care about trumpeter swans! Bet the motherfucker couldn't even tell a mallard from his own ass."

"Right. The *nerve*," said Risa. "I tried to get a recording of them on my phone. I got a little of it, the part that sounded most like a bribe. But I'm pretty sure it's totally illegal to wiretap or reed-tap or whatever. So we can't use it, exactly. But we know they are up to some shady-ass bird shit."

We got back to the Nature Center, where Richard was waiting with Louise.

"We got the stuff," I whispered.

Richard's eyebrows shot up like a macaroni penguin's. "Oh yeah?" he said.

I showed him the pictures and Risa played her recording. The words played surprisingly clear.

"Those *cads*," breathed Louise. "They know it's a bad idea but they want to do it anyway. And what for? Why do they want to use this land specifically?"

"Maybe it's cheap?" said Risa. "Or it belongs to the city already somehow?"

"Maybe this goes deeper," I said. Gran loved detective shows; this seemed like something that might happen on one of them. "Dirty politicians. Money. Corruption. *Murder*."

"Okay, rein it in there, Miss Fisher, master lady detective. Seems rather dramatic for little ol' Shunksville, but not outside the realm of possibility," said Louise. "One of the state reps is from Shunksville, and that guy is in with the governor, who is probably going to run for president one day. I bet all of this is tied together somehow."

"Totally," I agreed.

"I think we need to find out more," said Risa. "They mentioned that stuff would be filed and people could come look at it. There's also going to be meetings. I think it's pretty crappy to do it in June and July, when everyone is one vacation. Hardly anyone goes to those meetings to begin with. No one is going in the summer!"

"Maybe that's their plan, too. Allege to put it out there, no one pays attention, and then they just do what they want."

"Infuriating," said Louise. "Some things never change." She winked at Risa and me. "You girls feel like a little social action?"

"I'm in," I said instantly. Gran would be so proud of me; she loved this kind of shit. She used to walk around topless to protest men or something back in the day. (I probably should have paid more attention to all those stories. Maybe she was protesting sexism? Damn it, I'd have to ask Mom.)

"Protesting is for the birds!" said Risa.

"Indeed it will have to be," said Richard. "Come on, Lu. Let's go see if Jerry knows anything about this." They walked off toward the Nature Center.

"So what do we do?" I said to Risa.

"I already have a plan." Her eyes took on a wicked gleam.

"Are we going off the trail again?" I said.

"Me? Off trail? Always," said Risa. She reached out and squeezed my elbow.

Risa's tank top inched above her cargo shorts a little, but

that was secondary to the fact that heat shot through my arm from where she touched me. There was something about her eco-spying techniques that were so damn attractive. But this was Risa, photography saboteur. Maybe. Why was there heat in the first place? It spread to my face.

I was glad there were no wood ducks around this time. It would have been decidedly anti-conservationist to have incinerated them in the ball of awkward fire that now threatened to consume my face.

FIELD JOURNAL ENTRY
MAY 31

Shunksville City Hall stood across Main Street from Shunksville Central Park. Both had grander names than they deserved. City hall was really only a small, squat building flanked on one side by a construction site and on the other by a Coney Island Hot Dogs. The park was a few benches circled around a tiny stage for concerts and an even tinier fountain in the middle. Risa, Sophie, and I sat on a bench directly across from city hall, watching.

"What are we waiting for, exactly?" Sophie asked. I'd convinced her to come along so I could spend as much time as possible with her before she went off to art camp the next week.

I wiped sweat from the bridge of my nose. Risa had insisted all of us wear sunglasses, "to blend in."

"Anything suspicious," I said.

"Don't we think everyone has gone on vacation?" said Sophie.

"Maybe," said Risa. "But those guys said stuff was going

down over the summer, so I just have a hunch that this is the place to be today."

"Are your hunches generally correct?" said Sophie. I could tell her eyes were boring holes through Risa's head behind her dark shades. I might have gone a little overboard last year with my Risa-surely-sabotaged-me rants. The collision of my two worlds was getting kind of weird.

"I'd say about eighty percent. Eighty-five, maybe," Risa said. She pulled off her glasses and looked through her binoculars at city hall. "Plus Jerry texted me this morning. He said there is going to be a press conference in the park at ten. They usually do press conferences on Friday so that nobody notices them. They get lost over the weekend."

"Yes. That might seem to indicate your hunch is correct. You know, we could just go in. It's a public building," said Sophie. "The binoculars might give away our investigative intentions."

Risa smiled at her. "But I'm a birder." She pointed to the camera slung around my neck. "Another known birder. This is what we do. Bet you have your sketchbooks in that bag. Another non-surprise. No one is going to think we're weird. There's an owl who lives in the bell tower on the church down the street. We'll just say we are trying to get a glimpse of him."

Sophie glanced over at me. I could see her throw me the side-eye behind the sunglasses. She raised her eyebrows and gave me a little kick. I tried to kick her back without attracting Risa's attention.

"Look," Risa said. A van with an antenna sticking out of the roof pulled up to a meter across the street. Another one arrived a few minutes later. A bunch of bored-looking people climbed out and began unloading things from the backs.

"That's Bill Andrews from Channel Four Action Live," I said. "Gran's a fan."

"I think that other lady does the lunchtime news on Channel Eight News. Boy do they look thrilled," said Sophie.

The reporters and their camera crews strolled across the street, in no hurry to broadcast whatever city hall meant to announce in a few minutes. Risa, Sophie, and I stared at a few common grackles who hopped up to us. People on benches often fed them. One hopefully ticked his head in my direction. When he saw that I had nothing to offer, he squawked to his friends and they flew a few benches over to an older couple to try again.

At 10:05 a.m., a few people emerged from city hall. I recognized Edgar Snyder, the mayor, and Michael Ross, the deputy mayor. A woman rolling a small wooden podium across the asphalt followed them, as well as two of the guys who I'd photographed at the pond.

"I think those are the bad guys," I whispered to Sophie.

"Assholes," she mouthed back.

We watched the small crew walk over to the bandstand/gazebo/stage and greet the reporters.

"Might as well go over," said Sophie.

We moved to closer benches. A few other people joined us. Grackles, pigeons, and doves pecked nervously at our feet. They were used to the polka fests and motorcycle rallies where popcorn and pierogi bits dropped for the taking. A few crows called their annoyance overhead. This was probably the worst jamboree they'd seen in town in quite some time. I probably should have thought ahead and brought some seed with me.

The mayor cleared his throat. Cameras swiveled toward him and all of us assembled gave our full attention.

"Welcome to the last press conference of the spring!" he said. "As you know, there have been several developments in the works for Shunksville this year that will really start to take shape over the next few months."

The mayor launched into a twenty-minute explanation about details for the new online billing system for municipal services like water and trash collection, and how all houses would have to have their number clearly visible from the back for recycling pickup. He devoted another twenty minutes to road and alley replacement. Our fellow onlookers began drifting away, and I watched as a cameraman began to nod off with film still seemingly running. Even the grackles got too bored to stay around.

"And I think that's everything. Oh, actually, one more thing." The mayor paused. "My deputy mayor, Michael, has a few words."

Michael stepped up. "As you know, an exciting development is coming to Shunksville. We have been chosen as the new site for the cooperative Greater Martintown-Shunksville-Richburg school district."

A murmur went through the newspeople. This caught their attention.

The deputy cleared his throat. "The cities have been examining sites and have chosen one based on its convenient location, possibilities for expan—"

"Pardon me, sir," said Channel Four's Bill Andrews, "But isn't the merger just Martintown and Shunksville?"

The deputy mayor cleared his throat. "Ah. Well, yes. That has been amended. The exploratory committees have come back with their initial reports, and due to unprecedented growth in the biopharmaceutical industry, it has been decided that it would behoove all of the districts—"

"Isn't Richburg nearly an hour away? They'd put kindergartners on a bus that long? When would they leave in the morning? When would they get home? And the labs are largely centered in Martintown. Why are they building schools in Shunksville?" That was Channel Eight. I thought I remembered her name was Ellie something.

"Obviously there are some details that need to be explained. The next community meeting will be held at its usual time on the second Tuesday of June."

"And doesn't the school board have to vote on the school location?" asked Bill Andrews of Channel Four.

"Yes," said the deputy mayor. Beads of sweat dotted his forehead.

"And when will that be? June?"

"No. July," he said.

"Can the public give input on this proposal?"

"Will other towns weigh in as well?"

"Will other town school boards have a say in this? Will the boards merge?"

"Why is this taking place over the summer?"

"There wasn't much warning for this. Are there larger political implications to a move like this?"

"Are other sites still being considered?"

Four and Eight were taking turns lobbing rapid-fire questions as the deputy mayor looked increasingly uncomfortable. He pulled a little on the stiff collar of his perfectly ironed shirt. I bet he wanted to loosen his tie or possibly just run away.

"Friends." The mayor stepped back to the podium. "These are all great questions that will be hashed out over the next months. The public is welcome to view all proposals in the records department in the interim, and attend the council and board meetings." He stepped away and nodded at the cameras, a clear sign that the press conference was over. The woman stepped behind the podium and wheeled it away after the mayor and deputy.

"Well," said Ellie Something of Channel Eight, looking at Bill Andrews of Channel Four. "That's odd."

"Is it?" said Bill Andrews of Channel Four, shrugging. "It's probably better for Shunksville, right? Having the school here? There will be construction jobs, more faculty and staff jobs. Local vendors will get contracts. More kids and families might attract other businesses."

"Maybe," said Ellie Something of Channel Eight. "Do you know if Em's is open today for lunch?"

"Wait," I said suddenly. "No, Bill Andrews of Channel Four Action Live Team!" Everyone turned to look at me. "There is more to this story."

"I'm sorry, who are you?" he asked.

"Um. A viewer. I was here for bird watching. But that's the point. The new location of the school—he didn't say it. It's in the Nature Center. In Sarig Pond and Jenkins

Wood. They want to build there, take out the pond and the wetlands. That is the new campus."

Ellie Something frowned. "How do you know that?"

I could tell them about our secret recording. About the pictures. The questionable legality made me think twice.

"There are rumors. And I bet if you look into the proposal, you'll see that's where it is. They ended it before anyone could ask. And they didn't answer any of your questions. Don't you think that's weird?" said Risa.

"They work at the Nature Center. People have been coming around looking at the place. Haven't they?" said Sophie.

Risa and I nodded. What would Gran do in this situation? I wondered. She'd probably tackle the newspeople until they listened to her.

"Bill Andrews of Channel Four Action Live Team," I implored him. "Look into this. There is a story here." I turned to Ellie Something. "And would you want Channel Four to scoop Channel Eight?"

"You can just call me Bill," Bill Andrews of Channel Four said. "They seriously want to take out the nature preserve?"

"Yes," Sophie, Risa, and I said at the same time.

Bill shrugged. "I'll look into it," he said.

Ellie Something narrowed her eyes. "So will I," she said. Girlfriend seemed like the competitive type. Good. Let them fight over this story and get it out into the world.

"Thanks," I said. The newspeople gave us curious looks but then started back to their vans.

"They should be going to city hall to look at the proposals." Sophie sighed. "I mean you *told* them."

"Seriously," said Risa.

"Well, we could go to city hall," I said. "We can photo-copy them and send them to Channel Bill and Channel Ellie." I nodded to myself.

Just then, two sharp little bursts of sound erupted from the canopy of park trees.

"Holy shit," I said. "Where was that? Do you see it? It is right here."

"I did!" Risa looked up and raised her binos to her face. "Is this the bird you were looking for the other day with the junco? You were right. That was a weird call. Dang it, where'd he go?"

I pointed my camera into the trees and snapped. The call sounded again from across the park. We broke into a run. We stopped at a maple.

"He's up there," I said, trying to catch my breath.

"I saw him! Sort of. I saw a tail. I think he's gray."

The call sounded, loud and clear, directly above our heads.

"Show yourself, motherfucker" I said. I knew Gran's mes-senger or soul or Patronus or whatever would be pissed I was swearing at it, but maybe it could make this shit just a *little* easier for me.

Guilt gripped my heart and squeezed. Here I was blam-ing Gran for something that was clearly my fault. I took a deep breath to shove the fist down where it couldn't choke. I could do this. I would figure out what Gran was trying to tell me. I could will things okay again.

As if to let me know that I should watch my language in the presence of avian astral projection, the bird sang out once again and then rustled leaves. It took to the sky. I clicked and clicked but only got a blurred speck against the luminous summer sky.

"Goddamn it, motherfucker," I yelled toward it. The old couple on a far bench clucked their tongues at me and I sighed.

"Wow. It's fast."

"Birds usually are." I slumped on her shoulder.

"Okay, so," said Risa. She stopped and looked at Sophie. She frowned and took a step back like we had pushed her. "Um . . . I think it was tufted."

"Wait, what?" I said, straightening up. "What do you mean *tufted*? Like, his head? Had a tuft of feathers? Or his tail? Or both?"

"His head. I totally think your bird has a crest."

"And he was gray? But that would make him a breed of titmouse? A cedar waxwing?"

"I don't know about the gray part. It's so bright."

"Yeah," I said. "Fuck."

"Fuck," Risa agreed.

"But crested helps, right?" said Sophie. "Doesn't that narrow it down a little bit?"

"It could. If it's actually crested," I said.

"I stand by that. It's the gray part I'm not sure about." Risa sniffed. "Get any pictures, Laurel?"

I looked at the viewscreen on my camera. "No. Maybe there's a tuft there. But then maybe this is part of the tree. The stupid leaves block anything helpful. The sky pictures just make him a UFO." Sophie put her arm around me. It would be hard having her gone for the rest of the summer.

"He *was* tufted," Risa said again. "Why don't you believe me?"

"It's not that I don't believe he might be," I said. "I think Gran . . . I mean . . . it's not what I'd think she'd . . ."

"But like you said it's bright," said Sophie to Risa.

"Sure. Right," Risa said. She tilted her head at me curiously.

I kept trying to breathe. I could make this okay. I could make this okay. I could figure out the tufted (?!?) bird. Sophie put a hand on my shoulder.

"Do you need—" Risa stopped. She raised an eyebrow at Sophie. "Actually, I should get going. I have stuff to do."

"Don't you want to go to city hall to see their proposal?" I said, getting ahold of myself.

"Um. I'll leave you to it?" she said. She didn't sound sure. But she looked from Sophie to me and back again and then turned away.

"Oh. Okay?" I said as Risa walked in the opposite direction toward the library.

"What was that about?" I said to Sophie. "Was it because I questioned her bird identification powers? I wasn't trying to be a jerk."

Sophie shrugged. "Who knows? Maybe she really did have something else she had to do."

"I guess."

"Let's go to city hall ourselves."

"Good plan. I don't want Bill Andrews of Channel Four Action Live to forget about us," I said.

Sophie and I walked up to the information desk and who should be sitting there but Birdie Bro in chief, Greg.

"Oh, hi, Greg."

"Hey, Laura. How can I help you?"

"Laurel. My name is Laurel. Same as it's been for the last decade we've been speaking to one another. And we are here to see the proposal for the combined school district. Or the plans for developing the school site. Or whatever."

Greg raised an eyebrow. "Which is it?"

"Which is what?" said Sophie.

"What do you want to see? Do you want to see the merger plans? Or the site specs? Or any of the other fifteen reports related to it."

"Um. How about all of them?" I said.

"Okay." He pointed. "You will need to fill out a form for each of the files that you want to request. I'll need the gold-enrod copy. You can keep the green for your records. There is a three-dollar fee per request. Each will be available in two to four operating business days. But this window is only open twice a week in the summer."

"Are you kidding me?" I said.

"What?" he said.

"I have to fill out one form per report? And I have to *pay* to see them?"

"Technically the reports are free. But it takes clerical time to pull them, refile them, et cetera."

"Aren't you a volunteer? Why does it cost money? You work for free." I knew the bros had private school service hours to work in the summer to make them More Responsible Citizens.

"That's beside the point," he said. "This is the policy."

"Greg. Buddy. They are trying to tear down the woods

and wetlands. Don't you know that? You work here. Surely you heard that." He looked surprised at that, but I figured appealing to the illusion that he had some sort of power and privilege might make him more friendly. "The birds. The nature. Could you do me a solid and just get a couple of the reports? I'll look at them right here and give them back." I had wanted to make copies, but it would make sense just to take pictures with my phone. "Dude. Think of the herons. Think of *Fauna*. Shunksville will lose its renown as a migratory site!"

He hesitated. I thought I got him with that last one. "Nope. Sorry. Rules are rules. I'll get in trouble. But I'm open for another half hour, so if you fill this out, maybe I can get you something."

"A half an hour? Then when are you open again?"

"Wednesday."

"How are people supposed to look at these reports if you can only get them once every other month for a million dollars?" said Sophie.

"Don't get hysterical, ladies. It's just the way it is. A few bucks and a few days have never seemed to bother anyone else."

"Goddamn it, don't you care about the pond?" I said.

Greg opened his mouth, but I didn't want to hear whatever he had to say. "Forget it. I have the form. I'll fill it out." I grabbed one of the carbon copy sheets from a tray by Greg's window. Sophie and I went to two spectacularly uncomfortable orange plastic chairs near the door.

"These chairs smell like puke," observed Sophie.

"This whole process smells like puke," I said. I scribbled in my name, address, phone number, and all of the other irrelevant information to my purpose for being there. "Remind me to register to vote as soon as humanly possible after I turn eighteen. And possibly run for public office. This is shit." I ran over to Greg's station. He was reading a comic book with his feet up on the desk.

"It costs three dollars to pull you away from *X-Men*," I said.

"I'll waive the fee this time. I have the authority to do that." He smirked. He took my form. "You didn't say what form you want," he said.

"Do you know what one I want?"

He thought for a second. "Well. That depends where you want to start. Probably the most helpful might be the sites survey? But there's one for each place. Maybe the joint school district proposal, too. But I don't know the report numbers. You'll need those."

"Well, how do I get them, Greg?" I said.

Fuck, did this kid have a future in bureaucracy.

"They'd be in the online database. Eventually. If they were filed within the last week or two, those won't be online yet."

A wall clock over Greg's window loudly ticked seconds of my life toward Greg closing at noon.

"Goddamn it, Greg. I'm trying to save fucking birds."

"You know, I hear that now. I do. But the file room is huge and packed. I hate it. I only know how to look stuff up by the numbers."

"Do you know how to navigate the site where these numbers are?" Sophie calmly chimed in.

"Kind of. It's not a great interface." Greg leaned toward

the screen in front of him and typed something on his keyboard. "Okay. I went by date range, because you probably want recent documents. There are six. Two have to do with the new pipes that everyone will have to pay to hook up."

"Maybe I should tell my boy Bill Andrews of Action Live about that, too," I said to Sophie.

"There are two new ones. One on record from Martintown about school site availability. One from here about the proposed school district merger. Which one do you want me to pull?"

"Can you do both?"

"I'm off the clock in ten."

"Damn it, Greg . . ."

"We'll take the merger one. Thanks," said Sophie.

"564199b," Greg said, pointing to the form.

I wrote the number in the little boxes for him. He ripped off the green sheet and handed it to me.

"Be right back," he said. He disappeared behind a dark wooden door and reemerged a few minutes later. "You have five minutes," he said.

I sighed and took the folder he held out in front of him. I got out my phone and took pictures of all twenty pages. Sophie took them, too, just for good measure.

I handed the folder back at 11:59 a.m. "Thanks," I said. He nodded.

"And you'll be back on Wednesday?"

"No. I'm only Friday. My boy Brett will be here, though. Bring cash or a money order. He can't waive the fees."

"Super. Thanks." Sophie and I turned, and I rolled my

eyes to her. "Do you think we'll find anything useful in all that mumbo jumbo?" I asked her when we got outside.

"I don't know. Maybe I should have gone for the Martinsville one."

"Don't second-guess yourself. Without you, I probably would have been arrested for trying to strangle Greg. I'm going to miss you while you're at your fancy art camp."

"Back at ya," she said. "Use the sadness in your art. Shoot weeping willows. Mourning doves. Et cetera. Or maybe take yourself a lover."

"Uh-huh. I'll get right on that," I said.

We grabbed our bikes from the rack at the park. Sophie waved as she turned onto her driveway. I debated about going to see Gran after grabbing some lunch at home. But then I walked into the living room to find Mom on the couch with some rando guy, looking disheveled. Like, just made-out-with-rando-guy-on-the-couch disheveled.

Barf.

"Oh, hello, Laurel!" she said, like it was a surprise I should be coming into my own house. "I wasn't expecting you to be home."

Clearly.

"Hi," I said. I looked Mom's latest up and down. Short. Salt-and-pepper hair, as Mom tended to like. Beard, as Mom also liked. Dude was one part miniature lumberjack, one part hipster. More downy than a blond-crested woodpecker.

That reminded me that I really ought to fill Gran's bird-feeders next time I got the chance. Bet the fucking *Sciurus* scourge had taken out the last suet batch I'd put out already.

"This is Brad," she said.

"Howdy, ma'am," he said to me, holding out a hand. "Your mama talks a lot about you."

Oh. Cowboy? That was a first. Guy named Brad? Notsomuch.

"Hello, Brad," I said.

"You can take a guy out of Texas, but you can't take Texas out of the guy," he said.

"Good to know," I said.

He smiled. He didn't seem too bad. I gave him about a week. Though it was still spring mating season, so maybe two.

"I was just stopping in to grab something," Mom said. "Brad and I are going out. I'll be right back." She looked at me hopefully, as if asking me to behave.

"Sure, Mom."

Mom disappeared up the stairs and the new dude and I looked at one another.

"So what do you for work?" he drawled.

"I go to school," I said. "I'm seventeen."

"Good for you!" he said. "Have you considered the 401(k) options there?"

"What's a 401(k)?"

"It's for retirement. I imagine you are thinking about that?"

"Can't say that I am. I think I have to graduate first. And that's like a year away."

"Oh. I see. Never too early to start planning, you know. Do much hunting? You look like the kinda girl who can take names when needed."

I didn't want to like this guy, but the accent made every-thing he said sound friendly. "I only shoot things with a camera," I said.

"Fair." He nodded. "I hate hunting, too. More of an opera guy, you know?"

I stared at him, baffled.

Mom clattered down the stairs with more noise than usual, warning me to her presence. She looked less disheveled.

"Done!" she said. "Everything good, Laurel?"

"We were discussing her investment portfolio," he said. "Nice to meet you, ma'am." He shook my hand again.

"Thank you for the sound financial advice," I said.

Mom gave a grateful smile and they left.

Mom is dating a hipster cowboy from Texas, I texted to Sophie.

Pictures or it didn't happen, she texted back.

Next time, I said, knowing that I might never see that poor fucker again.

I sank onto a chair, not wanting to put my butt on what-ever had been happening between Mom and hipster cowboy moments before my arrival. I scrolled through the pictures of the report. They were too tiny, so I uploaded them to the cloud and looked on my laptop. Words swam in front of me. It seemed that Shunksville was a "tenable merger site solution." But Martintown was central to both of the other districts. Richburg had more land and better public transportation. It had just built a new school five years ago and could build another close by. Shunksville didn't seem to have . . . anything, exactly. But at the end of the report, it suggested Shunksville as the town best suited for the combined school. A footnote to the last sentence read, "For site viability see documents 964392c; 837566a; 736450b." I wrote those numbers down on a Post-it note to look up on Wednesday.

Got a report from city hall. Maybe interesting stuff? I texted Risa. I cut and paste all of the photos into a PDF and saved it to the cloud. I texted her a copy.

She didn't reply.

I should really go see Gran. Or go out to take pictures. Or *something*. It was early on one of the first days of summer vacation. The temperate bird-perfect weather called from outside my window. But a piece inside me gave way from the constant pushing of forces outside me. The politicians and their stupid paperwork held hostage by Greg and goldenrod forms. Sophie going away. Risa being weird again. I tried to force my usual optimism to the front of my brain, but nothing felt good or right. I surfed the web, looking for inspiration. I stopped on the site for Jenkins Wood. Stones and rabbits and a robin eating berries greeted me. Gran and the birders were on the "Seen at . . ." page. After enough scrolling, I found a picture of a party at Gran's place. The Friends of Sarig Pond used it like a kind of clubhouse, having meetings and things there. I'd loved those, despite their vegan activist eccentricities. (They served kale and things with "live cultures in it, Laurel! It's so good for you!" and wouldn't take no for an answer.)

The house. It waited. Like Gran. Gran would always wait for me. In the form of an elusive-as-shit tufted motherfucking bird possibly, but still. Waiting. And there was something fishy going on with the mayor and deputy and guys in suits wanting to take out *my* woods and *my* pond. I couldn't wait. I had to act. I grabbed my camera and headed out to go back to the woods.

If I couldn't find the answer in my own head, there was always a chance it lay in nature, where the best things tended to be.

FIELD JOURNAL ENTRY
JUNE 4

It is nearly impossible to move some hospital beds. The kind that held Gran was designed to be moved; it had wheels. But it was also plugged into the wall. A lot of things now connected to Gran also required electricity, so there were a lot of wires to deal with. She had these massage things on her legs that undulated up and down, simulating the movement an active life ought to have been providing her. There were monitors for her heart, blood pressure, and oxygen. There was a vent to push the monitored oxygen in and out of her lungs. There were bags to collect various fluids. I don't know if they had electrical cords, maybe the body just shot pee directly into the bag, but there were several tubes that you had to watch out for. All of this meant that my grand plan to move her closer to the window wasn't going to be a one-woman job. And her nurse wasn't convinced that this would aid in her recovery.

"She's a birder. A nature enthusiast. Fresh air would do her good," I said.

"Honey, even if we wanted to, we can't take her outside."

"No, I know that. But maybe we could just push her over

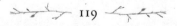

a little. So real sunshine could hit her face. Maybe the summer breeze?"

"We shouldn't open that." The nurse looked skeptically over at the window. "It's climate controlled in here, and there is an air filtration system. It's better for her this way."

I frowned. I wasn't going to win. "Okay," I said. The nurse checked Gran's roommate and walked out.

Nurse Joykill was wrong. There were no more potentially harmful pathogens floating around in the air outside than there were in the hospital, surely. People went in and out of patients' rooms all the time. Bringing food and changing sheets and giving medicine. All the gloves and hand sanitizer in the world couldn't stop *all* things from getting passed around. Outside might have weird crap from the mills or something, but Gran had managed to survive that for a buttload of decades; it wasn't going to end her now. Pollen was as good for the soul as it was bad for my sinuses. I decided to take matters into my own hands and get these ladies some ventfuls of summertime to help them out.

But then I realized the window was painted shut.

Utterly defeated, I went to work at the Nature Center. Risa had been away and incommunicado since the park incident. Jerry had said that she would be away on vacation with her family, but when I got there, she was weeding the Nature Center herb garden.

"There you are," I said. "Your hair . . ."

She looked up at me.

"Raven?" I said.

"Just felt like black," she said.

"No vacation?" I asked.

"Excuse me?" she said.

"Jerry said you were going vacation," I said.

"Oh. Right. Jerry. Yeah. I did say that."

"You aren't?" I asked.

"It's a long story," she said.

I plopped down on the ground beside her. A weird vibe hung in the air between us, and I wondered how it could be my fault. I automatically blamed the Birdie Bros. "Well, I have time."

"I don't really want to talk about it." She turned her back to me, and started ripping out weeds with gusto.

"Uh. Are you okay?" I said.

"I'm fine. Don't you have to go see your girlfriend?" she said. "Or mess with somebody's pictures or something? I gotta do this."

"Girlfriend? I don't have a girlfriend. You mean Sophie?" I laughed. "She's my best friend. We'd never be a thing. She likes dicks. Figuratively and literally, in my experience." It was true. Sophie liked penises attached to some of the biggest idiots I'd ever met. I'd introduce her to some of the cuter Birdie Bros, if it wouldn't surely cause a part of my soul to die.

Then the second part of what Risa said finally managed to register in my brain. "Wait, what? Mess with people's pictures? What the hell does that mean?" I said.

Risa raised her eyebrows. "You know what I'm talking about." She didn't sound convinced.

"Um, no I don't. Of anybody, I would think *you* might know something about messing with people's pictures."

"Why would *I* . . ."

"Birdscouts are here for the first tour of the day. Laurel, you are up," Jerry called from the Nature Center doorway.

Risa and I stared at each other for a second. I sighed and turned away toward my young birders. I didn't know what Risa was talking about, but I decided it wasn't my problem at the moment.

Karen, Fred, and their group stood poised at the edge of pond boardwalk. "What took you so long?" she said.

"Karen, I'm a full minute early," I said.

"Early bird. Worms. You know the deal."

The Birdscout moms chuckled.

"Follow me," I said. At the first outlook, we stopped. "Okay, so here's the deal," I said. "The Western and Central PA bird count is in two weeks, starting on June 21, and I want Shunksville well represented, you understand?" I said.

Little heads nodded around me.

"What's a bird count?" one kid asked.

"Shut up, Sidney," said another little girl.

"Everyone knows what a bird count is," said another.

"Now, Birdscouts! We do not shame people for asking perfectly respectable questions."

"I'm new." Sidney sniffed. "And I lived in Pittsburgh. All I ever saw was pigeons."

I really wanted to let him know that there were probably at least fifteen species in the city that you could see on any given day if you really wanted to, but the poor kid didn't know that.

"Don't you worry, my friend. First, I would be remiss if I did not mention the Great Backyard Bird Count in February, created by the Cornell Lab of Ornithology and the National

Audubon Society." I bowed my head and placed my hand reverently over my heart. The GBBC had its own photo contest and was the next nut I intended to crack, after I achieved *Fauna* domination. "But this one is just for us here in this part of the state, for fun. So many birds come back here in the warm months. We want to emphasize the copiousness and dissemination of our avian associates."

"What?" said Sidney.

"We count how many birds we see for at least fifteen minutes. You can do it one day, or you can do it on Thursday, Friday, Saturday, and Sunday," I said. "The Nature Center will be running bird counting groups in two weeks. You record how many of each type of bird that you see."

"But why do we do it?" asked another kid.

"Because ornithologists, or bird scientists, can learn a lot if they get information about where birds are hanging out. Bird populations don't stay the same; they are always changing." My voice rose dramatically. It was hard not to lose my shit entirely when talking about sexy, sexy bird counts. "And since there are so many of them absolutely everywhere, no one ornithologist or even group of ornithologists can gather data in a couple of days to analyze it. So the science people and even regular people who love birds record what they see and share it on the same day!"

Bird counts have also led to my best *Fauna* pictures in past years, but I left that part out.

"Cool!" said Sidney.

"Yay!" said Karen.

"I want to win the bird count!" said another kid.

"Well, it's not a competition," I said. That was totally a

lie. In my head, I always wanted Shunksville to have the most birds of anywhere. The Eastern PA summer bird count wasn't until July, because Philly had to be a dick about its birds. It was a shame that that side of the state had basically ruined all eagles for me. And fucking Martinsville always seemed to outpace us. Maybe they *shouldn't* get the new school. More elementary kids would mean more minions in the field counting birds.

Unless they ripped up the field to make the school in the first place. I shook the thought from my head.

"Okay, let's see what we can find! As Brian Michael Warbley says, 'We must count the birds we have now, so we always have our winged friends to count on.' Now let's go! Practice those observation and recording skills!"

I handed out little notebooks and mini pencils. My rallying speech had been a little too effective, because Sidney and Karen threw elbows to get to the front of the group.

"Roughhousing will scare the birds," I hissed at them. "We need to be quiet observers in nature." The group got the picture after a few minutes of ducks fleeing from us before we got close enough to really count them. By the end, my kids had counted robins, goldfinches, juncos, sparrows, jays, chickadees, bluebirds, catbirds, doves, grosbeaks, Baltimore orioles, and three black-backed orioles. Chicks had hatched and Mama squawked at the group as it went by.

"That's one off the life list, friends," I said.

"What's a life list?" asked Sidney.

Oh, city kids. They made me feel the most useful in this job.

Back at the Nature Center, I recorded the walk's data on

our big whiteboard. "This will be erased on the morning of June 21, and we will update totals for the official bird count. But you will be able to see data from your practice counts until next week!"

"Where will all of this go after that?" Sidney asked.

"We'll send it to the PA Audubon Society. It's our state version of the awesome national organization. It's like a club for people who love birds."

"And what do they do with it?"

"They use it to think about answers to bird-related questions. Like do changing weather patterns change bird patterns? Are there bird sicknesses affecting birds in a certain area? Is migration changing? Stuff like that. And the number of different birds changes every year. So some years there might be a whole lot of one bird, like finches say, and some years there might not be. They look for patterns and analyze what those patterns can tell us."

"We are totally going to win the most birds!" said Sidney.

"One hundred percent. In your *face*, Martinsville," said Karen.

I smiled. I saw a bit of little Laurel Graham in her. I should tell her mothers to get her a starter camera for her birthday. "That's the spirit. Kind of," I said. "Okay, Birdscouts. Mr. Jerry is going to do story time now!" I heard Jerry groan inside the Center. Tuesdays were his day whether he liked it or not. I'd helpfully set up an Eric Carle display earlier so that Karen would have easy access to her favorites.

Risa and I alternated groups until the afternoon, when the individual birders came. They preferred their practice counts in solitude.

I scrubbed the toilets and sinks in the ladies' room, put my signs outside of the men's, and scrubbed those, too. Usually Risa and I had to resort to rock, paper, scissors to decide, but I didn't want another encounter with her so soon. I emerged from the urinals, sparing her from having to smell like pine and bleach, and she didn't even say thank you.

After my shift, I decided to try to get some shots in for *Fauna*. The bird count got me thinking of all the contests I *should* be focusing on. With Sophie leaving for camp, and Mom back in the dating pool, and Gran either sleeping or flying around, my camera was really the one true constant I had to rely on.

Oh, Gran. You should be counting birds, too.

Shove the pain down, Laurel.

All

    The

        Way

            Down.

Outside, the air sunk heavier and heavier onto my hair and tank top. The perfume of freshly laid woodchips wafted over from the neat park just outside the gates of the nature reserve. The sky grew gray, then pink, then darker gray. The rain would start any minute. As I walked along one of the paths, I considered my options. I could go back to the Nature Center, but I was off the clock and there would surely be stuck children Jerry would expect me to help entertain. I could try to bike home, but Mom and Hipster Lumberjack or his replacement might be there. I decided the best bet was to stay with my trusty camera. Rain wasn't great for electronics, but droplets on ferns? That shit was *Fauna* gold.

I sat on an ancient, wide root provided by Grandma Maple. Elder Oak may have guarded the entrance of Jenkins Wood, but Grandma Maple watched over everything that happened inside it. I always thought of her as the real authority over the place. By Jerry's outside measurements, she seemed a century or two younger than Elder Oak, but Jerry was part of the Pennsylvania Recreation Department patriarchy, so I remained suspicious of his biases.

Plus I always inherently trusted grandmothers.

Dribs of water pattered onto leaves high above and slid through the canopy onto crevices in wood until it sunk into the soil beneath my feet. I covered my camera in my sweatshirt and closed my eyes. Sweet petrichor tingled my nose. I listened to the woods around me.

I could hear the short, brusque call of blue jays and the eponymous mating song of the chickadees. Sparrows sang to one another across branches. Birds didn't mind the rain, so neither did I. It beaded on my skin, cool and fresh after the humidity of the day. When it slowed, I pulled out my camera again and waited. Nature photography was all about waiting.

Gran (and Brian Michael Warbley) had taught me that.

I managed to get a few great shots of a fox that crept out from behind a tree. I captured a nose, then a snout, then his muzzle, then bright eyes and perky ears. His rust-colored fur repelled moisture, but the rain had given him a sort of unearthly glow. He looked at me and I looked at him through the viewfinder. He considered my potential as an apex predator and skipped away after a few seconds. I smiled as he bounded off into the underbrush.

A skunk wandered by and I sat rock still. No picture in

the world was worth scaring or pissing off that guy. A confused-looking beaver wandered past slightly after that. He grabbed a branch not far from my feet, glancing at me as if he'd been searching for that *exact* branch all along, and it was my fault he had to come this far from the pond to get it. Technically, he didn't even live in the pond. There was a river that turned into a creek that marginally fed Sarig, and he lived with his family about a mile away by the deeper parts.

"I had nothing to do with this branch, bro," I said.

He ignored me and started dragging it away. He stopped behind a tree and I heard him gnawing at it to cut it down to size. I considered trying to follow him to get a picture of whatever the hell he was doing, but a rustling from behind Grandma Maple distracted me.

"Oh," said Risa.

"Sorry," I said instinctively, like I'd interrupted her even though I'd been there first.

"Did you see the fox?" she asked.

"Yeah, then there was a beaver. I think they both left, though."

"I probably scared them," she said. She looked down at me.

"Hey, Risa," I said. "Earlier, what did you mean when you said . . ."

"Nothing. Forget it. My bad."

"No, listen. I want to . . ."

"It's fine. I was just talking. Gotta go." She turned and walked past me farther into the woods. I didn't try to stop her. That's how it was with Risa. One flight forward, two flights back.

I went back to see Gran before I went home. Her bed sat where it always sat, achingly out of range from the slants of waning dusk drizzle. I angled my digital over her face and scrolled through the photos, hoping maybe they'd register through her closed eyelids and neurons of questionable functionality. She twitched and her thumb moved in my direction.

"You wouldn't be in a fox, would you? You never cared much for them. They ate your vegetables."

Twitch. Twitch. Stillness.

I sat there and watched. Waited in case a miracle of nature would occur with open skies or petal bloom or *anything*. Instead, beeps and clicks and whizzes and whirs kept time with Gran's mechanically enforced breaths.

I rode my bike home slowly. Mom wasn't home and there was lasagna in the fridge. "Hope you had a great day at the Nature Center, honey!"

I microwaved dinner and uploaded the new pictures onto my laptop. I sent a couple of the best ones to Sophie. Sometimes she liked to paint them when she lacked inspiration.

Miss you! I typed.

I made out with a sculptor! she texted back almost immediately.

Good ol' Soph.

Rain came again in the night. I wandered in and out of dreams where tall grass morphed into cranes whose long necks struck out into a violent wind that would then just beat them back to the ground. They'd raise their fierce wings toward the sky that longed to hold them, but their feet would sink into the earth and then they had no choice but to turn back into plants. Then came the men in suits who set them on fire.

I woke with a start as thunder shook our little house. No birds had died; no reeds longed to fly. It was just my brain making up stories.

But as I drifted back into sleep, I couldn't help wondering if all the plants who felt the wind's rustle didn't long to waft freely, untethered, like the birds they saw do it daily.

FIELD JOURNAL ENTRY
JUNE 5

Mom hummed a little tune in the kitchen. I eyed her suspiciously.

"Good morning, baby!" she said.

"Summer vacation treating you well?" I asked. We hadn't really seen a lot of each other since both of our schools had let out.

"Mmm-hmm," she said, mostly to herself.

"When does your summer gig start?" Mom tutored in the summer and occasionally waited tables. She earned good tips but honestly I think she did it to find new dudes.

"Clients on vacation. Going to start up next week. Shift tonight. I'll bring back smiley cookies." She set a plate of eggs down in front of me. I always felt a little disloyal, eating eggs. But they weren't *fertilized* birds, and I forced Mom to buy expensive ones from a free-range organic famer Gran knew. So these eggs came from relatively happy chickens who I liked to think didn't want to have kids in the first place.

"To what do I owe this fancy meal?" I asked. Usually I was lucky if Mom remembered to buy cereal once a week.

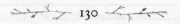

"Just enjoying the time off. The weather. Brad," she said, the last one almost a whisper.

"Ah," I said. So the hipster lumberjack *was* still around. Maybe I'd still be able to score a picture for Sophie.

"What are you up to?"

I shrugged. "Nature Center. Pictures for *Fauna*. Visiting Gran."

"Oh, that reminds me," Mom said. She picked up a pen and wrote something on the pad on the fridge.

"What?"

"Nothing." She looked right at me. "Are the eggs good?"

"Yes. Dippy eggs are always my favorite."

Mom's phone began to sing from the counter. She tended to pick the most mortifying sounds possible. I couldn't tell who the artist was, but it sounded like the lyrics included the words "let's get it on."

"Speak of the devil. That'll be Brad!" Mom said. She giggled and left the room.

Barfity barf *barf* to that one. I almost returned my perfectly good breakfast to my plate right there. I counted my lucky peacocks that Brad 2.0 wasn't *in* the kitchen.

Still, I was unable to eat any more. I scraped my remaining eggs into the compost bin and rinsed my plate for the dishwasher. I'd vowed to myself to go to city hall today to find the remaining reports referenced in the one I already had. I got my backpack and nestled my camera in the front pouch. In the back I put my school-issued tablet that I got to keep for summer homework. It didn't connect to my home cloud, but it'd be easier to just take pictures of the new reports with that so I could read and transport them. A thought occurred to me then.

Hey, Risa, I texted. *I didn't mean to sound like a jerk with the tufted bird thing. I really didn't. I believe in your identification skillz.* Maybe that was why she was acting so weird. Or thought I might be against her in her *Fauna* pursuit.

It's fine, she texted back.

Do you want to go to city hall with me today? I tapped. I waited a few minutes.

No response.

So maybe that was it? Sophie or I *had* offended her? What was she getting at when she said that thing about me messing with her pictures? Who could say. I gathered up my stuff to go and seize some reports. I caught sight of Mom's note on the fridge as I passed.

"Realtor and city rep, June 7, 11 a.m.," it read.

A Realtor? Chills rose up my spine and knotted in an icy ball at the base of my neck. That sounded *way too much* like Gran's house was about to sell. It was empty and Mom hadn't brought it up in a while. I thought she'd dropped it for the time being, since Gran seemed stable. I put a reminder in my phone to show up to fill the bird feeder at 11 a.m. on June 7 in the likely event that Mom was betraying me at that time and date.

I pedaled to city hall in record time, spurred on by my Mom rage. How could she still be seriously considering this? Gran had insurance, didn't she? And some supplemental old people money. Surely that would keep her until she woke up. Goddamn it, I needed to find out who the strange bird was and I needed the fucking pond and woods to stay intact so the Gran bird wouldn't leave before I could.

As I caught my breath, I tried to straighten myself out before I cajoled Brett (another Birdie Bro, dumber but nicer than Greg) to give me reports. I wiped off my sweaty face and brushed my hair so it didn't look quite as smashed from my helmet. I even put on ChapStick for good measure.

Walking as casually as possible up to the counter, I pulled a few of the request sheets from their bin and began to fill them out. Brett noticed me from behind his glass window.

"Oh, hey," he said.

"Hi, Brett," I said. "We've met in the woods. I work there. At the Nature Center."

"Yeah!" he said brightly. "You were there for the black-backed oriole! Reports came in of an indigo bunting and a black-throated blue warbler this morning."

"Shut *up*," I said, looking up from the forms. "An indigo bunting? Where?"

"Outside of the Sheetz. The one by the high school? Like a half an hour ago."

"No way," I said.

"Way!" He grinned. "I'm outta here at noon, and me and the guys are going to try to get some shots in. You gonna try? *Fauna* deadline coming up."

"You know I am," I said. "But first I am after something. Could you find me these?" I slid the forms through the opening in the window. "I know it takes days to photocopy or whatever. But last week Greg let me look at them here. I promise to stay where you can see me and not run away with them."

He laughed. "I trust you. I know allllll these files would go for the big bucks on eBay." He ripped off the top copies for me and took the green ones. I had him searching for

964392c, 877566a, and 736450b, since the other report suggested it. None of those were on the database online, so of course I couldn't *order* them online. But I had the day off and I just wasn't in the mood to dodge hipster lumberjacks, as would be the likely outcome of staying at home.

He typed at the computer for a few minutes and then disappeared behind the other door. He emerged with three file folders.

"Here you go. They look just as dull as all the rest of them," he said.

"Thanks." A Post-it note fluttered down to the floor from one of them as I pulled them through the window. "Here," I said. "I don't want to lose it if it's important."

Brett looked at it and frowned. "Thanks," he said to me. He then left his little office and walked off down the hall.

I got my tablet out and got to work. I figured I could just read most of it at home. I clicked on page after page in file 964392c. "Construction Viability: A Snapshot" was really long. Files 877566a and 736450b, both reports about potential school sites in Martinsville and Richburg, were fortunately much shorter.

I double-checked to make sure I got all of the pages and slipped my tablet back in my bag. I settled into the orange puke chair to start reading one of the shorter files. Just then, Brett rounded the hallway corner with none other than Deputy Mayor Michael Ross.

Brett stayed a few steps behind the deputy mayor. He shrugged at me. "Sorry," he mouthed from behind Michael Ross's back.

"Pardon me," he asked. "Our staff member here alerted me to the fact that you wanted copies of this report?" he said.

"Oh, well, not exactly. They weren't in the online database, so I know there's some reason they can't be copied? The, uh, staff member last week told me that." As much as Greg annoyed me, it seemed like a bad Birdscout move to get him in trouble with his internship. "But there was one report I could get last week and it referenced these three in the footnote. So I came to read them here."

"I see. Well, these aren't for the general public, I'm afraid. There was a note that indicated that on them."

Maybe that had been the Post-it that fluttered away. But that had only been on *one* of the reports. I wondered which one.

"Aren't all of these files for public review?" I said. "They have to do with the new school. You said at your last press conference that they'd be made readily available for, um, constituents." Had he said that? Whatever he'd mentioned behind his little podium sounded like that at least.

"You're a voter?" he said.

"Well. No. Not yet. I'm only seventeen. But I will be," I said. Was there an age limit on files? That didn't seem to make sense either because Greg and Brett were my age and they were in charge of the records once a week for three hours.

"Why do you want to see them? They are really dull. They aren't written for anyone. It's full of technical jargon and things for architects and planners."

"I want to know about the new school, that's all. I'm, um, passionate about education."

Brett slowly backed away from this conversation until he got safely behind his glass partition. I didn't blame him. Up close, Deputy Mayor Michael Ross came off a little like a turkey vulture.

"I just don't think you'd be interested in them. That's all," he said curtly. He took the two folders from the table. He stuck out his hand for the one I was holding.

"Is it against the law for me to look at this?" I said.

"It's not meant for the inexperienced eye."

"That isn't what I asked. Am I *allowed* to see this if it's a *public* record?"

"Young lady, I will need you to give that back to me. Right now." Deputy Mayor Michael Ross loomed over me, his shadow blocking out the light from the outside.

I pushed my lips together. Something told me I was allowed to look at these all that I wanted, but it wasn't worth it to me to argue with the guy.

"Fine," I said. I handed him my folder.

He looked at me. No. What would a turkey vulture do? He *leered* at me. I didn't like this guy. I vowed right then and there that one of my first acts as an eighteen-year-old would be to vote against him. I might even try to be one of those people who go door-to-door.

"Did you have time to read any of this?" he asked.

"No," I answered honestly. Since I'd been taking pictures of all the pages, sir. "Your staff member got you right away."

"Good," he said. He leered once more at the folders in his hand and then turned and walked briskly back down the hall from which he came. His shoes clicked with a neat crispness across the wooden floor, which would have been a pleasant sound if it hadn't been made by a turkey vulture asswipe.

After he'd turned into an office at the end of the hall, I went back over to the counter.

"Sorry, sorry, sorry, sorry," Brett said, getting out of his chair and coming over to me. "There was a note on the folder." He held it up to me.

"Please contact DP MR immediately if anyone requests this form," it read.

"Could I have that?" I said.

"Why?" I asked.

"He was kind of mean," I said.

"Yeah," said Brett. "Okay. Here. I'm sorry you didn't get to read the reports. I didn't want to get in trouble. I have, like, one thing to do here and I don't want to fuck it up."

"No worries. I understand." I took the Post-it note from him and attached it carefully to the inside of my tablet cover. Poor Brett was a few eggs short of a full nest and didn't seem to realize that this could be proof of some kind of school-planning conspiracy. Or maybe he just wasn't suspicious enough as a person and I was actually the ridiculous one for wanting a random Post-it note in the first place.

As I was talking to Brett, I noticed a black orb attached to the ceiling by the door. That could mean a security camera. That could mean someone, somewhere, would know that I'd made a copy of this form. While I still didn't think that was illegal, sticking around to find out what Deputy Mayor Michael Ross thought about it seemed unwise.

"Maybe I'll get my mom to try another day," I said to Brett. "She's of legal voting age."

Brett nodded at me. "Go try for the indigo bunting. 'Cause who really needs an excuse for a Sheetz Shmuffin anyway?"

"Truth," I said.

Brett waved goodbye. No one tried to stop me from walking out the door. I left city hall, mounted my bike, and rode away as fast as my legs allowed. I wished Sophie were with me. She'd have more insight into this present weirdness than I did. Painters were naturally more suspicious of people's motives, I've found.

FIELD JOURNAL ENTRY
JUNE 7

There were no birds at Sheetz yesterday or today, save the tasty, tasty unfertilized or already dead ones in the sandwiches. I felt disloyal to Gran getting any, so I opted for hash browns. Sometimes deep-fried potato-like foods get the job done.

I'd spent last night and most of the morning trying to wade through the dense files I'd photographed at city hall. I texted Sophie some pictures of the more boring pages, thinking she could do an artistic interpretation of bureaucracy. Most of it turned out to be the geographical survey of our area that assessed whether Sarig Pond and Jenkins Wood would make a good school site. A familiar ache settled behind my eyes seeing Gran's address listed on an appendix labeled "Property to Acquire." Basically none of the land was good for much other than birds. The land was low and the area around the pond formed a natural kind of basin. City planners long ago thought it would be most usable for public recreation space, or maybe a reservoir if they flooded the space around it from the creek. The city abandoned the reservoir idea because a coal family's estate sat too close. The Jenkins family (owners of the estate) bought the land instead, and donated it with the suggestion (not a *mandate* the report pointed out) that it become a park. The rich people were happy their big house was safe, the city was happy it had land, the birds were ecstatic they had a migratory habitat.

I live texted most of this to Risa, who either didn't see it or ignored it. Richard and Louise were off on a bird vacation somewhere cold, because that is what they did in the summer. I decided I'd go tell Gran.

Wait. Shit. Gran.

I looked at the clock. 10:45 a.m. Thank the doves, I hadn't missed Mom's meeting at Gran's house.

I tucked my precious fancy suet from Jerry into my backpack, hopped on my bike, and spun over as fast as I could go. Sure enough, Mom's car was in the driveway. Two cars sat parked against the gravel lining Gran's yard. I debated whether filling the feeder first would look more legit. I opted to carry the suet in with me, making it look like I came with a definite purpose totally unrelated to spying on Mom.

I creaked the door open as quietly as possible. It didn't matter, since Mom was standing in the middle of the empty living room with Mr. Hughes, the Realtor I'd met weeks ago in this same spot, and the podium-pushing lady from the press conference with Deputy Asshole Michael Ross.

"Laurel?" my mom said, guilt sliding around in her mouth like dry crumbs. "What are you doing here?"

I held up my bag. "Downy woodpeckers," I said. "I just haven't seen many this year. Bird count is coming up; maybe that's significant. But they like this stuff. I came to fill the feeder."

"Ah. Go right ahead," Mom said.

"What's going on here?" I asked. I glanced at Mr. Hughes, who busied himself with his phone. Podium Lady smiled at me.

Mom sighed. "You might as well know, Laurel. The house sold. The city closes on it at the end of the month."

"Mom, no!" I said, dropping my bag. Thank god the seal held because it is a bitch to clean up suet. Jerry refuses to buy the solid blocks for reasons no one comprehended.

"Honey. We've talked about this a half a dozen times. It has to be this way. Grandma needs long-term care. That costs money. She won't be able to come back to this house, which also costs money to maintain. The city offered well over market value."

"Because they want to build new schools here! They want the combined district houses on this basically unusable land for . . . I don't know . . . reasons. Shunksville government people are going to destroy our nature reserve. Gran would never want that. Never, never." I stomped my foot like a toddler in the middle of a tantrum.

"Why do you say that?" Podium Lady said.

"The last press conference said Shunksville planned to move forward with its bid for the new school. I saw the reports you talked about at city hall. It's a bad idea, developing this area, and I think someone is trying to cover that fact up. This house was one of the last standing in your way. Maybe *the* last."

I didn't tend to cry out of sadness. Nor out of fear or pain.

Frustration, though, served as my kryptonite. I could feel the tears coming.

Podium Lady, for her part, seemed impressed that some rando teenager freaking out in her grandmother's ~~former~~ living room knew all of this political intrigue.

"Sweetheart," Mom said. I let her wrap her arms around me. "I love your grandmother more than I could ever say. I know how important this home is. I grew *up* here. It holds the last real memories of my dad, who I know died before you were born, but he would have loved you. And I also realize how important Sarig Pond and Jenkins Wood are to you, to Grandma, to the town. But the only way I can take care of *us* is to sell this house. I'm so sorry. Feed the birds, honey. Okay? I have to talk to them." Mom looked over at Mr. Hughes and Podium Lady.

There was no point in arguing. The worst, worst thing was that I understood. The utter correctness of Mom's argument loomed the most frustrating thing of all. I filled the feeder with suet mixed with grief. A hungry squirrel eyed my work from an electrical wire overhead.

"Don't even think about it, motherfucker," I growled at it.

The bastard didn't even have the decency to look scared.

FIELD JOURNAL ENTRY
JUNE 11
NOTABLE LOCATION: SARIG POND
LIFE LIST ENTRY 3,286: INDIGO BUNTING

"Let me get this straight," said Richard, "there are reports?"

"Reports with proof they want to destroy this place *and* that it's a bad idea?" said Louise.

It was their first day back from the birding trip on which they'd logged seventeen new artic species to their life lists. Gran should have been on that trip.

"Yes," I said. I was hitting them with a lot of information. I looked over at Risa, who stood with her arms folded at the edge of the birders. "The mayor and his people talked about it at a press conference. I looked for the plans. They tried to keep me from said plans. But I took pictures, which I will email to you when I get home. Basically they want the school here. I don't know why because all of the papers seem to agree it's a bad idea."

Richard frowned at Louise, who frowned at Owen, who frowned at the knitting ladies, who frowned at Karen, who frowned at her mom, who frowned at Risa, and it would have been a complicated continuous Möbius frown strip, only Risa avoided my gaze and it ended with her.

"Wow. Okay, then. Still, this gives us enough to protest," Louise said.

"What do you mean?" said Risa.

"The nature reserve is needed. Building here is a bad idea. We can protest the use of the pond and woods as a merged district campus on what we know—what we have concrete evidence to support," said Louise.

"How do we do that?" asked Karen's mom.

"Let me think on it," said Louise, smirking at Richard. "It's been a long while since we've made trouble."

"*Too* long," agreed Richard.

"And, um, there is another problem," I said.

"Oh?" said Louise.

"Yeah, Mom . . . Mom finally sold Gran's house. To the city. After June 30, they can do what they want with it. Which probably means tearing it down." I looked at my shoes and the faded boards under them. I hadn't really spoken to Mom since the time at the house. We'd visited Gran and talked to her and eaten near each other. But then she went out with the hipster lumberjack and I'd immersed myself in local government red tape. Talking wouldn't undo the sale of Gran's home or the reasons why it was necessary, so we avoided bringing it up.

"Understandable. The only one who wanted to buy over there *was* the city. And I know Aurora's care can't be cheap. I'm sorry, Laurel," said Louise.

"Yeah," I said.

"What does make trouble mean?" Karen said. "I'm not allowed to do that."

Richard and Louise chuckled with Karen's mom and started to explain social protest movements.

I wandered off down the boardwalk to stave off the returning frustration. I noticed two of Greg's Birdie Bros walked by off path next to me. I thought about yelling at them, but then two sharp chirps sounded overhead, followed by the familiar strange coo I'd come to know. Gran's mystery bird fluttered overhead. I caught a glimpse of the movement of its wings. I lifted my camera and clicked as fast as I could, just as it took flight.

"Of course. Missed it," I said out loud to myself. But I hadn't, not really. It was still in the tree.

"I have my binoculars," said an equally elusive voice behind me.

I turned and looked at Risa. She was carrying a tripod and her camera, with binos strung around her neck.

"Here," she said, untangling them from her body.

"Thanks." The summer sun conspired with azure blue as I adjusted the thumbscrews and independent focus. "I see him! Kind of! He is tufted. I think. Damn it," I said. "He moved *again*. This is ridiculous."

Just then, a sweeter song erupted just a few branches away. I swung the binoculars around toward the sound.

"Whoa," I breathed. "Risa, look!" I gestured her close to me. I handed her the binos and pointed to the thin, bouncing limb just a few feet away.

"The indigo bunting," she said. "Here." She shoved the binos into my hands again. She deftly unfurled her tripod in one silent, fluid motion. She screwed her camera into the base.

I stared at the exquisite little creature staring back at us from his tree. He tweeted until a female glided to his side.

"Oh my god, there are two of them." The male, of course, stood vibrant lapis in sunlight, indigo in the shade. His chest, a golden brown fading into white, puffed up in song. The female, with less need to show off, contrasted with her wheat and copper feathers. Together they hopped up and down on the branches in a kind of dance.

"Shit," Risa said next to me. "Shit, shit, fuck. Fuckity, fuck, fuck," she said.

"You okay over there?" I said.

"My damn camera is two seconds from dead. I forgot to

charge the battery. I of course left the other one in the camera bag I didn't think I'd need."

"Go get it," I said. "The buntings might still be here. They don't seem in a hurry."

Risa bit her lip.

"I mean, why not?" I said.

"Yeah," she said, glancing at the tripod and at me. She gingerly ran down the boardwalk, trying not to make noise or move in a way to freak out the birds.

The buntings, for their part, ignored her. They seemed happy in each other's company. I wondered if they would still be around so that we could count them in the official bird count. Would it be cheating to include them if it was only a week away? Probably.

A sharp cry echoed from behind me. I whirled around, my mystery bird the closest it had ever been.

"Gran, come *on*," I said. "Is this about the house? I have zero control over that. Less than zero, even. I make seven dollars and a half pound of suet or soil an hour. I can't buy off the city for your house."

The bird called again.

I tried to follow it. It moved from canopy to near my head. I could hear the way in which his song grew long or soft, near or far. I followed it clear to the other side of the pond. No matter how hard I pressed the binos to my face, no feathers or beak or legs or even telltale movement came into focus. At one point, an eastern blue jay peeked around a tree I could have sworn held the exotic bird.

"Get out of the damn way," I said.

The blue jay ignored me, as they tended to do, because they were pretty big dicks in the avian world.

Finally, after about ten minutes, I realized yet again that I wasn't going to find the fucking bird. I sighed. I should get back to Risa and the buntings before she thought I had run off and stolen her binoculars. It was a shorter distance to just keep walking the rest of the way around the back to return to where I'd started.

A thought worried me as I saw a titmouse, a cardinal, two chickadees, six ducks, and a male swan. (Swans were dicks, too, and he chased the ducks.) Every time I saw Gran, she looked less and less like herself. Like her spirit, her *Granness*, was evaporating into the air around us. And I thought maybe that meant that she was possibly becoming more bird than human, because who really knew what happened as you died? I'd learned in physics that energy is neither created nor destroyed, so who says that your energy doesn't join something else like another animal who could use it? The energy needed something to stay in, or it got wasted. You don't want to leave the lights on when no one is home; it's bad for the planet. Maybe Gran didn't want to stay in a body that didn't work anymore. Now that her house had sold, that was one less thing tethering her to the earth. So her energy had even *less* reason to stay put. I'd thought that telling her what our bird was would keep her here. Maybe it was the one last thing that would let her be truly free.

Because she'd know what she was to become.

I shook the thought from my head as I headed back to the beginning of the boardwalk. The buntings had moved closer to the edge, and the rule-breaking Birdie Bros stood off path snapping pictures of them.

"Excuse me," I said. "You aren't allowed to be over there. There's poison ivy." I pointed to the patch of three-leaved plants in which they were standing. "Though, it appears it's too late for you." I fought down a giggle. Serves them right.

"I think we know what poison ivy is," the one said. His companion didn't look so sure. He picked up his leg and shook it. Both wore only tennis shoes and ankle socks.

"Get back up here," I said more forcefully. I startled the buntings, who flew up higher to avoid the human drama.

"Bitch, please," the first one said. "You scared the birds."

"Did you seriously just call me a *bitch*?" I said. Jerry had actually nicknamed the small section of wetlands they had chosen to go rogue in "death valley." Because there was a distinct possibility the idiots had wandered through poison ivy and sumac and maybe even oak. Jerry never tried to get rid of it because it always came back, but also because the threat of it was enough to keep most reasonable people *on the fucking path*.

"Fine. Itch forever in hell. I don't care."

I left them, wishing I had my phone or camera to take their picture for Jerry's wall of shame. I could have them banned from the Nature Center forever for this kind of rap, and the world would be better for it, because the Birdie Bros didn't deserve close-ups of buntings.

I got back to Risa. "Hey, sorry, not trying to swipe . . ." But I stopped short when I noticed her bone-white face.

"How. Could. You?" she kind of choked out at me.

I realized then that Risa was standing over her fallen tripod, her camera still attached.

"Oh no! Did it hurt your camera?"

Risa's jaw dropped. She stared at me.

"I'm sorry I left it. I followed my mystery bird. I heard it call around the pond, but all I saw was a jay. How the hell did it tip over? Surely there's no way the wind did that?" Risa owned the same tripod I did, which I knew to be the sturdiest on the market.

"Don't even try this," she said. "You did it once and I fucking let you do it again. I can't even believe how stupid I am."

"What? Do what?"

"Ruin my setup! Last time you just fucked up my time-lapse of the hummingbirds. But this time you cracked my lens. It took me a year to save up for this one." Risa balled and unballed her fists.

"Risa, I had nothing to do with this. I mean, I left it alone. That was my bad. But there was no one even here to mess with it. I swear!" I stared at her. "Wait, is this what you meant before when you said *I* ruined *your* shot?"

"Like I should believe you, I—"

"And hold up a fucking second," I said. "How about *you* knocked over *my* time lapse of the sunrise over the pond. The hummingbirds like the corner that lights up in the morning. I wanted to catch them midflight against the pink sky."

If I had gotten them mating, I swear I would have won *Fauna* forever. The judges love that smut.

"What are you even talking about?" she said.

"You were the last walk-around shift. I know you were, I

checked the fucking schedule. My camera wasn't visible. You'd have to know exactly where to look to find it. And all my pictures were jacked up because someone messed with it. And you were *the only one who could have done it*." My heartbeat picked up with every decibel level.

"You are blaming me for that?"

"Of course I am. And you are blaming me for this shit? What makes you think I would risk ruining your fucking lens? I know how expensive this shit is. And I bet Jerry gave you birdseed instead of money, too. I know you can't just buy it. I don't fuck with people's equipment!"

Risa paused. She looked down at her poor camera. She clearly had been blaming me for her *Fauna* loss as long as I'd been blaming her. This was ugly, because it'd taken me months to even speak to her last year. My picture concept had been one of my more brilliant ideas (if it had worked). Mom wouldn't let me go out by myself to sunrise at the pond or get up that early herself, and Gran had convinced me to try time lapse for the sake of learning technique. But someone messed with my timer, and I *knew* it wasn't my mistake because I checked it at least a dozen times before leaving it there. I'd gotten nothing. The second and third times I tried, someone knocked my camera down, just like here.

"If it wasn't you," she said, clearly trying not to start screaming at me, "then who was it?"

"I was wondering the same thing about you."

We stood there, looking at her tripod. There had been no one else nearby. Then or now. Unless some dick swan had . . .

"Wait," I said. "The Birdie Bros."

"What about them?"

"There were two of them. Off path. I saw them before I saw you earlier. And I saw them shooting the buntings when I came back around."

Risa sucked in her cheeks. "If someone was going to do something dickish, it would likely be dicks."

"Is the camera itself okay? Do you think it caught anything?"

"I don't know. I was too pissed off about the lens to check. The battery was almost dead, so I doubt it."

Risa unscrewed the dial on her tripod and wiggled the camera free. She swapped out the battery with a new one. I walked over to her and stood behind her shoulder.

"I guess I left it on. I got one of the buntings." She smiled in spite of herself.

"Oh, look at them," I said. "It's crystal clear. Jealous!" I grinned.

"And here are . . . huh. What are they?"

"They look like skin. Fingers, maybe?"

That didn't clear my name, as I had fingers with which to screw with a camera.

"And one with black. With part of a white shape. And a half of a gold star or something. It looks kind of familiar, but . . ."

"That's because it's the Steelers logo," I said. "Look at it!"

Risa turned her camera. "You are right. I don't suppose one of the guys you saw was wearing one?"

"I don't know. But I bet you money they are still off path where I last left them."

They weren't. Instead, we found them defiling the good name of the home team right in front of the Nature Center.

Risa took a picture of them before she even said anything. "For the wall of shame," she said to me.

"You boys are going to pay for my fucking lens," she yelled at them. Then she yelled at them a lot more.

Several summer-unterm, unschooler mothers pulled their kids away in horror.

The Birdie Bros tried to run away, but Jerry had come out to see what was going on and made them stay until Risa explained the yelling and the banned-at-the-Nature-Center language. He made them call their parents, which was pretty much the best part of my day.

I waited for Risa outside of the Nature Center. She walked out carrying her camera and tripod, looking pleased.

"These are yours," I said, holding out her binoculars.

"Oh, I'd forgotten about them!" she said.

"I figured. Everything cool?"

"Yeah. Jerry was so pissed about the boys tramping on plants that he didn't even write me up. Both dude bros' moms were pisssssssssed. One has the same camera and she told him to give me his lens. It's not the same kind, but I'm pretty sure this one is better? At least for long-range shots. It's still a win."

"Good lord. Never a dull day at the pond!" I said.

"Seriously." She paused for a second. "Hey. Sorry I yelled at you. Stuff at home is weird. This was just one more thing that sucked. And I'd always thought it was you who . . . um . . ."

"Tried to ruin your *Fauna* entry?"

"Yup," she said.

"It wasn't." Man, Sophie was going to eat up this development like chocolate cake.

"I believe you. It was probably the Birdie Bros, since messing with equipment to win seems to be their MO. And they were stupid enough to be caught on camera this time."

"Agreed. I'm sorry I thought it was you. I probably should have just asked," I said.

I looked up at Risa. She hauled all her stuff a little closer to me. "Friends?" she asked. She stuck out her hand.

"Birds of a feather," I said, taking hold of her hand.

She grinned. "See you later."

"Later," I said.

I watched her move to her bike and neatly pack everything in her basket. She waved and set off for home. I could still feel her fingers on my wrist. I felt like that spider from Karen's favorite nature storybook.

It had been a fucking, fucking busy day.

FIELD JOURNAL ENTRY
JUNE 13

Life was more pleasant, but much stranger, now that Risa and I no longer blamed each other for *Fauna* failure, as well as now held a common, renewed cause to resent the Birdie Bros. Our morning bird walk canceled, we'd been scooped by text alerts of a Ross's goose sighting (confirmed) on the other side of town. Part of me was pissed I was missing a fucking Ross's goose and another part of me knew I could probably go look, too, but I'd miss time alone with Risa, which I found I now craved.

Risa also made no moves to go see the goose.

So, instead of walking the woods and pond, Risa watched me trace an outline of Sarig Pond and Jenkins Wood on a sheet of butcher-block paper I had taped over the art table. I needed a visual representation of where I heard the calls.

"Cartography. Bold. Ancient, yet new," said Risa.

"Mmm," I mumbled. I was pretty sure she was making fun of my art skills, which were sadly lacking. I should have convinced Sophie to do this as a camp project instead.

"Is there a particular reason you are doing this?"

"There's still a bird out there with my name on it," I said. I didn't have the energy to make up something creative to keep her from bothering me. I could just curl up and sleep, right there on the table, actually. All of my spare time had been consumed with Gran. I barely shut my eyes and terrible dreams about her being hit by a car barreled through my brain.

"Tattooed on its butt, or something?"

"My grandmother's bird. The one the other day at city hall. I think it's her messenger. Or maybe just her. I don't know. We heard the new call right before her accident. Now it's all over. There are more of them, and I can't see them or find them. I think it's her."

I could feel Risa's eyes on me. I met her gaze, waiting for the sarcastic reply.

"Ah" was all she said.

"You thought it might be tufted," I said. "But how could it be? Wouldn't I have figured out who Gran was sending by now if it was? You know?"

I could tell Risa considered this. "Where all did you hear it, again?"

I drew an "x" in all the different locations and pointed. "There. I'm kind of on a deadline here." My nose started to burn involuntarily. I'd used the word "dead."

Risa nodded.

"Aren't you going to make fun of me or something?" I said. "Because I said something weird?"

"Why would I do that?" she said.

"Oh," I said. "I mean, it seems like a reasonable response."

Risa shrugged. "Nah. It's cool. Though. Question . . ." She paused. "That you don't have to answer. But . . . why do you think your gran is in a bird?"

"She reacts whenever I talk about the mystery bird. More than any other time. Mom and two nurses and a neurologist said that it's just reflexes or whatever. But I swear, she only does it at certain times. And there *is* this new bird. It's too weird not to be connected to something. Don't you think?"

"The doctors said so, too? That it's probably not her paying attention to you?" Risa scrunched up her face.

"I mean. Yeah."

"I've seen shows like this. People are kinda trapped and no one knows they can hear and feel stuff around them. But they *can*. So why not your grandmother? And why not birds? It doesn't hurt to try to solve the mystery for her."

I smiled at Risa. Amid the suckiness, the girl got me.

I noticed then that Risa's gray "I stop for water fowl" hoodie really brought out her eyes.

Maybe I could be a fashion photographer instead. Gray hoodies suddenly seemed pretty inspiring.

Risa cleared her throat. I realized I'd been staring at her way too long.

"I like your sweatshirt," I said. Oh my god, Laurel, get it *together*. This was about *Gran*.

"Thanks." She full-on blushed.

"Sure," I said, turning back to my map. I suddenly decided that I should note specific bird positions to remember what my mystery bird *wasn't*.

And also to maybe stop noticing Risa's fetchingly ripped jeans.

Looking at the map, I noticed that the bird seemed to like the entrance of the sanctuary.

"I am going over to the iron gate," I told Risa.

She nodded and, to my surprise, followed me out of the Nature Center.

"A little help, please," I whispered to the universe.

Chirp, chirp, question mark? No. Exclamation point?

Thank you, universe!

"There you are," I said to the branches above me. "Come down here, won't you?"

It answered from several trees away.

"Of course not," I sighed. I looked up and waited. Nothing.

"It's an elusive little fucker, isn't it?" said Risa.

"What are you doing tomorrow?" I asked. She usually had the day off.

"Um. Nothing?"

"Would you watch birds with me? I need to find her. It. You know." I looked up at the sky. "You could shoot for *Fauna* at the same time."

"Of course," she said. She walked up to my side and looked up at the sky as well. Sunlight filtered through the leaves, and only the recognizable calls we heard every day echoed through the wood.

Usually when the Gran bird slipped away, I felt a hole filled with guilt slosh around. But with Risa there, looking up, the empty places echoed with a more hopeful song.

FIELD JOURNAL ENTRY
JUNE 14

At five in the morning, I shivered by the nature sanctuary gate, and watched Risa stroll up the path carrying a travel mug in each hand.

"Coffee?" she said. She thrust one of the mugs into my mittens.

"Um. Sure," I said. I didn't really like coffee. It tasted like burning. But it was nice of her to bring it. I tried a sip. This was some fancy kind. Hazelnut and vanilla or something.

I sipped some more. I wrinkled my nose.

"Not a fan?" said Risa.

"It was a nice thought?" I said.

Risa laughed. "Understood. I live and die by coffee. Early birders get the early birds and all."

"I think my body produces its own caffeine," I said.

"This would not shock me to learn," said Risa.

Just then, a flutter-swish worried the leaves above our heads and my call sounded.

Risa got out her phone. "I have a new bird identification app. There's still cars nearby, so you get more noise pollution here than you would think. So, it's not running at one hundred percent. But it's something."

We sat on a bench, still and silent. The bird called out, as if telling us it knew we were still there. Risa held up a finger to her lips and then raised her phone toward the brightening sky. The bird called again and again.

When it stopped, Risa spoke. "Decent recording. App thinks it's a northern mockingbird. But it's only a thirty percent match. That's the thing about mockingbirds, though. They can imitate others. So maybe that's it, and maybe it's not."

"Let's walk around again. Try to get a good look at it. Try to get a *picture*," I said.

Sparrows and grackles and a hawk made appearances to Risa and me. The app positively identified every one of them. We saw mallards arguing with Canada geese and that was fun until about eight in the morning, when my bino strap was starting to cut into my neck and Risa's phone battery approached death.

"This was not as successful as I had hoped."

"We heard him! And maybe we have an ID. Seems positive to me," she said.

"Gran would have recognized a mockingbird."

"But . . . ," Risa started.

"They imitate, I know. But she was interested enough to go after it, which meant that she had no idea. Maybe she wouldn't have. I don't know." I leaned against a tree, defeated.

"I have a friend at the Science Museum. The one who told me that they were giving away the wing movement statue. Maybe he could help us," she said. She put her hand on my shoulder. The warmth of it crept in.

"Yeah?" I said.

Risa laughed. "I have a car we could use if you want to go. They have a killer bird section. I mean, not just predators. But a really good one. They have a bird call library, too."

I felt encouraged by this. She was practically drooling at the thought of the exhibit.

"That good, huh?" I said.

"Totally." She looked relieved that I seemed less likely to burst into tears. "You busy Sunday? How about we go? A couple of hours at most."

"I want to," I said. It was an incredibly generous offer, particularly from a person I thought I hated and who I thought hated me until fairly recently. "I should go see what they are doing with Gran. Can I text you later?"

"Sure," she said. She moved toward me and held out her hand like she was going to shake mine.

My blank stare amused her.

"You still have my travel mug."

"Oh! Right! Sorry," I said, handing back the sloshy coffee cup I'd wedged in my coat's deep pockets.

Risa took it from me and we both kind of stared at each other, close up.

Man, her hair looked great. And gray really was her color.

"Okay. Well. Bye," she said. She leaned in toward me. She casually slipped one arm loosely around my back. Having someone so warm and solid up close caused the tension in my shoulders to involuntarily relax.

She pulled back. "See you, Laurel," she said.

"Bye." I think I said it. I tried to say it. But I had lost the ability to communicate in words.

I watched her even, easy stride shrink him into the distance. I shivered a little bit, even though the sun warmed the earth and leaves around me. Surely I didn't now *like* Risa? I mean. She was still my sworn *Fauna* competition even if she was no longer my enemy. And relationships were a bad idea in general, right? They just left you crying on Wednesday morning. Though, to be fair, none of the people that Mom rolled through the house had spent their free mornings staring into the sky in search of heavenly song, either.

That's what Gran called birdsong. Heavenly.

Oh, Gran.

I shoved off on my trusty Trek, plodding my now well-worn path to meet Mom at the Place People Get Better or Die Trying. I still didn't know into what category Gran fell, but there was nothing pretty about her new setup. We sat for an hour in silence. I could only really talk to Gran if it were just the two of us.

Before Mom and I left, I turned the television on to PBS, in case *Nature* came on. Gran also had a thing for *Nova*.

"How's co-op?" Mom asked once we got home.

"Fine," I said.

"Is it really?" she said.

"I guess." I shrugged.

Mom rubbed her temples. Headaches were her new tears. "I just hope you are living life amid all this, Laurel."

"I am living my life!" I said, ready to launch into the great things I was pursuing to change her world and mine, but stopped. I looked Mom up and down. She had her clean hair up. Red lipstick artfully curled around her lips, a gold eye

shadow peeked out when she blinked. She'd opted for her red
dress, the one with the fun belt.

She'd been living enough for her, Gran, *and* me lately.

"Are you going somewhere?" I said.

"Laurel, I need a little time for myself. To relax. Just a
little, tonight. And I think you should focus on your photography again."

"Time for yourself? Relax?"

"It's only dinner," she said. "Maybe a movie or something."

"Oh. Okay. Wow. Brad? Good for you?" I said.

"Yes! Thanks, honey. I knew you would understand." She
beamed. "I just need to freshen up a little."

She didn't need to freshen up. She'd gone to see Gran
looking like a million dollars.

I smiled, not knowing if I actually understood. I wanted to.

Sophie was in the throes of camp, so I couldn't complain
to her. I looked at my phone.

*Did you really mean the thing about going to the museum
together?* I texted to Risa.

Ten minutes later she texted back. *Car secured. It's a go.
Text me your address.*

I did.

See you Sunday! she said.

Gran was living in the same room next to a stranger, Mom
was all about Brad, and I was making plans with Risa. The
world had turned upside down.

Though for some reason, that night I dreamed I was the
mystery bird. Flying above the canopy of leaves, singing a
song no one had heard before I chose to sing it.

I wrote Mom a note early in the morning. I didn't know when she had come in the night before. Since that was the level of parental supervision I was working with, I didn't think she'd care much about my wild day out to the Science Museum.

Risa pulled up to the curb in front of my house and clicked the locks open. "Ready for all the knowledge?" she asked.

"Always," I said. I couldn't think of anything else to say. We drove the rest of the way into the city in silence.

I forked over a good portion of my Nature Center earnings to pay for parking at the Science Museum. Risa said I didn't have to, but it felt fair.

The inside teemed with tired parents being pulled from exhibit to exhibit by bouncy little kids. The flashy exhibits, like the live animals and the dinosaur skeletons, attracted most of their attention. The bird room was decidedly quieter.

"Ah," said Risa. "Heaven."

I laughed.

"Come on," she said. "I called ahead."

"Oh, did you get us a reservation in the cafeteria?" I said.

"Better," she said.

It should be noted in the interest of scientific observation that Risa also had fantastic dimples. Like all of the world's joy fit into tiny little indentations in her face when she smiled.

I should similarly note that I shook off that thought in the name of the mission in front of me.

We walked through the Hall of Ornithology, which was a giant arched tunnel painted the color of an autumn sunrise. Flocks of every imaginable species filled each inch of wall, and rows of consoles offered buttons to hear different calls.

"My friend George is going to meet us in a half an hour or so," said Risa, looking at her phone. "For now we should try this. You start down there on that end. I'll go down here."

I obliged. Squawks and honks and whistles and cheeps echoed around the room from speakers suspended from the ceiling. My favorites were the thrushes—smooth like water over rocks in the summer. Gran and I would sometimes sleep outside in her yard in the July heat. I'd fall asleep to a cricket symphony and wake up to the thrushes' liquid song. Their breasts were speckled like the honey and cinnamon oatmeal we'd make in Gran's fire pit. They liked to hide, but would come out if you sat really still and threw enough birdseed out onto the lawn. I closed my eyes and listened to their song over and over again.

"That sounds a little like it," said Risa next to me. "But it's less harsh. We need a harsh bird. Like a raven. Only more complex. Though, crows are pretty complicated, aren't they? They remember the faces that feed or chase them. They find things. Anyway, thrushes sound more like a flute."

I opened my eyes and threw her a look. Was she *nervous*? To be here with me?

"None of these match," I said.

"Agreed." She cleared her throat. "Hey, George is ready for us."

I followed Risa out of the hall, through the taxidermied horror of the main display, and into a little room at the back that I'd never noticed on the million school trips I'd taken here.

"Hey!" said a large, bearded man. "See anything?"

"Here? Everything."

George laughed. "You have a friend."

"Hi. I'm Laurel," I said, sticking out my hand.

"And you have a mystery for me, I'm told."

"I do," I said.

"Well, let's hear it, then!" said George. "You could have just sent the digital file, you know."

"What fun would that be?" Risa's dimples said.

"Well, send it to me now, because that's the highest sound resolution we are going to get. A copy of a copy isn't going to get us anywhere."

Risa emailed George her sound file. George brought it up on his computer and listened.

"Hmmm," he said, stroking his beard. "Interesting." He played it a few more times. "A mockingbird is a good guess. I don't recognize it, exactly, which is saying something. It sounds like some sort of pigeon, mixed with a loon? No. Something like it. It's a dense call, I'll give you that. Let me feed it into the database."

I watched George click and drag the file into a folder and bring up a few screens.

"It'll take a few minutes to scan," said George. He glanced over at me. "Been a while since we got a new one from around here. I'm pretty psyched."

"Lots of birds depend on Sarig Pond and Jenkins Wood

as a migration stop," I said, reciting the words from the wooden sign at the gate leading to the walking paths.

"Kind of early for that, though. And only one? Most peculiar," he said. "Excellent. All done. No exact match! This is fantastic!"

I frowned. "How is that fantastic?"

"It's a challenge. We love a challenge. My buddy isn't in today, but let me talk to him. I'll have this bird for yinz in a week."

"Okay," I said.

"Thanks, kid," he said to Risa. "Totally worth coming in on a Sunday."

I wilted a little as we walked past stuffed peacocks and turkeys and *Tour of North American Migration* exhibit.

"Cheer up, Laurel. We got some of the best people on the case now."

"I know. You're right," I said.

Risa grinned.

I noted her dimples for posterity one more time.

We drove back silently listening to "Warbley's Classic Birdcalls" on the way home. Risa dropped me off and I noticed Mom's car was gone.

"Hey, Laurel, I have something for you," said Risa as I opened the car door.

"What more could there be after the trip to the Science Museum?"

"This," she said, holding out a book.

"*Warbley's Birding Basics—A Field Guide and Life List*," I read aloud. "This is the limited-edition version—and it's signed. Risa! I can't accept this!"

"No, it's cool. Seriously. Warbley did an event and my aunt got me one, and unbeknownst to her, my uncle got me one, too. People know I have a theme, so I have way too many bird-related items in my life. My room is an unkindness already."

"What?"

"You know, of crows? A group of them is called an unkindness? And don't even get me started about the Audubon Society clock. Instead of chiming, it bird calls on the hour. Right now it's"—she checked her watch—"quarter past song sparrow."

"I know this clock well," I said, thinking of the two Gran used to have in the downstairs alone.

"We'll find your bird. Birdscout's honor."

"Those are strong words there, invoking Birdscout honor."

"I know it."

"Well—thanks. This is awesome. Have a good night, Risa," I said. I watched her drive away.

Inside, the house loomed dark. Mom had left *me* a note that she'd gone out on another "I need to live my life" date. She left dinner in the fridge. After I ate it, I got into my pajamas and flipped through Risa's book. I heard my phone buzz from my coat on the floor. I picked it up and noticed about twenty missed texts from Sophie.

Hellllllo, are you alive?

Camp boys are killing me.

Are you out with the birds?

Did the birds kill you?

OMG TEXT BACK YOU HAVE BEEN EATEN BY AN ANGRY GOOSE.

You are right about geese, they are the ones who would take me out. Or turkeys, maybe. Toms are assholes, I texted back.

Sophie called right away. "She lives!" she said. "I was starting to worry."

"Mom went out on a date," I said.

Sophie groaned.

"Right? So, I, uh, went to the Science Museum. Um. With Risa. From co-op."

"Wait, Risa? Risa Risa?"

"Is there another one?"

"Things warming up between you two since you figured out you weren't ruining each other's work."

"She's being helpful with the bird stuff."

"Bird stuff. Got it."

"As Brian Michael Warbley says, 'A friend in birding makes the heart take flight.'" I rubbed my finger across that quote, gold-embossed across the back of my new journal.

Just then, I heard the door open downstairs.

"Mom's back, gotta hide," I said to Sophie.

"But wait, I need you to quote the bird guy to me some more," said Sophie.

"I'll text you later," I said. She was lying; she already had more of Warbley's wisdom in her life than she wanted. But I was not one to pass up an opportunity to share him with the world. For now I quickly flicked off my light and put my phone on its dock. I did *not* want to hear about ChetBrett or whoever it was Mom would want to talk about.

Mom padded up the steps and I heard the door creak as she peeked into my room. I closed my eyes and tried to even out my breathing. She crept over, kissed my head, and smoothed my hair. She wedged part of my comforter out from under me and pulled it up around my chin like she did when I was a little girl. I involuntarily snuggled into it. Mom pulled the door shut, leaving it open just a crack.

The day swirled around behind my eyelids. Mom could drive a person batty sometimes. But then her love tucked me in and kept me warm. Gran balanced that all out. Without her nearby, I tipped daily from one side to another. But tomorrow Richard and Louise might have some answers, and that could bring it all back to stasis again. I could record my observations in my sweet new bird journal.

It was worth a shot, anyway.

FIELD JOURNAL ENTRY
JUNE 17

After I showered, I made a mental to-do list for the day. The field trip with Risa (or maybe just Risa) had refreshed my weary spirit. I thought maybe I could go to city hall and try to get my hands on a few more reports.

(I didn't think I'd know the person at the window, which might be a good thing given my recent run-ins with the Birdie Bros.)

Then I'd go visit Gran, and then I'd try to meet up with the dusk birders in case Richard or Louise had any new ideas. Along the way, I could try to get some shots for the *Fauna* contest.

I was going to make it a great day.

I walked into the kitchen fantasizing about chocolate cereal to find Mom and Brad 2.0 gazing into each other's eyes, deep in conversation.

"Oh," I said.

Both of them looked startled.

"Honey!" Mom said.

"Just. Um. Getting breakfast before I go out for the day," I said.

Dudes didn't usually sleep at our house. At least, not to my knowledge. Maybe Mom got some under the radar (ew), but had enough courtesy to keep that far away from my line of vision or even thought. Though now, for some reason, Beardy McBasic warranted a spot at our table.

I could tell from his rumpled clothes and tousled hair that he probably hadn't just dropped by.

"Hi, Laurel," said Brad.

I stared at him. "Um. Hi, Brad."

"Well, I should get going." He looked at Mom, then at me, then back at Mom, as if he wanted one of us to tell him to stay.

"Okay. Cool. Bye," I said.

"I'll walk you out," Mom said to him.

I sat at the table and soaked little chocolate wheat squares with almond milk. Normally this brought me a lot of joy, but today it just tasted like disappointment in Mom.

Mom returned to the kitchen just as I was finishing up.

"Do you want to tell me what that was about?" she said.

"Wait, *what* was about?" I said.

"You. Being weird with Brad. You are usually a morning person."

"Mom," I said. I gave her a look of my own. "Since when is it okay for your boyfriends to spend the night in this house? Do you even really know him? What if he tries to kill us in our sleep?"

She looked hurt. "You're nearly an adult now, Laurel. I didn't think this kind of thing would bother you."

"Nearly? One second you're telling me I shouldn't worry about adult stuff with Gran. I should focus on photography and fun and whatever. But when you feel like doing whatever you want, then I am making a big deal. You date a lot of men, Mom. And you know what? Whatever. You do you. But I don't want to know about it. At all."

"You make it sound like I'm out every night with a different guy and that's not fair. I've barely had a serious relationship in more than a decade. I've tried to focus on us. But Brad is the real deal. And I don't appreciate your tone."

"Mom. Are you serious right now? If we count the guys I've met, you've brought at least five home in the past year. And those are the ones who stopped by. I know there are more who didn't get that far. Brad is the *third* one *in a year* you've called 'the real deal.' I'm just saying that I'd rather not have random guys in the house. They weird me out."

I resisted the temptation to point out she'd even dated more than one *Brad* in six months.

Mom sniffed. "I think you are exaggerating."

"Oh my god, text Gran right now. She'll back me up. She's met the last three . . ." I stopped when I realized what I said. Gran, my witness, would not be able to talk sense into Mom. Sophie knew, too, but she was at art camp and Mom wouldn't have been pleased to learn my best friend could recount tons of embarrassing details about Mom's love life.

Mom and I looked at each other for an eternity of seconds.

"Okay, well, I like to date. It relaxes me. And I know they don't seem serious. But Brad is different, Laurel. You'll come to see that, sweetheart. You will. He is all that is keeping me going with all that's going on right now."

I frowned.

"Well, and you, of course. But you are so busy . . ." Now she trailed off.

"You know what, Mom," I said with as much forced brightness as I could muster. "I understand. It's fine."

"Honey . . ."

"No. Really. I'm sure Brad is nice. But I should go. Work and stuff," I said.

"Okay." She didn't sound convinced.

I flashed what I hoped was my most winning smile and exited the kitchen before she could say anything else. After all, what problem did I have with Brad 2.0? Was it the beard? Was it that he took Mom's attention? Was it that I knew he would be gone soon and I'd have had yet another brief glimpse of a father figure?

It was probably the beard.

Once outside, my spirits lifted. A bluebird bounced on a slender ribbon of electrical wire coiled around a splintered pole at the end of the street. He chirped to a friend in a pine not far away, who chirped back. House finches and brown-headed cowbirds pecked at crusts of bread thrown by the baker downtown. The park starlings caught wind of the buffet and tried to give chase to the other birds. As I parked my bike in the rack, all species had settled in and around one another, warily sharing. Birds weren't so different from humans when it came to dividing resources. Both kind of sucked at it.

Since the office didn't open for another fifteen minutes, I walked over to the park. I sat on a bench and looked up into the trees.

"Hey there," said Risa, coming up beside me. "Funny meeting you here."

"Birding in the park?" I asked.

"Yes. Kind of. I thought maybe . . . um . . . your bird might come back. And I could get a better look."

My heart grew several sizes in that moment. Risa had been a lot friendlier since we'd uncovered the Birdie Bro sabotage plot.

"That is very kind," I said. "I believe he had a tuft. It just doesn't make sense. What kind of bird is he?"

"Oh, you know what, I have news!"

I laughed. "What? He didn't really have a crest?"

"Oh, no. That was for sure. No. It's my friend. At the Science Museum? I heard back from him."

"Really? What did he say, then?"

"The vocal pattern *is* unique. *So* unique, in fact, that it's probably a mockingbird. Or a bird that is a master imitator. It's a completely new call, not in any database. Which, unless he flew up here from the bottom of the ocean or some remote jungle, is super unlikely. So it must be an imitator bird who heard a call and changed it."

I thought about that. "Then why haven't we seen it, if it's a common bird? Or heard more of the call in general?"

"It does seem to be spreading. Are you hearing it more often?"

"Yeah, a little," I said.

"Me too. Owen and Karen hear it a lot more now, also. Louise and Richard texted me twice last week about it. Even Jerry mentioned it. I think it's spreading. It could just be that the handful of birds who use it have been sneaky so far."

"Oh." It disappointed me, a little, that it could just be an ordinary natural phenomenon. If it wasn't special, it couldn't be Gran.

Risa sat down close to me. Closer than we'd ever been, in fact. She squeezed my chin between her thumb and index finger. "Cheer up, kid," she said. "You never know. Discovering a new call is something, isn't it? You could name it in honor of your grandmother."

That made me smile. "She'd like that."

The fact that Risa had touched me registered. This, along with the new reality that she had never been the source of my past creative failures, shifted my sense of balance. Her face hovered mere inches away from mine. What's to say that I couldn't just lean over and brush my lips against . . .

"Hey! Heyyyyyyyy!" called a screechy little voice behind us. "I know you! You aren't at the pond!" Karen ran up to us. "Why aren't you at the pond?" she accused me. "And you aren't at the pond." She glared at Risa. "You are here instead."

"You are here, too," Risa pointed out.

Karen's mom caught up to her. "Hi, girls." She grinned. "We decided we'd try to do some digging into the city records ourselves."

"We are going to go to the city council meeting in July!"

said Karen. "It's my unproject for summer. Down with the man!" she said.

Karen's mother rolled her eyes. "Her other mother taught her that."

"Look! Richard and Louise are here!" Karen pointed to a shiny black scooter that had parked on the street. A cotton-candy pink one pulled up behind them. And another one.

"Mr. Jerry?" Karen said. Sure enough, Jerry tugged off a helmet and attached it to the front of his scooter.

"Did you know Jerry was in some sort of motorcycle gang with the other birders?" Risa whispered in my ear.

"Um," I said. I tried to come up with something witty, but I'd just noticed Risa had a tiny tattoo of a dove behind her left ear. At that moment, most of the words I knew skidded and ran into each other right there on her neck.

"Fancy meeting you lot here," Jerry said to Karen. "This lot convinced me to take ol' Glinda out for a spin."

"Jerry has a pink scooter *named Glinda*," Risa whispered again. "I could die happy knowing that."

I swear the dove on her neck winked at me.

"This is good," said Richard. "It will be harder to ignore a group of us."

"Though I wonder," said Louise. "It might overwhelm the staff. You know how they are in there. Kids running the front desk. Maybe we should go in one at a time. Space it out."

"We checked online. We couldn't find case numbers like Laurel said we needed. But we found references to different report names. I hope that will be enough. No one ever picks up the phone when we call. I think the admin staff are part-time in the summer," said Karen's mom.

"All the tax increases, you'd think there'd be more ser-vice," muttered Jerry. Not unlike Karen, I was a little taken aback that Jerry existed out of the context of the Nature Center. I'd never seen him in town in all the years that I'd known him. Even when I'd seen him birding with Gran, he'd always just sort of appeared in woods on the other side of town. Or the state. I always thought he was some sort of gruff wood sprite who couldn't stray far from the trees. (Though, he *had* rid-den in on a pink scooter named Glinda, so my theory might still hold.)

"I want to go first," said Karen. No one argued with her, because she had a small and powerful unschooled army a few calls away. Her mom grinned at the civil action teachable moment of it all, and followed Karen inside.

The rest of us looked at each other.

"Read your reports," said Richard. "The ones you pilfered."

"I didn't pilfer them," I said. I might have. I had never heard that word before. "I exercised my right as a person related to a taxpayer and took pictures. Nothing left that build-ing except images."

Richard winked at me. "Sure. Either way, the facts add up to any Shunksville location having six or seven things going against it. And the other two options have several compelling arguments *for* putting the new combined schools there. Frankly, reading it all over, I don't know that we really need a new district at all. Each town is growing, even if it's slowly."

"Each town could use the economic growth, too," said Louise. "It's not like Richburg or Martintown are rolling in coal or steel money anymore. Surely they are fighting for the new schools."

The door to city hall burst open. "No, Mommy, no," said Karen. She stopped on the top step and stomped her foot. "No fair, no fair, no fair."

"What happened?" asked Risa.

"Well, we went up to the guy at the desk, who was very nice. I filled out a form for a 'Letter of Intent to Develop Shunksville,' a city plan we found from several months ago that includes proposals about schools. Apparently it's checked out or in use in the building. The guy wasn't quite sure. So we went for copies of the mayor's remarks at the last city council meeting. My wife had gone with Karen because they were talking about all of the businesses they want to bring back to downtown with the new labs being built in Martintown. I know those should be on file because we've gotten them before. And then the deputy guy came out—"

"Deputy McMean Face!" said Karen.

"—and said that they'd instituted a new policy where you had to request any file online. No requests could be filled in less than forty-eight hours."

"So why do they still have someone working the desk?" said Risa.

"And they are barely open. When can you even *get* the reports like that?"

"That's what I asked. Particularly because they don't update the online database."

"Then I said I thought he was hiding the reports all for himself," said Karen. "Because I think he is."

"She kind of screamed it," said her mom apologetically. "So the deputy mayor suggested we leave."

"Always that guy," I said to Risa. She nodded.

"Well, us old-timers will try next," said Louise. "Maybe Jerry can charm them."

Jerry grunted.

"Come on." Richard clapped him on the back. "Remember when you got the snapping turtles away from the Boy Scout troop? And those geese away from the college students studying nests? You're good with difficult creatures."

Jerry grunted again, but followed Richard and Louise into city hall. Karen huffed around incensed until her mom convinced her to get a doughnut down the street. Risa and I watched them go.

"We should get doughnuts," I said.

"Yes. Doughnuts after information," she said.

We looked at each other.

"Ready for the bird count?" I said.

Risa grinned. "You know it! Are you going to be there all weekend?"

"Totally." I couldn't help thinking about the tiny bird behind Risa's ear. "I like your tattoo."

"Oh!" Risa's hand flew up to her neck. "You noticed that?"

"Yeah. Did it hurt?"

"It wasn't too bad. Needle on bone is the worst," she said.

"You have more?"

"One on my ankle. A nuthatch, since they like to climb. Or it was supposed to be a nuthatch. Not much flesh on the ol' ankles. I cried and made them stop. It's more of a random bird silhouette just like this one."

"If I find out my mystery bird, I'm going to get a tattoo of that," I said, suddenly deciding it to be true. "For my gran."

Risa grinned again. "That's a great idea! My birds are for my mom and dad. I'll take you to my girl in the city. She's the best. Are you eighteen soon?"

"October. Your tattoos are for your parents? What did they think of that?"

Risa opened her mouth like she was going to say something but then closed it. She did it a second time. "They never saw them," she said.

"Would you get in trouble?" I said.

"Maybe. I mean, I live with my aunt and uncle. They would be so pissed. My parents died when I was little. Dad was a runner, so hence the ankle. And Mom used to kiss my forehead and cheeks and give me an extra behind my ears, so. Um. Yeah."

I had no idea Risa's parents had died. I hadn't really known her until high school.

"I'm so sorry. That sucks," I said.

"I thought about getting 'fuck you' on my knuckles in honor of the aunt and uncle," Risa said. "But they still have control of the money. And my sister."

"You have a sister?" I said. Good grief, did I know anything about Risa at all?

"It's a long story. She's a couple years older than I am and is kind of in prison." Risa looked out over the park for a few long moments. "Or just in prison. You can't kind of be in there." She shook her head. "Wow. Hey, I'm sorry I'm in a TMI mood today, I guess."

"No. It's okay," I said. "I think I started it." I stepped closer to her. Part of me wanted to throw my arms around her. Or maybe find her mean family and throw some angry ducks on them. "You know your entry to *Fauna* two or three years ago? The robin's nest?"

Risa cocked her head. "I sat in a tree every day for two weeks to get that shot."

"That's one of my favorite pictures ever. Because you got that chick pecking out. Its little beak—"

"That *was* one of my best," she said.

"I just thought I'd tell you," I said. My skills at comforting others needed work.

"That means a lot coming from you. I really respect your work." She cleared her throat. "Where's Sophie these days?"

"Art camp." I sighed. "She always goes to art camp. She finds some dude or four and then forgets about me for a month. It's part of her artistic process." I shook my head.

"You are really just friends?" said Risa.

"Of course," I laughed.

"You are just always together at school," she said.

"I had a thirty-five millimeter phase in my youth. I found out her dad had a dark room in his basement. We just kind of stuck together after that."

"Huh," she said.

Silence fell again. The urge to hug her—or at least touch her—still poked at my brain. But we didn't have that kind of relationship.

Did we?

Could we?

She *had* just shared major life drama. She already knew most of mine. But I'd gone the change-the-subject-to-something-good route. She seemed to have liked that, at least.

"Hey, do you . . . ," I said.

"Would you think . . . ," she said at the same time.

We both stopped talking.

"What?" I said.

"No, you can go first," she said.

"Oh. Okay. I was going to ask if . . . um. In theory . . . no I mean, maybe sometime we . . ." I had zero plan about how to do this. I'd asked people out before. On dates. But was that what I was doing? Should I go a different direction? Suggest a creative collaboration?

I was saved from my thoughts by Louise, Richard, and Jerry emerging from city hall. I heaved a sigh of relief.

Risa sighed, too. But it had a distinctly disappointed air to it. Or that could have been my wishful thinking.

"What's the word, bosses?" I asked.

"Well, the nice boy in there seems annoyed with people telling him what to do. So I gave him three dollars and he got us one record." Louise waved her phone. "And I got pictures, inspired by you, young lady."

"That took all that time?" I said. It felt like I'd been standing on the corner with Risa for years.

"Well, then Jerry asked for the charter for the establishment of Sarig Pond and Jenkins Wood Nature Sanctuary."

"I've seen it before. I think we have a copy in the archives. But it's buried someplace since the intern from the college quit," he said.

(Jerry had fired the kid for throwing cigarette butts by Elder Oak, but this hardly seemed the time to remind him of that.)

"Did you get it?" asked Risa.

"No he did not," said Richard. "Kid at the desk said that report was flagged and then he wandered off. Brought the mayor with him this time. We had a civil conversation, and then we left."

"When the mayor refused his request, Richard called him a heartless paper-pushing meat-eater," said Louise, "so then we were told that the desk was closed."

"It doesn't close until noon," I said.

"That's what the sign said. I pointed that out," said Richard.

"And then the mayor asked us to leave."

"Can he do that?" asked Risa.

"Well. He did," said Jerry. "Something smells in there, and it's not just those pleather chairs."

"Let us try," said Risa. "It can't hurt."

"Are we going to ask for the charter?" I said.

Risa shrugged. "Do you have any other ideas?"

"There was some decree about Pennsylvania wildlife months ago. They dedicated the pond to some statewide project. I didn't really pay attention, because Jerry said it was mostly for a research grant or something," I said. "But that might be on file here?"

"We'll go for any of it," said Risa.

I followed her into city hall, the weirdness of our random conversation fading as the familiar municipal office odor wafted toward me.

"Hey, Greg," I said.

"Seriously, Laurel?" he said wearily.

"What?" I said.

"Are you with those other people?" he said. "Who were just here? From your pond?"

"She's only here with me," said Risa.

I liked the sound of that.

"There's a Post-it here about you," he said to me. "You are blacklisted from city hall."

"*Excuse* me?" I said.

"I'm supposed to go get the deputy or the mayor or Vern the security guy if you come in. Apparently you create a disturbance."

"Dude. I've never done anything here except come to the window and ask for reports."

"Yeah. I kinda figured. Because that is now the new definition of 'disturbance,' here."

"Is it legal to ban someone from public property?" said Risa. "That's not right. Listen, we are here for—"

"Don't bother," said Greg. "I'm going to sweep the file room. Window is closed early. I know you know Jerry. And those old birders and the little angry birder who was here earlier. And I don't know what you are trying to do, but I gotta make service hours before my folks take us to the beach next month. So I'm *not* getting fired."

"There's something wrong here, Greg," I said. "You have to know it. Why else are they flagging records? Why are they banning me? All I do is ask questions."

"And that's enough of a problem." He shrugged. "I don't know if it's wrong or just a hassle. I don't care. See you." With that, Greg hung a Closed sign on a suction hook on the window, and slid the venetian blinds over the glass.

"Are you fucking kidding me?" I said.

"Unbelievable," said Risa.

We went back outside to the group and reported our utter lack of progress.

"Well. That settles it, crew. We need to keep on this. We need to take this to the next level."

"What's that? Clearly city hall is in on it."

"Oh, I have an idea," I said.

Maybe I'd failed at my plan to make it a great, productive day. And maybe I wasn't able to change stuff at home, with Mom-the-mostly-absent and Gran still in her holding pattern. But I might know someone who could challenge even city hall.

There was still hope.

FIELD JOURNAL ENTRY
JUNE 18
NOTABLE LOCATION: CHANNEL 4 ACTION NEWS
LIFE LIST ENTRY 3,287: SCARLET TANAGER

"Richard and Louise's skepticism about my plan convinced Jerry it wouldn't work," I said to Gran. "But like you say, persistence goes a long way."

I watched her face. Monitors beeped, her leg compressors undulated. A finger twitched. Daily she looked paler, like the border between this world and whatever came after it thinned and the light of beyond lit up her face more and more from within. It seemed more plausible that she could be soaring in the breezy summer sky, so vacant was the once-lively body.

Gran's roommate still had pink cheeks and warm-looking skin.

"Risa's going to meet me at the Channel Four building today. Funny thing about Risa . . ." I paused. "I think I like her. *Like* her, like her. It's a possibility. I don't know. But I'm focused on you. On us. Obviously. As Brian Michael Warbley said in the most recent issue of *Fauna*, 'Focus on what is most important in the present, to prevent the extinction of a beautiful future.' That's me, Gran. I'm focusing on our bird to figure out what you are trying to tell me."

Unlike *some* people who spent every waking moment with Brad. Possibly non-waking ones as well.

Barf.

"So that's where I'm going. I'll keep you posted." I leaned over and kissed her forehead. "Wait for me, Gran," I said. "I'm really trying."

Outside, I hopped on my bike and sped over the hills to Channel Four Action News. Risa was already waiting for me, leaning against the warm gray stucco, legs crossed so that her green cargo pants looked like a curved vine. She'd bleached her hair for the occasion.

"Is that bad for your scalp? Changing color that often?" I greeted her.

"I had to go back to blondish to get another color than black. This is my transition phase. It's not great for the hair. But I think I'll shave it off and start over at some point."

"Ah." I wanted to ask her more about her family. Or *something* about her. But in the moment I could never work up the nerve. If Gran had been conscious, she could have given me a pep talk.

"You ready?" said Risa.

"Ready as I'm going to get," I said.

"Hard same," she said.

We passed through the sliding double doors side by side, our hands almost touching. A sliver of electricity shot through my arm when her hand brushed against mine. Had that been on purpose?

We stopped at a desk just inside the entrance. The place had the air-conditioning cranked; I wished I'd worn layers.

"We are here to see Bill Andrews," Risa said. "He should be expecting us."

"Names?" the bored receptionist said.

Risa gave her our names. She printed out name tags and handed us a clipboard to sign in.

"Someone will be with you in a second," she said.

Risa and I wandered over to a small fountain.

"I'm surprised it hasn't frozen over," I said.

"Seriously, penguins could live here," she said. "Do you want my hoodie?"

"Aren't you going to use it?"

"You are wearing shorts. At least my legs are covered. I'll be okay." She unzipped her sweatshirt and handed it to me.

"Thanks," I said, slipping it on. It smelled like the woods and rain and faintly of bleach.

She raised an eyebrow. "It looks better on you than it does on me."

The heat from my face swallowed any chill left in my body.

"Hey, girls," said Bill Andrews of Channel Four News.

His head popped out from behind a door on the far wall. "Come on back."

Risa and I walked after Bill Andrews. We followed him into a small office off a bustling hallway.

"How can I help you?" he said.

"Well, like we said in the email, there is something funky going on with city hall and possibly the school board. They want to put the new school in Jenkins Wood and get rid of the pond somehow," I said.

"We have several documents showing that Richburg and Martinsville are better sites. We have a survey that argues that, while it's possible to use the land for other purposes, it's not a great idea to build there. We have several papers written by students at Shunksville Community College about the animals and birds who rely on the site for survival," said Risa. Louise had gotten the latter from her granddaughter who taught there. "I printed them all for you."

"And we have a copy of the charter for the nature reserve. The original landowners were explicit in their wishes that the city only use it for public space." I'd spent all weekend searching through boxes of dusty archives to find it.

"Is a school a public space?" said Bill Andrews of Channel Four News.

"Well—" I paused. Richard had said that the school could, indeed, qualify. It specifically said in the combined school district plan that the new public spaces would be designed for use by the three communities. "Yeah."

"But that doesn't change all the other stuff. And maybe that's a loophole, but it doesn't change the *tone* or *intent* of the charter," Risa said. She handed over a folder of everything Jerry had printed out.

"Both you and Channel Eight usually report on the bird count weekend," I said. "This would make the story more compelling, don't you think? You could *save* the bird count."

Bill Andrews chewed on his pen. "Have you brought this to any other news outlets?"

"No," I said. "We started with you."

He smiled. "Why me?"

"Because my grandmother likes you," I said.

He chewed on his pen some more. "Are you going to give it to anyone else?"

"Possibly," said Risa. "Because everyone should at least know about this, before they rip out our woods."

Bill Andrews nodded. He paged through all the printouts.

"Okay. I'll see what I can do. Thanks, girls," he said.

Risa and I stared at him.

"Are you going to do the story?" I asked.

"I have to pitch it. I think there's a strong case. But no guarantees, I'm afraid. Do you remember the way out? Here. Have a Channel Four pen." He stood up and held out non-chewed versions of his. I could tell the conversation was over. Bill Andrews exuded a no-nonsense, zero-small-talk kind of vibe.

Once back outside, Risa and I walked back to our bikes. "I don't know if he believed us," said Risa. "But fuck me if this isn't a nice pen."

"Seriously," I said. I held it up for a better look. The weight of it balanced perfectly between my thumb and middle finger. "This is some fancy shit."

A rumble of thunder threatened in the distance.

"Balls," said Risa. "We'd better go. Jerry wanted me there early anyway. You on today?" She swung her leg over her bike.

I shook my head. "No, I'm going to check Gran's yard," I said. "It's not ours anymore in less than two weeks, but her feeders are still there. Might as well fill them."

Risa stopped and looked at me. "Do you want company? I could call in. Make up an excuse about birds. It wouldn't even be a lie."

Even though the impending rain cooled the air around us, the now customary heat rose to my cheeks.

"Oh. Thanks. That's so nice. But it's bird count prep, you know? Jerry might actually kill you. And me, if he uncovered my involvement."

"True," she said. I looked at my sneakers. I could feel her studying my face.

"Next time?" I said. "I'll have to go back again to check the yard, anyway. You can see the feeders. I keep hoping the woodpeckers will come back."

"It's a date," Risa said, grinning.

My god. Her dimples.

We rode in silence toward the Nature Center. I waved as I turned to Gran's road. There I found the feeder empty and hungry fucking squirrels watching me unearth the bag of suet from the storage bench next to the porch.

"Don't even think it, motherfuckers." I unhooked two of

the feeders from their curled iron rods and poured suet into the holes. For the millionth time, I cursed Jerry for not springing for the neat blocks, but this was the cheapest way to get the good stuff. I uprighted the feeders, and in two seconds a squirrel sauntered over, undeterred by my presence.

"Are you actually serious, motherfucker?" I said. "This is not for you!" I lunged to chase him, but a strange song wafted over from Gran's spruce.

"Hello?" I said at the tree.

It wasn't the mystery bird, exactly. It resembled the mystery bird. Or it possibly resembled a hoarse robin. I crept slowly to the left, hoping not to scare whatever it was. I changed my mind and backed toward my bike. I debated for a second between binos and camera, and opted for the camera. I moved back toward the sound.

"There you are!" I said as a flutter erupted from the needles. Red body. Black wings. "Another one! " I said to them. Yellow body. Browner wings. They resembled one another, so it must be a male-female pair. The two of them made their way over to the suet. They talked to each other, pleased with the discovery.

I moved around them and kneeled on the ground to get a better angle. I snapped and snapped them eating, stopping only to throw an occasional dirty look at the squirrels hungrily eyeing the suet.

Just then, lightning cracked across the sky, scaring the shit out of girl, birds, and interloping squirrel alike. The pair took flight and I ran to the porch just as the heavens opened up.

I sat on the porch for a few minutes. There was no way I was going to bike home in this. I opened my bird identification app and looked for their features. It located the scarlet tanager easily, and I confirmed the yellow female.

"Sweet, another one on the life list!" I said to Gran's porch. Even better than that was when I scrolled through my camera and found my shot of the birds framed by lightning. Streaks of light highlighted the serious "WTF" look on the birds' faces.

"I just might have a winner here, Gran," I whispered.

Eventually my camera battery died. I swung back and forth on the porch swing, the rhythm of it reminding me of countless days there from when I was a little girl. Gran and I used to love to watch the rain, just like this. I curled my knees under my chin and wrapped my arms around my legs. I drew in a deep breath, ready for the deep, profound loneliness to swallow me whole. But then I smelled the rain mixed with—woods. And bleach. I realized I was still wearing Risa's sweatshirt.

Instead of lonely, I felt warm.

FIELD JOURNAL ENTRY
JUNE 21

"This is the big show," I said. "Everything has been a rehearsal for today."

"Binoculars at the ready, Birdscouts," said Risa.

"I want more birds than Pittsburgh," I said.

"They can shove their three rivers," said Risa. "Our water fowl outnumber theirs even on a good day."

"They do have Penguins," said Karen.

The kids around her laughed. I resisted the urge to tell her

that unless Pittsburgh won something for their small, flight-less, fish-eating penguins, I wasn't interested.

"Go," I said. "You are round one, day one."

"Find! Those! Birds!" said Risa.

Fourteen Birdscouts and their chaperones took off down the path. That kind of noise was going to frighten the shit out of almost anyone perched nearby, but maybe most of our birds were used to it by now.

"You girls go watch them," said Jerry. "We don't want no kids getting poison something by going off path."

"Yes, sir," said Risa and I together. We followed after the raucous birders slowly.

"Sparrows on the left. Four male and one female," I said.

"They blend in. Do you think there are five?"

"Six. One is up top there." I pointed to a stealthy female on a higher branch.

"Got them," said Risa.

"There's an oriole. Nope, two. Oh, and a nuthatch! He's on a reed." I sipped hot chocolate from my stainless steel tumbler. Normally early morning birding didn't bother me, but bird count weekend required a special diligence. Sugar prevented me from throwing the more enthusiastic Birdscouts to the swans.

"Blue jays. Male and female. Right there," said Risa, more to her binoculars than to me.

"Got it," I said.

Risa stopped walking and stared through her lenses. "I . . . ," she began, but didn't say anything or move for several moments.

"You what?" I said.

"Nothing. It's just—his crest."

"Oh, the jay? They are indeed crested. Actually, that one is particularly blue, isn't he?" I made a notation of that. The jay squawked at us. Their call is harsh, somewhat belying their dickish nature.

"It kind of reminds me of your bird. The bird we saw in the park. Like, his silhouette. I mean . . . I think your bird could be a jay."

"What? There's no way. Listen to them."

The jays flew from tree to tree around us, angrily calling to one another, or possibly other birds farther away who answered. Short, brusque sounds. Each sound they made was as far from the mystery call as possible.

"I know," said Risa slowly. "Yeah." She sounded skeptical. She watched the jays flutter up to the canopy and stay there.

My bird *did* prefer to be up higher, generally. I closed my eyes and tried to fix my attention on their sound.

Not my bird.

"I'll have to look up crested birds again," I said. "I listened to every call I could find, and none of them matched."

"Jays are master imitators," said Risa. "They are in the crow family. They are wicked smart."

I frowned. There was just really no way Gran could be something so . . . *common*. What kind of message from the universe would that be? Jays are everywhere. Fucking jays steal from other birds just for the fun of it. They take out other birds' young if given the chance.

"But you're right. There is no call I recognize as yours here," she said.

I nodded. I'd surely have had visual confirmation of a shitty blue jay by now. They were all over. In fact, there were sixteen of them around the pond. The buntings were there (suck it, Richburg!), but no tanagers. Risa and I collected an exciting owl pellet (no owl that I could see, though), three bluebirds, two herons, two swans, four cormorants, five juncos, seven orioles, eleven wood ducks, twenty-five mallards, and one Channel Four reporter Bill Andrews.

Bill Andrews stood in suede dress shoes and crisp khaki pants, staring up at Elder Oak. Elder Oak watched him, unimpressed by his inappropriate footwear choice.

"Hello there," he greeted us.

"Counting birds?" I said.

He leaned toward Risa and me. "Those documents you gave me were sure something."

My eyebrows shot up. "Are you doing a story on them?"

"I believe I am," he said. "Want to go on camera?"

"Um." I glanced over at Risa. I wasn't really an on-camera person. I much preferred to be behind it.

Risa shook her head slowly. "Let me get our boss. He'll talk to you," she said. She ran into the Nature Center to grab Jerry.

"A reporter," Jerry's voice boomed from inside the small center. "About time."

We couldn't hear Risa's response. But the wooden screen door banged open and Jerry charged toward Bill Andrews.

"Do you have a microphone, sir?" Jerry asked with loud deference. "I'll give you the what-for."

"I do . . . ," said Bill Andrews. He gestured to his camerawoman to point the lens toward the stream of consciousness pouring out of Jerry's mouth and into the microphone Bill Andrews barely managed to get in front of him.

"For twenty years I've worked here. The city pays my salary. It's not big, but it's enough. It lets me have a staff." He gestured to Risa and me as we backed farther and farther off camera. "It lets me do programs for the kids. Birders from all over come here because of the migrating populations. I swear to god one August we once had a Kirtland's warbler and a gyrfalcon. And last September we had a whooping crane. *A whooping crane, I tell you.*" Jerry pointed to Bill Andrews to emphasize his point. "Those birds have little business in Pennsylvania, right? But they were here. This one got a picture of the crane." He gestured again toward me.

I had. It was true. It was silhouetted against a cloudy sky. I hadn't had my settings right to get it, because who can think straight when a whooping crane flies by?

"And now these suits show up, walking around like they own the place. Maybe they do own the place, technically. But all I know is that these woods are bigger than they are. And so is the pond. And the sky don't belong to nobody but the birds. So maybe just leave this place alone." With that, Jerry nodded to Bill Andrews, turned, and stomped back to his office.

Bill Andrews shot a neutral look at the camera. "What's his last name?" he asked us.

"Fern," I said.

"Seriously?" said Bill Andrews.

"Yup," said Risa. "One hundred percent. He's the Sarig Pond and Jenkins Wood programming coordinator."

"All right, then." Bill Andrews wrote his name and title

down in a notebook he took out of his pocket. Several Birdscouts emerged from the boardwalk. "Pardon me," he called to them before they headed down the path into the woods.

Risa and I watched him interview Karen. We couldn't hear what she said, but it involved a lot of jumping up and down.

"Do you think this will help the cause?" I said.

"All publicity is good publicity, right?" said Risa.

I shrugged. A sweet smell wafted over the grass and from the air.

"It's going to rain again soon," I said. "Oh, that reminds me, I still have your sweatshirt."

"That's okay. I have tons. We get two every year from this place. I have at least four that still fit."

"Okay. I kind of like it. It smells like you."

Risa glanced over at me.

"I mean. Wait. Maybe that sounded weird? Not that I seek out clothing that smells like you. Of course you don't smell *bad*. It reminds me of the woods. And your hair. Uh. Never mind."

Stellar, Laurel. Fantastic, even. Get the microphone from Bill Andrews and have that shit recorded.

But Risa smiled. "I kinda like that you have it."

"Oh. I like it, too. Having it. Wearing it is like having your arms around me." Gratitude for the damp earth mixed with horror at what I was currently saying out loud. Without it under my feet, I would have ignited the forest floor with the heat coursing from my head to sneakers.

"I—" started Risa.

"No listen . . . ," I interrupted.

But then a commotion from Bill Andrews's direction made Risa and I turn around. Deputy Mayor Ross had shown up with his own cameraperson.

"Hello, everyone!" said the deputy mayor, speaking into a mic and looking only into the camera. "It's a great day for a nature walk. We at city hall are here to honor"—he glanced down at an index card in his hand—"bird count weekend!"

"Well, this is a first," I said. "I don't remember city hall caring about this before."

"Seriously," said Risa.

"That's the mean man who kicked me out of his house!" said Karen to Bill Andrews.

"City hall," said her mother. "We were in city hall."

"We went to see papers for my project. But they wouldn't let us see anything." Karen glared at the deputy mayor.

Hell hath no fury like a seven-year-old, brother. Don't even try to engage. But like the deputy mayor would heed my psychic warnings even if he could hear them.

"Honey, I'm sure that's not true," he said into his mic. "Even our youngest citizens are always welcome."

"Liar!" yelled Karen. "You said I should leave!"

Karen's mom grabbed the hood of her sweatshirt and gently tugged her away from the mic. I appreciated the hell out of that kid. Jerry would have to give her a special commendation on the Birdscout Wall of Fame.

Drizzle fell on Bill Andrews and Deputy Mayor Ross as they stood with their microphones. Bill Andrews offered his to Ross, who took it and spoke to him and his camera.

"This is important, this land. But more important is the

whole community, and jobs, and education. The founders of this park loved Shunksville and wanted to see it thrive. Obviously we take the preservation of this particular legacy quite seriously. That's why, if Shunksville becomes the home to the new combined school district, we will make sure to remember what stood here."

"So, the school is going to go here, on this site?" said Bill Andrews into his own mic.

"That hasn't yet been determined."

The rain picked up. Droplets stuck to my eyelashes, blurring the world.

"Come on," said Risa. She grabbed my wrist and pulled me under the Nature Center awning. She'd been smart enough to wear a baseball hat. "You'll get soaked," she said.

"How can he really not care?" I said. "A whooping crane, you know?" I shivered.

"Do you want another sweatshirt?" Risa said.

"Your other one is inside. I brought it back to give to you. But I guess I'll just put it on again."

"Girls, the second Birdscout troop is here," Jerry said from inside the Center. "Well, a couple of 'em anyway. Take 'em out."

"Yes, Jerry," I said as I leaned inside the door to grab Risa's sweatshirt and two garbage bags for makeshift ponchos, handing one to Risa. Bill Andrews and Michael Ross still stood in the rain, talking. I couldn't pay much attention to them, since I had birds to count and Risa's clothing once again on my body.

"You even look good in a garbage bag," I said.

"You too," she said.

The ridiculous thing was that I had meant what I said. The even more ridiculous thing was that it seemed like she meant it, too.

Risa's shift ended one troop of birders earlier than mine, so I didn't get to say goodbye. It was just as well.

The rain let up, so I was able to bike over to the hospital to see Gran without wiping out in a puddle. There greeted me the same acrid, antiseptic floor. Same stiff white sheets, same glowing, beeping pauses. Everything that Gran shouldn't be and so completely was, barely tethered to life.

"Gran," I said. "Surely you aren't a blue jay, right? Maybe blue was your favorite color. You wore a lot of it. But I just thought that was because of your eyes."

Twitch.

"You liked purple or green more, though. The colors of your name, you said. The aurora borealis? The northern lights? Waves of green across the sky. You saw a snowy owl and a king eider in Greenland. And then at night the aurora came. You said you'd take me to see it. You have to wait, Gran. You have to stick around to show me the aurora."

Tiny shudder.

I sighed and sat down next to her. I turned on her TV and adjusted the volume on the speaker attached to a moveable call button on her bed. I flipped idly to the Discovery Channel, but didn't want to watch the scary fishing show. I landed on Channel Four just as the opening music to the five o'clock news chimed from Gran's speaker.

Bill Andrews and another anchor talked about sewer lines and a house fire not far from my house. A commercial came on for soup and my stomach growled. I thought about heading home early for dinner. Mom would surely be out with Brad. The benefit of this was that since they ate out so much, there were generally pretty good leftovers to steal in the fridge.

"Gran, do you want the TV on?" I tried.

Nothing.

I fumbled with Gran's speaker thing to turn down the sound. When the news came back from commercial, though, the second anchor looked into the camera and said, "Tonight, we have a special report from our own Bill Andrews."

"Thanks, Gail. It's the annual Western PA bird count weekend, and there is some controversy taking flight."

Oh, Bill Andrews. Bird puns. This could be promising or a portent of bad things.

His camerawoman got Elder Oak at a good angle and must have followed some birders when I wasn't watching because she got a great shot of Grandma Maple as well.

"We want what's best for the community. We want jobs. We want education . . . ," he started. The face of Michael Ross cut off Grandma Maple's screen time.

"There has been some resistance to proposed plans to place the unified school district at the site of the Sarig Pond and Jenkins Wood Nature Sanctuary. But development of the city-owned land would save taxpayer dollars while creating sorely needed employment opportunities," said the deputy mayor. "We learned last night that Shunksville was picked by the committee as the site for the new school. We've gathered bids preemptively and are confident that the special July city council session will see our proposals pass."

My mouth dropped when they cut back to Bill Andrews in the studio. WTF?

"This sounds like a great opportunity for Shunksville," said one anchor. "Why are people opposed to it?"

"Because it will sacrifice an important ecological site," said Bill Andrews.

"But it's not like Pennsylvania lacks for trees," the other anchor said with a laugh. "Just ask my husband in fall, when he has to rake all the leaves."

Bill Andrews agreed, laughed, and they went to commercial.

I stared at the screen. No Karen, no Jerry, no birders. Just the deputy mayor. Bill Andrews, how could you? I felt betrayed. He had the documents, he knew this was a bad idea, and he chose not to say it?

"Gran, you liked *that* guy?" I said.

Surely my imagination chose to play tricks then, but Gran looked kind of pissed.

"I can't believe this shit," I said.

I rode home to my empty house, where I wolfed down some spicy chicken pasta from a Styrofoam container. I didn't even bother heating it up. I called Risa, but she didn't pick up. I texted Sophie.

You are not going to BELIEVE what is going on, I typed.

Sophie called. "Hey! I'm on break and have reception for once."

I kind of shouted the weeks' events she'd missed. "I'm blacklisted from city hall! Bill Andrews is a dirty traitor to the man! No one cares about whooping cranes except Jerry and Risa!" I finished.

"Could we go back to the part where you told Risa you wanted her arms around you?"

"That's not the point here, Soph."

"I think it should be. We were aware of the government corruption and their lack of regard for the environment. What is surprising is the fact that Risa didn't destroy your work and that maybe she is gonna be your lady friend. Is she your woman? Are you going to kiss her? I hooked up with another guy here. He's into woodworking."

"There's a lot I could say about that. But no, listen, Bill Andrews . . ."

"Laurel, you listen to me. Go find another reporter. Someone will listen to you. You printed documents. You have a folder. There are plenty of newspeople who would be all over that shit. Call Rachel Maddow."

"Who is Rachel Maddow?"

"She's on at night. My parents watch her. National cable news."

"I don't think this is exactly national news. Yet." It probably could be if Jerry had seen Bill Andrews's report. His head might have exploded.

"Well, how about that chick who was in the park that day? Ellie, something."

"Yeah. True," I said. My phone buzzed. Risa was texting, too.

"The woman is texting," I said.

"Good. You need to get some. This will chill you out," she said.

"Your priorities are so out of whack right now," I said.

"You can save the world and still make out with a hot girl, is all I'm saying," said Sophie. "Also, send me your lightning bird pictures. They sound cool."

"I hate you," I said.

"Love you, too. Bye." She hung up.

You called? Risa had sent.

Did you see the news? I said.

No! Was Jerry on?

Nope. Bill Andrews is a dick. We need to regroup.

Okay. Home stuff tonight. See you tomorrow?

I stared at my screen. I wondered if I should say something about home stuff, since I knew it wasn't that great.

How are you? Anything I can do? That seemed safe. Thank the herons I hadn't called or I probably would have complimented her boobs or something.

Don't strangle Bill Andrews. Until tomorrow anyway. She ended with a heart.

We were in heart territory? What did that mean?

It's an emoji, Laurel. Keep it together.

Still.

A heart isn't something to give to another person lightly.

FIELD JOURNAL ENTRY
JUNE 23

The bird counts were flowing, and we pulled ahead of the Pittsburgh region by a nose.

Again. I knew it really wasn't a competition of numbers.

But if we were going to record the most birds, this should be the year. It legitimized the fight to save the land.

I stopped at the grocery store before heading into the Nature Center. My elusive mother had texted and asked me to get food to feed myself. She'd left money on the counter.

Spending time with Brad and Gran left her little time for me, which suited me. She'd sold Gran's damn house and, I mean, *Brad*. He'd lasted longer than any other of the recent dudes, but that wasn't saying much.

I spotted Mom's preferred brand of nine grain and snagged the last bag on the shelf.

I walked down the next aisle. Two women stood talking quietly next to my heavenly chocolate wheat squares.

"Pardon me," I said. They glanced at me and moved over a fraction of an inch. That was a little weird, but it was early and maybe the cereal they wanted hadn't been stocked. I went to the counter and the woman who has worked there since the dawn of time checked me out. I handed her my money. She took it and looked at me. She rolled her tongue around in her mouth.

"You know," she said, the cash drawer shuttering open. "Mill's been gone from this place for a decade."

"Um. Yes," I said. Everyone knew that.

"Blooms gone, too," she said. That was the food manufacturing plant that'd shut down a few years ago.

"Yes," I said.

"The way I see it, bringing in a couple of schools with all those kids is a good thing. No matter where they put it. Lots of jobs with new schools."

"Uh . . ." I didn't know if that was true. It seemed like the teachers who already had jobs in the individual schools would come here. Or other staff. And teachers needed training to be teachers. Who else would get jobs? Janitors maybe? And how many of those would the schools really need?

"Maybe you shouldn't try to stop jobs."

"I'm sorry. I don't really know what you are talking about," I said.

"You were on the news. With them people at the woods."

"I was?" I wondered if Bill Andrews had been on the air at eleven on Thursday. Or if he'd reported it again yesterday. Maybe he had a different report with different footage. I had tried not to be in any shots, but I might have been in a couple with Jerry.

"You are easy to spot. Your gran was always real nice to me. Bringing you here since you were a little girl. And your mom. She's a teacher. This is good for her. You shouldn't go poking your nose into stuff like that."

"Okay," I said. I took my change and groceries and got the hell out of there as fast as possible.

I stopped at home and shoved everything into the refrigerator. I rode over to the Nature Center. Risa had gone to see Ellie King of Channel Eight yesterday on her day off. Given her our folder of all the documents. Hopefully she would be less of a dick than Bill Andrews.

"Hey there," said Risa, coming over to the bike rack. "Major drama."

"What? Bird-related?"

"Kinda. We have protestors."

"Protestors? Are they loud? They better not piss off the swans. No one wants that."

"You'll see."

We walked away from the gate to Elder Oak, where a few people were gathered with signs. "Schools mean jobs," one read. "Education > Preservation," read another.

"What is even happening?" I said.

Richard and Louise stood talking with two of the men with signs.

"Education and preservation aren't mutually exclusive things," said Richard.

"Isn't preservation essential so that children have a world in which to *live*?" said Louise.

"Yinz don't know what's even going on here. It's bigger than you know. There are union contracts at stake. People high up want this and they are going to get it. Birds don't live in one place. They fly all over," said a woman.

"Risa," I whispered. "What is this?"

"Last night. Apparently our governor earmarked this project for Shunksville because some of his donors are from around here? And they are connected to other donors who might fund him to run for president one day? And our mayor and deputy mayor are his friends. Richard and Louise and Jerry were kind of shouting it in the Center before all these people arrived. It's scaring the unschoolers."

"Damn it, we need their numbers," I said. "It's a four-day average!"

"There were three red-bellied woodpeckers. Or one that people saw three times. Hard to tell."

"Oh good," I said. Damn it, the squirrels had probably eaten all of Gran's suet again. I'd have to fix that tomorrow.

"Jobs, not ducks! Jobs, not ducks!" the group stared chanting. They formed a line and started marching around Elder Oak.

"This is the saddest, stupidest protest I've ever seen," said Richard, walking over to us.

"They can go duck themselves," muttered Jerry.

"If they try to chain themselves to Elder Oak, his spirit will eat them," said Louise.

"What did the news say?" I said.

"Well, they showed Jerry. But they edited him to make it sound like he was against any new school anywhere. And anti-Shunksville. Bill Andrews cut to himself saying how we haven't had development here for years. And this is our chance to be back in the game."

"We're regional. They get these broadcasts in Martinsville and Richburg. What are they saying?" Risa said.

"They apparently don't have an in with Bill Andrews," said Louise.

A dad with three little boys walked toward us from the gate. All four of them looked at the protestors stumbling around Elder Oak's roots, yelling about jobs. The smallest boy started to cry and buried his face in his dad's pant leg. The dad looked down at his boys, then at the protestors, and ushered the kids back to the gate.

"No, wait," I called after them. That dad totally had a pair of binoculars strapped to his chest. He didn't even have a neck band. This guy was the real deal. "We want your count!" I caught up to them. "I'll walk you past them. They won't bother you. Go count birds."

"Well . . ." He looked unconvinced.

"I saw a scarlet tanager," I said. It wasn't here and it was days ago, but those were irrelevant details at the moment.

"Are you serious?" said the dad.

"Yes, sir."

He didn't even hesitate. "Okay." He picked up the littlest boy and followed me past Elder Oak to the woodland path.

"If he's not here, try around the pond next," I said.

The dad nodded.

I walked back to Risa, Richard, and Louise. "Almost lost that one," I said.

Risa grinned. "You are a real asset to the cause," she said.

The familiar heat pinged the back of my neck. "Yeah, but the cashier at Food World kinda told me off this morning about this." I waved at the feeble protest. "Bill Andrews has people thinking that the Pond and Wood are coming for their children and careers."

Louise sighed. "That guy. He's drinking buddies with the deputy mayor. I would have thought he'd be dedicated to the truth. But no. Disappointing."

"So what do we do?" said Risa.

"We talk to her," said Richard, pointing at Ellie King. She walked up to the protestors.

"Hi there," she said to them. "Anyone want to speak on camera?"

Oh, did they ever. Everybody seemed to think that the only thing keeping Shunksville from being great again was nature. After listening to the protestors talk about jobs and access and opportunity, Ellie King wandered over to us.

"Hey, Risa, thanks for the tip," she said.

"I'm sorry we went to Bill Andrews first," she said.

"It was my fault. He seemed so trustworthy," I said.

Ellie King shrugged. "No worries. He took the information . . . in a different direction. But he's not on Sunday nights. I am." She smiled at us. "Want to share your thoughts on the matter?"

I cleared my throat. I should really be helping children

quietly observe color variation on male and female avian species. But next year at this time, there might not be any avian species *to* observe. "Okay," I said.

Humidity plastered my hair to my scalp and I probably should have worn cleaner shorts, but surely the camera need not pan down that far.

Besides, I was wearing Risa's sweatshirt. It made me feel brave.

Ellie King came close to me.

"Ready?" she said.

"Yup," I said. I wasn't. Not even a little. *Gran, help me,* I thought.

Sure enough, a mystery call sounded from Elder Oak, loud and clear. Wide-eyed, I looked at Risa.

"On it," she said, and ran straight toward the protestors.

"What's your name?" Ellie King asked.

"Laurel Graham."

"And you work here at the nature reserve?"

"Yes. My grandmother lives . . . um . . . lived on the other side of the woods until recently. She took me birding since before I could walk. I went to nature camp every summer until I was old enough to volunteer. This is my junior co-op for Greater Shunksville High School. I was allowed to extend it through the summer."

"Would you say the pond and forest are important to you?"

"Um . . ." I bit my lip and looked over to Risa gazing up at the sky through her binos. "This place is my life. It's the life of Shunksville, too, even if people don't know it. The diversity of swimming things and crawling things and flying things rely on plants and the plants rely on them. And we rely on the plants. Honeybees hide in the sunflower field at the edge of the woods on the southern side. Blight is wiping so many bees out. Our colonies in Shunksville have been growing. If someone paved part of the wetlands, or tore down any of the maple or oak or spruce . . . it wouldn't be pretty. We might not realize it right away, but a few years down the line, this place would be a little grayer. A little dimmer, and hotter, and worse. This place is already a school for so many children. Putting up buildings *here* is not needed."

"But what about the construction jobs and development the new district could bring?"

"I've seen the reports about building here. I don't think this land is suitable for development. It would be more trouble than it's worth in not much time. The natural space does us more good for longer. And how many jobs would really be created? Construction is just temporary. Would businesses come if the unified district were built here? Would more people want to live here? Strip malls? This space makes Shunksville worth living in."

"Thank you," said Ellie King. Her cameraperson put his camera down. "That was great."

"Are you going to ignore me and just agree with the mayor?" I said.

"Oh, no. That's my friend Bill's job. Noon and weekend anchors do what we want," she said.

The dad and the three little boys emerged from the other side of Jenkins Wood trail. "Saw the tanager!" he shouted at me, scaring one protestor who hadn't seen the dad emerge.

"Excuse me," said Ellie King. "Going to try to talk to him."

Risa huffed out from the path a few minutes later. She jogged over to Richard, Louise, and me. "Followed"—she breathed hard—"the fucker. Couldn't"—she inhaled sharply—"catch it. Damn it. Now going to see"—she breathed in again—"tanager. Will text if I see your bird." She ran off.

"Thank you for trying," I called after her. I figured she wouldn't be able to get it. Ghost jay or something else, the little shithead delighted in remaining hidden.

Fortunately the protestors got sick of no one really paying attention to them and they left before lunch. Grateful for the returned silence, I agreed to read books to Karen's crew for a full half hour until my shift ended.

I thought about asking Risa if she wanted to hang out, but my phone buzzed in my pocket. *Come home!* Mom said.

Everything okay? I texted.

Mom didn't reply.

Shit. This was it. This was the end of Gran. The accident I'd caused had finally killed her.

My phone buzzed again. *Everything fine. Gran okay. Just come home.*

I sucked in the cool June air. Okay, Mom, jeez. Way to practically give a girl a heart attack.

Risa was still out looking for the tanager, so I waved to the three of them and ran over to my bike. I rode home wondering what was happening. Maybe Mom didn't have to sell Gran's house? Maybe we were going to move in? It was smaller and less convenient for her than our place, but I could live with that. I could sleep in the loft. I'd have to build the loft first . . .

I pulled into our driveway and noticed the lumberjack's car in the driveway. Was he going to help move us? He could be useful in some instances.

My bike fell in a heap against the side of the house and I took the front steps two at a time to get in quicker. Inside, Mom and Brad sat on the couch, calmly gazing into each other's eyes. Mom looked up and grinned at me.

"Are we moving to Gran's?" I said.

"Honey, what?" said Mom.

"Are we moving? Is that your news? Did you save the house?"

Mom's face fell. "Oh, no. That's not . . . I'm sorry. It still belongs to the city on Friday."

"Wait, this Friday?" How was it the end of June already?

"Technically I guess it's July first, but figured why worry about it over another weekend. No." Mom looked at Brad. "We have some news."

I shivered then.

I balled my fists around the cuffs of Risa's sweatshirt.

Mom had said "we." Not "we" as in "Laurel and Mom," since there had been no real "Laurel and Mom" since Gran's accident. That meant that "we" meant "Brad and Mom." Mom was forty-seven, so the statistical likelihood that Brad had gotten her pregnant remained blessedly low. The alternative to pregnancy, however, was . . .

"Brad proposed!" Mom held out her hand. A shiny diamond glittered in the sunshine sneaking in through the front door.

"Oh," I said, unable to spin this to positive effect in my head. I looked at Brad.

"Guess I'll be your stepdad, kiddo."

"Oh," I said again.

I took a step back from them. And another. And another. I only stopped because my back hit the door.

"That's—really something, guys. Yeah. Wow."

My body glued itself inconveniently to the door, so I couldn't open it and run down the street screaming. Mom was *marrying* this rando? Was she out of her mind? She'd known him for weeks? Granted the man had gotten my name right, but . . .

"We're thinking of eloping. Maybe in August?"

"August. This August? Wow."

"Are you happy, honey?" Mom got up from the couch.

Happy? The woman was seriously asking me if I was happy? This could only end in disaster.

"Sure, Mom. Sure."

"Oh, Laurel." She unpeeled me from the door. "Thank you. I need this. We need this, baby."

Now "we" seemed to mean "Mom and Laurel," for reasons beyond my comprehension.

"Yeah. Great. Cool," I said. "Congrats, Mom. Congrats, Brad."

Brad got up, too.

Mom let me go and put her arm around him. Brad was smart enough to sense that he was not in the hug zone with me and came no farther. He tilted his head, considering my face. Mom believed I could be happy for her, but this guy seemed more canny than that.

Go figure.

"Okay, welp. I should go. I have more, um, stuff to do. Yup. Stuff. Great news! Keep me updated. Bye!" I said. I rounded on the door and threw myself out of it. I got on my bike and pedaled. Away from there. Away from Mom and Brad and my house and my stupid life. Without really paying attention to where I was going, I found myself at the start of the bike trail up the mountain. The one that crossed over the site of Gran's accident. Where I'd ignored her and let her be nearly killed until she was trapped in the body of a bird or maybe just a coma patient. That was my fault. Somehow that meant that Mom's mistake with Brad landed on me, too. Without Gran's accident, she wouldn't be looking for comfort in a well-maintained beard.

The bike path ends at the top of the mountain, at the sidewalk adjacent to Grandview Cemetery. I stopped at a water fountain near a bench and then sat down. I called Sophie.

"Hey," I said.

"What's up?" she said. "Great timing, again! Any Risa news?"

"Mom got engaged."

"Are you serious? Your mom? To the lumberjack?"

"Yup."

"Well, fuck me. Didn't see that coming. You okay?"

"Yeah. No. I don't know."

"Shit. I gotta go. It's my day to help with the younger campers and we just finished lunch. I'll text you as soon as I can. Hang in there, okay?"

"Miss you," I said.

"Miss you, too."

I held my phone in my lap and it buzzed again. I hoped Sophie actually could talk, but it was a text from Mom. *Brad and I going to celebrate. We know you are busy! See you later, honey. Yay!*

I shook my head. Mom. Honestly. What the ever-living fuck?

I rode around some more, stopping only for ice cream downtown. I pedaled over to the hospital to sit with Gran. She smelled clean. Someone had washed and combed her hair, neatly separating the thin silver strands. I tucked them behind her ears. She preferred her hair in a bandanna or artfully poofed into an old lady halo, but that required equipment and a sense of purpose that I lacked.

"Mom's engaged," I said.

Beep. Wheeze.

"Maybe she told you. Have you met Brad? He has a beard. It's his most distinguishing feature."

Twitch.

No more words came into my head. Gran's hand sat cool in my own. Cooler than before? Hard to say. It seemed like it. Her skin paler, face more slack. How many days would this happen? How many days would the indomitable Aurora Fowler continue to waste away like this?

"I just can't find the bird, Gran," I said. "You're too fast. It's too fast. Maybe there is no bird. Maybe it's a squirrel."

Goddamn it, the suet. I vowed I'd do it this week for sure. At least once before the city came for the house and yard and garden. Gran had some "Squirrel-B-Gone" in the storage bench. I'd show those assholes. It'd be my last act before the end. I'd sit there until a downy woodpecker showed up even if it meant I waited there for days.

Anything beat having to share space with the soon-to-be newlyweds.

An hour passed. I stroked Gran's cheek like she used to do when I was little to wake me up. It soothed me, even if Gran didn't move.

"Time for the Sunday news, Gran," I told her. "I might be on." I found her remote thingy and tapped the TV button. It lit up and I flipped to channel eight.

The catchy news music crackled from Gran's speaker.

"Gran, it might be that Bill Andrews filled my heart with hate, but this theme song crushes Channel Four's," I said.

"Good evening," said Ellie. "We start tonight with updates on the Hornerstown sewer line project."

Sewers were big news in Shunksville. Ellie and Man Ellie talked about sewers and a coming heat wave and a shooting and the planned Fourth of July parade route. I looked at my watch.

"It's six twenty-five, Gran. I guess I'll get going. Visiting hours are over soon."

"After the break—city hall is for the birds!" said Ellie King.

"Okay, I'll stay," I said to the TV.

After a tampon commercial and Red Lobster ad, Ellie King was back. "Plans for the united Shunksville-Martinsville-Richburg merger are moving forward at the July tenth school board meeting," she said. "The special summer session was seemingly called to specifically get the merger underway without much local opposition or input."

"Ellie King is my queen," I said to Gran.

The news showed shots of protestors and an interview with a construction worker who hadn't had a job in several months, even though spring and summer used to be the busy season. Ellie King explained that even though there were problems with the Shunksville site, there were also possible economic benefits.

"But is progress at the expense of our environment really worth it? Especially if the available land will end up causing problems down the line?" Ellie King asked.

And then.

I appeared on screen.

"Shit, Gran," I said. I turned up the volume as high as it would go.

". . . A little dimmer, and hotter, and worse. This place is already a school for so many children. Putting up buildings is not needed," I finished. They'd played every word I said.

"Ohhhhh, shit," I said.

The camera showed the studio again.

"Couldn't have said it better myself," said the guy anchor.

"Food for thought, that's for sure," said Ellie King.

"That's all for Sunday. Now it's time for *NBC Nightly News* with . . ."

I switched the TV off. They'd put my full name under my talking head. (My hair looked pretty good, all things considered. Fuck me if I'm not vain enough to care.)

My phone buzzed.

HOLY SHIT, texted Risa.

You saw it? I wrote back.

OF COURSE I DID.

A lot of people probably don't watch news on Sunday, right?

Nah. Probably not. You did great though!

You think?

Yeah, the camera makes people ten times hotter, she said.

My cheeks burned, even though I was alone with Gran and her roommate.

I hadn't heard that.

Truth, she said.

I slid out of Gran's room and kept looking over my shoulder as I followed the yellow line on the floor to the exit. No one seemed to notice me leaving. This was good. People were at work. They barbecued or swam or mowed their lawns. No one watched Ellie King.

Most probably tuned in to Bill Andrews's weekend counterpart, anyway. At least they did if Channel Four's "the tri-county area's most watched local news" ad was true.

Outside, I rode home with a golden post-solstice breeze brushing my face. I let myself into the dark Momless house, ate the rest of the leftovers in the fridge, took a shower, and went to bed. The sun hung in the sky for hours. I just lay in my bed, watching the shadows dance on the floor as my curtains billowed in the wind.

I fell asleep with Risa's sweatshirt tucked under my chin.

FIELD JOURNAL ENTRY
JUNE 26

The best part of Wednesday was learning that Cambria County had pounded Westmoreland into bird-count *dust*. The

worst part of Wednesday was learning that people not only watched Ellie King on Sunday evening; they liked her on Monday and Tuesday and Wednesday at lunch as well.

Some of those people were kind.

"You did real good, kid," said Jerry. "Real good."

"Brilliant. You were brilliant," said Louise.

"Truly," said Richard.

Random strangers had started to come up to me on my way in and out of the hospital as well. Ellie King stirred up a lot of positive feelings for the nature reserve. Birdscout sign-ups shot up over four hundred percent from last year.

Those feelings ran rather heated on the other side, too. More disaffected workers with posters showed up and practically took over Elder Oak until Jerry forced them away from the path. When I walked by, they legit *hissed* at me, like geese. Then Bill Andrews, the mayor, the deputy mayor, and even one of the state senators stopped by to get on camera saying how the environment remained a priority, but so did jobs.

"Why is it either-or?" I said. "Why can't they find some other place in Shunksville to put the stupid schools?"

"I don't know," said Risa. "Probably something to do with saving money or because they can or because they don't understand about migration. They really shouldn't fuck with the honeybees, either."

After four bird walks, that afternoon as I was leaving I found someone had slashed my fucking bike tires.

"Seriously?" I said to my bike. "Are you ACTUALLY serious right now?"

Jerry heard me and banged out of the Center. "Whoa,"

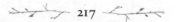

he said. He glanced at me. "This isn't right. I'm sorry, kid."
He went back inside, though that was the most sympathy I'd
ever heard from him.

"How'd they know it was your bike?" said Risa.

"I always ride it. It's the only lime-green one." I looked
over at the protestors. "I am the Laurelax. I speak for the birds.
And my bike. Leave both the fuck alone."

"Language," Jerry called from inside, but the reprimand
sounded half-hearted at best.

"This is a mess," I said to Risa. "Guess I'll walk home. I
have spares at my house."

"I'll come with you," she said. "I'm done here, too."

"Oh. Sure. Isn't your bike here?"

"Eh. I'll get it tomorrow."

"Okay. Cool." Words left my brain. We walked in silence
past the hissing protesters, through the gate, through the field,
until we reached the path.

"We could take the sidewalk. It's faster," I said.

"Are you in a hurry?" said Risa.

"No. No, I am not," I said. I smiled.

We headed into the trees and followed the dirt path that
wound its way up the side of the mountain and nowhere near
my house.

"How's your gran?" said Risa.

"Same," I said. "Not great. Trapped in the body of a bird.
I don't know anymore."

"Ah," she said.

"How are you? How's your family stuff?" I said.

"Same. Not great. Mom and Dad still gone. Sister still in
prison for another twelve to eighteen months. Don't steal a car

and then crash it and almost kill another person. Tip from me to you."

"Wow," I said.

"Yeah. What's really messed up is that our parents died in a crash, you know? I was only three, so I don't really remember. She was eight. My aunt and uncle aren't awful, but they don't like us that much. They just hoped enough therapy would take care of our issues until they could legally stop. At least Mom and Dad had life insurance, so my aunt and uncle aren't going into debt over us or something. Though, pretty sure most of my college fund went to big sis's legal bills."

This was probably the most she'd ever said about herself, ever. I stopped walking.

"I'm really sorry," I said.

She shrugged.

"No. I am. I'm sorry I hated you because I thought you were out to get me in the *Fauna* contest. And I was always kind of mean because of that," I said.

Risa smiled. "Oh. I hated you, too, for the same thing. No biggie. Birdie Bros, you know?"

"Yeah," I said.

A black-capped chickadee called above us and his mate answered. Wind rushed through the canopy and down over branches and limbs until it reached Risa and me in this strange clearing of new honesty.

"I always thought you were cute, though," I said.

"I always thought you were dating Sophie," she said. "And that you were both cute."

I grinned. "Never tell her that, she'd never shut up about it."

"Well"—Risa moved toward me—"you're cuter."

"Definitely don't tell her that. She'd *really* never shut up," I said. I reached my hand out to hers. "It's been a while since I had anyone to walk with me in the woods."

"Same," she said.

"We should do this more often," I said.

"I'm cool with every day," she said.

"Same."

We wandered like that, hand in hand, up the mountain to where the stone angels watched. Then along the creek to the river with its pale cement walls and chalky currents high from all the rain. Then to the end of my street, where there stood one vast elm that could hide two people sharing their first kiss.

"This is where you live," said Risa.

"Do you want to come in?" I said.

"Nah, gotta go Weedwack the yard. Tomorrow?"

"Okay," I said.

I watched her jog off toward town.

As I got out my key to let myself in the house, I noticed a piece of paper sticking to the mailbox.

Quit the school shit, it read. *Or else.*

I stared at it, not quite sure what to do. Should I call the police? Should I text Mom?

I went inside and tossed the paper toward the coffee table. It floated off toward the floor, where I left it. The house was empty (of course) and quiet. Safe. The people of Shunksville surely wouldn't be violent, would they?

I shut myself in my room for the rest of the day and for once was grateful when I heard Mom and Brad come in. Their voices carried and it sounded like they weren't going out again. Eventually I got too hungry to hide and came down the steps.

"There you are," Mom said. I noticed the paper she held in her hand. "Laurel, we need to talk."

"Uh-huh," I said. Maybe they'd decided to go to Vegas. Fuck me if I'd be going with them. Although, that could net me several grebes or a blue-footed booby (not named Brad) for the life list. I wandered past her into the kitchen. A good toaster-oven English muffin pizza would hit the spot right about now.

"You didn't tell me you were going to be on the news. You didn't tell me you were involved in blocking the new school."

"The interview wasn't planned," I said. "And I'm not blocking the new school."

"You went on the air and went on and on about how bad it would be if they built it," she said.

"I talked for about thirty seconds. That's hardly going on and on. If you want that, I suggest you tune into Bill Andrews on Channel Four. Deputy Mayor Michael Ross will take care of your needs in that arena." I slid the English muffins out of the bread drawer. I hoped the mozzarella I'd hidden in the back of the fridge hadn't molded.

"Laurel, look at me when I'm talking to you!" Mom's voice rose. It'd been a long time since she'd been angry.

Or wanted my attention, for that matter.

I stopped my search for pizza sauce in the cupboard under the bread drawer and faced her.

"Young lady, this needs to stop. I understand you were upset about Grandma's house. But there are people in town who this affects. There are children . . ."

"Mom . . ."

"I'm serious." Mom's face grew redder and redder. "I'm a teacher, Laurel. My job depends on the actual presence of a school in which to teach. The new district will be letting people go. If it's here, I'm in much better shape than if it goes somewhere else."

I considered this. I vaguely knew that Mom's job could be in play.

"Several of my colleagues have called and texted asking what game you are playing. They aren't happy. My principal called. If I didn't have tenure, I might already be out of a job. If the merger doesn't happen, I'm gone. If it does, now I'm probably gone. Did you think about that?"

"This isn't a game," I said.

Brad shifted uncomfortably. I looked over at him, daring him to say something.

"Are you trying to punish me for Grandma's house? Because this will hurt you, too, you know. College costs a lot. And . . ."

"Stop!" I said. "Just stop."

The little, positive voice inside me yelled to try to be kind. To understand where Mom was coming from. But the light that I tried to find at the end of any tunnel had flickered and dimmed. The little voice inside my head had grown hoarse from all the shouting. "You know what," the voice said instead. "Fuck it."

"I . . ."

"No! Not 'you.' Not right now. Shunksville needs the nature reserve more than it needs to house the school. I have the reports, Mom. There are better spots. Building on that cheap, available land would mean big trouble down the line.

Combining the districts doesn't even make sense. It's all there, in the paperwork city hall doesn't want you to see. That they have actively tried to hide."

"Maybe . . . ," Brad tried to cut in.

"This isn't about you, Mom. Not everything is, believe it or not. This isn't about the house. Not really. And it's not about me, either, only maybe it is a little because of who I am. I *am* the pond. I am the woods. I am an indigo bunting and last year's fucking whooping crane. So is Gran. If you stopped looking at Brad for a second, maybe you'd notice that."

Mom just stood there, taking in my words.

"And since we're doing this here, in front of him"—I nodded over at Brad—"you might as well know this, too. Gran is in a coma because of me. I could have stopped it. I could have saved her, but I kept going. And it's my fault. All my fault." I started shaking then. A small tremor started in my leg and worked its way up all the way to my shoulders, as if I'd run five miles straight and my muscles had decided to rebel.

"Laurel, there's no way that's possible."

"Yes, it is, Mom!" My voice shook now. "She was on the mountainside looking for a strange bird we'd heard call earlier. I saw her on the side of the road in the rain and I knew it was dangerous. I told her to get off the road but she didn't listen. I knew, I *knew*, it was dangerous, but I didn't go back. I let her stay. I let her stay." My legs would soon give way. I could feel their wish to buckle to the floor right there.

"Baby . . ."

"No! It's true and it's my fault and you can hate me. Hate me for that. But the fucking school shouldn't take out the nature reserve. If I hadn't killed Gran, she would say the same thing to you over and over until you couldn't ignore her!"

That was it. That was all I had. I stumbled away from her and practically crawled up the steps to my room. I slammed my door, not because of my rage at Mom and fucking *Brad*, but at myself. Because the truth of what I'd done crashed down around me. I curled into a ball and rocked back and forth until the shaking let up and I fell asleep. Usually I dream about common grackles or sometimes house sparrows.

This time I dreamed of lightning.

FIELD JOURNAL ENTRY
JUNE 28

The day began with Mom shuffling outside my door. I heard her there, making noise. Maybe she was hoping to wake me up. Or possibly she was willing herself to knock on her awful daughter's door before telling me she hated me and wanted me to move out to the woods, though at this point the woods were too good for me.

Whatever her motivation, she moved on after a few minutes and left for work.

I texted Jerry and told him I wasn't feeling well.

I got up and moved stealthily through the house, in case Mom had staged an ambush to punish me for causing her and Gran all this torment. My head throbbed, my chest pounded, even my feet burned when flesh touched Teva. The walls of the box inside me strained, the one with the accumulated knowledge of my active participation in Gran's ruin threatened to burst and course through my blood like non-eco-friendly poison. I forced a smile onto my face. Sometimes smiling alone could put you into a better mood.

My face ached.

I had to get out of the house. The fragrant breeze brushed my cheeks. It should have been pleasant but felt like razor blades in the moment.

I biked to the hospital but couldn't go in. I biked to the Nature Center, but then Jerry would know I'd faked being sick. I biked to the library, to the river, to the stone angels on the top of the mountain in the cemetery. They stared at me with empty, accusing eyes.

Nowhere in all of Shunksville wanted me. What I'd done to Gran pushed against the seams holding my body together. Muscle and bone and skin flexed, as alive as Gran was almost gone. Life continued as if to spite me, me who had selfishly left my one vital organ unattended and then she'd gone and gotten so terribly hurt.

I couldn't bring myself to text Sophie, killing her joy at art camp. And what would Risa think? I biked home. In our front yard, where my bird feeders belonged, stood a white board tied sloppily to a wooden stake. *STOP* was all it said. I pulled it out of the ground and tossed it into the recycle bin out back. I found someone had toppled our garbage cans as well. Fortunately my recycling efforts meant there wasn't a lot to scatter, but the message was clear. The front and back doors had brown smears all over them.

I put on Mom's thick yellow gloves and scrubbed the doors with bleach. I deserved this. Really, I had done this to myself. Maybe not for the school; that was right. But for Gran. If she had been here, I was sure she would have stopped the development of the nature reserve in its tracks. Then she would have taken on the haters and we wouldn't be dealing with this. Maybe this bleach was strong enough to clean off the truth of what I'd done. The fumes burned my eyes.

After I was done, I searched around the house for my feeders, but they were gone. I wondered if Gran's were still at her place. Mom would be home soon, so I'd have to go to bed to hide from her. But I vowed to check it out tomorrow.

An oriole called overhead and another responded from across the street. They probably wondered where their easy dinner had gone.

"Sorry, birds," I said. "This is all my fault."

I fell into my bed. I, unlike the birds, had no need to eat. My stomach was stuffed with the guilt of all I'd broken.

FIELD JOURNAL ENTRY
JUNE 29
NOTABLE LOCATION: THE HOUSE THE CITY OWNS

The house was quiet when I woke up the next morning. The Grahams were great at avoidance, so Mom had probably gone to one of her summer jobs without leaving a note. Brad might have gone to cut down trees or tell people about bands they'd never heard of, or whatever it was that hipster lumberjacks did.

Normally sleep made things better. But sleep had done nothing to improve my mood, mostly because the truth was out now. Mom knew it was my fault. The worry about paying for college didn't matter now, since she'd probably already disowned me. Worse still was the fact that I now knew it to be true. Saying it out loud made me realize the dark reality of it all.

I'd killed Gran. Slowly. In the worst way possible. She was stuck in a lifeless shell, trapped in a way I knew she'd never have wanted to be. Her house gone to the city to pay for the care I made her need.

Fuck. The house. The city closed on it, or took it, or whatever they were going to do with it today. I needed to feed the woodpeckers.

I pulled on a pair of jeans and my "That's Hawkward" T-shirt and didn't bother with my hair. I grabbed my bag and clipped it to my bike after I'd changed my tires. Hopefully people wouldn't get in the habit of slashing them, since it'd cost too much to replace them again. My phone, which I'd left in my jeans overnight, buzzed with the last of its battery.

Busy today? texted Risa.

Phone dying. Going to Gran's. Woodpeckers, I replied. The screen went blank. I sighed. I'd have to charge it later.

I reached Gran's yard. The grass was too long, the garden weedy. I hadn't done a good job mowing last time. Still, tomato plants climbed and I could see the sweet corn had somehow started to grow. Had Gran planted that? Had I? Did seeds somehow fall on their own and wait for their chance? It didn't matter. The squirrels would probably rejoice.

I walked over to the bench and threw open the top. It banged against the side of the house with such force that paint flaked away at the corners. Gran would be so pissed about that; only, no, she wouldn't because I'd put her in a coma. The city would be tearing the house down anyway, so what's a few old paint chips?

"Hey," said Risa behind me.

I looked up, startled.

"Sorry," she said. She smiled shyly. "I figured when you quit texting that your phone had died, and that I'd find you here. Is that okay?"

"Yeah," I said. Great. Now Risa would know I was awful, too.

"Are you okay?"

"I . . ." No. I sucked. A lot. I found the new bottle of Squirrel Fire™ that Gran had bought but never gotten to try. I grabbed the bag of suet. "I need to feed the woodpeckers."

"Oh, be careful with that stuff. Did you read the directions?"

I glared at her.

"Did I do something wrong? I thought . . ."

"No. It's not you. Trust me. It's alllll me," I said, unscrewing the top of the squirrel repellent.

"Laurel, seriously, be careful with that stuff."

"Risa, I killed my grandmother. Maybe that's why we can't find the bird. She doesn't want to be found. She's just been trying to tell everybody what I did. I saw her on the road that day. She was probably looking for the fucking mystery bird. I could have made her get into the car with me but I didn't. And then someone else hit her because it was raining. And my mom is marrying fucking *Brad*"—I poured Squirrel Fire™ all over the suet—"even though she's known him for like a *day*. And she is mad at me for speaking up against the school even though it's the worst idea ever. Oh my god, you have it so much worse than me and I shouldn't even be complaining and do you see that?" I gestured with the Squirrel Fire™ and some sloshed onto my hand. "That fucking squirrel is watching me. It knows, too. It knows I'm such a fuckup." I mushed the suet around to make sure it got good and coated. If it was the last shitty thing I did at that house, at least I'd feed the woodpeckers.

I hadn't cried before then. Not in the hospital over all those weeks, not over Mom and what's-his-beard, and not over the pond and woods and house. But now the tears of true frustration came in front of Risa and the squirrels. I sniffed as I poured the suet feeders. I couldn't see very well, so it kept falling.

"Let me help you, please," said Risa softly.

"I can't even do this right," I said. A sob flared from deep in my chest. I reached up to wipe the tears.

"Oh god, don't do that," Risa said.

Pain. Sizzling, horrible, blistering pain scorched my eyes and nose and mouth.

"What . . . ," I gasped.

"Is the house open?" said Risa.

I coughed.

"That hose, is it attached to water? You know what, let's find out."

I doubled over. The tears kept flowing, but the more they did, the farther down my face I could feel fire.

A cool gentle stream started flowing down my forehead.

"Just try to breathe," said Risa. "Try to avoid inhaling the water, obviously. But stay bent over like that so I can rinse your face."

I still didn't understand what was happening, so I listened. The water eased what felt like my eyes sizzling out of my head. After a few minutes, the water stopped.

"Give me your hands," Risa said.

I stuck them out in front of me. I watched a blurred Risa turn the nozzle and blast my hands. I turned them over for her to do the back side.

"Do my face again?" I said. I started coughing, but she obliged before I had to try to repeat myself.

A few more minutes later, she stopped. She took off the bandanna tied around her hair and dabbed my face.

"That anti-squirrel stuff is wicked," she said. "You basically Maced yourself."

"I can see now why it is effective."

"Does it still hurt?"

"Yeah."

"A lot?"

"Kinda. Less than it did, though. I can mostly see. And breathe. Now that I think about it, that shit burns your hands, too." I tapped my palms gingerly. Pinpricks traveled up my fingers. "Ouch."

"I'm sorry, babe. I probably should have tackled you when you were pouring it while upset," said Risa.

"I deserved this," I said.

"No way. No one deserves that shit in their face. Well. Maybe Bill Andrews or Michael Ross, but I'd hesitate to do it to them even."

I scrunched up my nose, but it only made it burn again. More tears dripped from my eyes, though I couldn't tell if it was from life or the Tabasco facial I'd just given myself.

"Laurel," said Risa. She reached an arm around my waist. "Listen to me a second, okay?"

"Okay," I said.

"All that stuff . . . it wasn't your fault. Your grandmother. I knew her. She did what she wanted to. If she wanted to be on that path looking for a bird, she was going to be on that path looking for a bird. You didn't harm her. And now, looking back, it seems like your fault. But how many times had she probably gone on that same road and nothing happened? Or how many times did you stop her from doing something that could have hurt her? You just don't know. This one time something really bad happened. But maybe it would have happened sooner if you'd acted differently in the past."

"You're just being nice," I said. I sniffed painfully.

"No, I'm not. I mean, I'm not trying to bullshit you. I really believe this. It's easy to want to take all that blame and pack it inside your brain. But if you do that, you have to take credit for all the stuff that you've done. But the thing is, half the time we don't know what we've done, because we don't see the effects." She squeezed me to her.

This would have been a nice moment if my nose didn't feel kinda like exploding.

"Do you hear what I'm saying?" Risa said.

"Yes."

"Do you believe me?"

"I think so. I get it. It's just . . . it's hard not to feel responsible."

"I get that."

"I saw her. I saw her right before."

"Yeah."

More tears came and I sat there, wrapped up in Risa.

"I must be a mess," I said.

"Nah," she said. She wiped my face with a paper towel.

Birders. Always prepared.

"Still being nice," I said.

"Look." She pointed. Two downy woodpeckers flew to a feeder. Both pecked tentatively at the food. One called the other and they flew over to the yard, where the suet bag lay splayed on the ground.

"I think I might have made the other stuff too spicy," I said.

"Well," said Risa, looking at the feeders. "The squirrels are avoiding it at least. And there are downy woodpeckers eating in your grandmother's yard *right* now. That's a win, right?"

I shook my head, smiling in spite of everything. "Yeah, sure." I started to laugh until Risa did, too.

"Hey, who is Brad?" she said after a while. "Do we hate him?"

She said "we."

Sophie would love that.

"I don't know. I barely even met the guy. Mom . . . Mom doesn't always make good choices."

"Ah."

I leaned into her. She squeezed me again. Under different circumstances, we would probably have started kissing by now, but I got the distinct impression Risa was avoiding getting anywhere near my face.

"Do you have to go to the Center?" I said.

"Yes. My shift starts at ten."

"Mine too."

"You up for it?" she said.

"The face. It feels ablaze. But I think it's better to stay busy."

"Good idea," Risa said. "Richard and Louise have a plan for the city council meeting. Karen's mom told me they were coming by today to tell people about it."

"They want us to go to the meeting?" I said.

"I think so? Or make our own signs and stand outside it, maybe? We'll have to go find out."

"Okay. I'm in." I reluctantly untangled myself from Risa's arms.

"Do I look decent enough?"

Risa grinned. "You look beautiful."

"I do not."

"Your skin does kind of glow."

"Yeah, in a hot-sauce kind of way," I said.

"It works for you."

"Stop." I shoved her.

"Do you want me to clean up the suet?" she said.

I hesitated, watching two new woodpeckers who had just shown up. Word had gotten out about the smorgasbord. So this is what it took for them to finally come around. "Nah," I finally said. "Leave it."

"You okay to ride your bike?"

"Will you be my bodyguard? My peripheral vision is still kind of, um, burny."

"You got it."

I rode away from Gran's house, maybe for the last time. But at least the woodpeckers were there, and the squirrels would probably fear the place for a little while.

And I felt better. Risa's words finally filtered through the pepper-induced fog. If anyone would know something about sucky life circumstances, she would. That alone almost made nearly boiling off my face worth it.

Almost.

FIELD JOURNAL ENTRY
JULY 2

Memorial Day was huge for birding. Near Independence Day, not so much. Risa and I sat alone on the dock next to the pond, looking out at several preening black-crowned night herons.

"How's your *Fauna* entry?" she asked. "Got anything?"

"I think so. I had a stormy encounter with some tanagers. You?"

"A couple, I guess. They are ho-hum."

We pointed our cameras at the night herons, and then I turned my camera on her.

"You inspire me. I'll submit you."

"This is my natural habitat." She laughed.

"It's almost time for the meeting," I said.

We got up and brushed off the dirt from the dock. Louise and Richard now held daily meetings to prep for the city council meeting. A school board meeting had been hastily thrown in right before. None of this usually took place during the summer, but it had been advertised, and even with all of the publicity, I think Deputy Mayor Michael Ross and company were still hoping no one would come out to see what was really going on with the development of the nature reserve.

Richard and Louise, however, would have none of that.

All of the birders gathered in the clearing next to Grandma Maple. Jerry, the knitting birders, Owen, Karen, both of her mothers, and several other Birdscouts and their families sat in a circle looking at Louise.

"We think we've come up with a viable option," she said.

"Our brainstorming thus far has been good, but none of the ideas strictly feasible. But Owen here had a revelation that I think everyone will be able to get behind. Owen, I hand over the forest floor to you," said Richard.

Owen blushed. "Well, thanks. Um. So, I'm an Eagle Scout."

One of the knitters whooped.

Owen grinned. "And for a badge once, we studied social justice movements. What strategies worked to change stuff. And I was thinking about all the marches and nonviolent protests of people like Martin Luther King Jr. I had to read a series of graphic novels called *March* by a senator named John Lewis that got me thinking about that again. When they wouldn't let Black people eat in restaurants, the protestors would just go in and order lunch. Because that's what anyone should be able to do—go into a restaurant and order lunch. It was dangerous, because the white people who didn't think everyone should be treated equally got mad. But they still did it."

Heads around me nodded.

"People still do stuff like that now, too. There was a mom who tried to feed her baby, um, with her breasts and mall police showed up and told her she wasn't allowed. So all these moms went at the same time and fed their babies with her, because it's totally legal to feed babies in public. They called it a 'nurse-in.' I thought we could have a 'bird-in.'"

Owen stopped talking and looked around at the group. Finally he sat down next to his dad. Karen started clapping, and then everyone joined in.

"So what would we do, dress up as birds?" said Karen. "I have a flamingo costume."

"Or bring birds to city hall? Spread birdseed outside? That would bring them," said Risa.

"Or maybe unleash birds *inside* city hall? In that room where they have all their meetings. It's always needed more sparrows, in my opinion," said one of the knitters.

"Well. I hadn't exactly gotten that far. I hoped for ideas like these," said Owen.

The group sat thoughtfully for a few moments.

"I think this needs to be a multipronged approach," said Louise. "I like the birdseed-outside idea. And people are allowed in the meetings, but I don't think birds will be allowed in. It would be disruptive to the point of police to capture and let birds out inside the meeting. But . . ."

"Don't say it," said Richard.

"Richard and I . . ."

"I don't even fit into them anymore . . ."

"Have bird costumes also. Ravens, to be exact. I look good in black."

Richard sighed. "I—" He paused. "Fine. Yes. I could dress as a bird. For the cause."

"I don't have a bird costume," I said. "But I have pictures. Of most of the birds you can see at Jenkins or Sarig. Or backyards around here. And binoculars."

"If you don't have a costume, you could just bring your binos! Brilliant. And we could blow up some of the pictures from the pond and bring them."

"Most of the kids aren't in school right now at the community college. So, the teachers are probably away, too. But

I bet a lot of them are around, and there are summer session students. Some of them were here the other day tagging squirrels," said Jerry.

"Okay. This is what we need to do. We put the word out to our networks. Get the people to that meeting next week. Dress as your favorite bird. Or fox. Or, uh, marmot. Any creature who lives around here. Or wear your binoculars to watch the meeting up close and personal in the room. If you don't want to do that, Risa and Laurel will print some of their pictures, right?" said Richard.

We nodded.

"We'll bring the birdseed," said Louise. "Cover all the bases."

"We should tell other people?" said Karen. "The unschoolers?"

"Everyone," said Louise. "Their game plan all along seems to have been to keep people from being interested. To try to get this done under the radar. We are going to fly this up to the top and shout it from the canopy." She practically glowed with joy.

"Birdscouts on the count of three," Jerry yelled. "One, two, three . . ."

"Birdscouts!" the assembly called. Several annoyed cardinals hurried away from the noise.

Afterward, Risa and I walked back to the Nature Center and cleaned the bathrooms together.

"Do you think this can work?" I said. "A bird-in?"

Risa shrugged. "Can't hurt. It will create a scene at least. And I bet Michael Ross won't be able to stand that."

"What if they don't even let us in?" I said.

"Well, then. That will create an even bigger one, then, won't it?" Risa grinned.

"Yeah." I smiled with her.

"How's your eyes?"

"Oh. Better. I keep rinsing them. It still kinda burns now and then. I feel like that stuff hides in your pores."

"You know what, I'm willing to take my chances."

Risa leaned in and her lips gently brushed mine.

"There's nothing like romance in a public restroom."

"A *clean* public restroom," she pointed out.

"True," I said.

"Want to go get some ice cream after this? It's on me. We get paid today."

"Jerry giving us actual money?"

"I believe so. Someone donated money to expand the Birdscout program. I heard a rumor he's trying to butter us up so we'll stay on next year even after co-op ends."

We walked outside, carrying our bleach and brushes. I stripped off my rubber gloves and threw them into my bucket.

This time, I kissed Risa. Her thick, long eyelashes tickled my cheeks.

"I'll buy next time."

"Deal," she whispered.

I hadn't been able to save Gran, or her house, and maybe even her beloved woods and pond. But at least I had a plan now to try. Maybe my pictures could have some impact for Gran, even if they didn't bring me *Fauna* greatness. As Brian Michael Warbley says, "A picture can be worth a thousand words to another person, even if you don't think it says anything at all." I didn't know if a bird-in would do the trick, but sometimes just the hope that you can do something is enough.

FIELD JOURNAL ENTRY
JULY 7

I sat at Gran's right side as usual. I swept my fingers through her hair and stroked her face. She wasn't there, she wasn't there, she wasn't there. But her heart beeped on the monitor. Her lungs expanded in and out. Tubes with clear liquid that glistened in the midday sun drifted lazily into her veins taking the place of food in her mouth.

"Gran," I said. "I know you said you'd wait for me. We'd have a Big Year together and add kakapos and condors and Honduran emeralds and red-crowned cranes to our life lists. We'd go to Iceland or Greenland or the artic and see the aurora borealis. But . . . maybe you shouldn't stick around for that. I don't think you like being this way. Stuck here. Even if you might occasionally be a bird."

Twitch. Flutter. Same old story.

"I'll be okay. I promise."

The machines remained the only sound in the room, besides my own voice.

I sighed and walked out of her room. The July air felt heavy. A few nights ago, I'd watched fireworks with Risa on the old bridge next to Shunksville Creek. The light in the sky above us bloomed like flowers, and lightning bugs blinked their thoughts around us. Still, Risa was the brightest thing burning against the darkness around me.

I parked my bike in the driveway. Mom's car was there,

but Brad's was not. We'd barely spoken since our big fight. Most of the time it was Mom-and-Brad time, but when she was nearish to me, it was like Mom kept trying to find words to say to me but then didn't have the heart. I figured it was because I'd probably killed Gran. I couldn't blame her.

I walked in and Mom was on the phone. She waved at me with the pained expression she'd been wearing the last three times I saw her. I grabbed an apple and went upstairs to my room, where I shut my door to hide. I finished emailing Jerry the pictures he was having blown up and printed.

"Laurel," I heard Mom call from downstairs. I heard her feet on the stairs, her weight creaking the boards in the hall. She knocked. "Honey?"

"Busy, Mom," I said. Neither one of us was good at talking about our feelings with one another. Mom usually just burst into tears and I just wanted her to cheer up. Not the greatest system, as it turned out.

"Okay. I'm going out. I . . . I'll see you."

I listened to her retreat down the stairs, the jingle of her car keys as she lifted them from the hook on the wall, and the front door whine, wood on wood, as she pulled it shut.

My mystery bird called outside the window. I opened it wide and gazed out at the houses and trees and wires and clouds. The bird called and called.

Come see me, I thought at it. *Show me who you are just once, please?* But nothing came. Two robins, a grackle, and a jay flew past.

I was as alone here as I was at the hospital.

Gran wasn't really there. But there was still a chance she was outside somewhere, waiting for me to find her.

The morning of the bird-in dawned bright and hot. It was already eighty degrees by nine in the morning. I'd refilled my water bottle twice before Risa even made it to the Nature Center.

"Holy balls," she said. "Summer decided to kick in."

"At least city hall is air-conditioned," I said.

"Thank god," she said.

Jerry walked down the path carrying two huge bags.

"I got the stuff," he said, and went inside. Risa and I caught up with him before the Center door even had a chance to close.

"Can we see?" I said.

"Show us the goods, Jerry, my man," said Risa.

Jerry set the bags on the floor.

"Wow, you sprung for—what—two-feet-by-three-feet signs?" I said.

"Yup."

"Holy shit—sorry, Jerry. Holy lightning—that's your picture you were talking about?" Risa pointed to my lightning tanagers. "This. This is going to get you first place and *Fauna* glory forever."

"Thanks," I said. "It was mostly luck I had it on the right setting for it to show up. I didn't know it was going to happen. We should take pictures of the protest. *Fauna* loves this kind of thing. As Brian Michael Warbley says . . ."

"'When people flock together, change can happen'?" Risa finished.

"Yes," I said.

"Figured the house counted as part of the Wood. It sits right on the far edge of the woods," Jerry said. He busied himself with papers on his desk, which I think was his way of avoiding any feels Risa and I might display.

"Is this one yours?" I said. I held up a stunning pink sky with three herons taking flight in a neat row.

"Yes," said Risa. "Heron-tastic."

"Herons are the shit, Risa. And I would bet money you are the only loon who got up early enough to get this shot." I snorted. "See what I did there?"

"Wow, Birdscout in chief. Good one." She rolled her eyes.

The bird whisper network had attracted attention from all over the county. I refilled my water bottle a third time and took a group of nine college students on a bird walk. The chickadees were out in force, and our oriole and blue jay game was pretty strong as well. Risa took the second tour. I was emptying the recycle bins when the recycle dumpster whispered to me.

"Laurel," it said.

I peered around the corner to see Birdie Bro Greg standing there, rubbing his hands together.

"Uh. What the fuck, Greg?"

"Listen. I'm not going to stay here long. I, um, shouldn't be here. But I needed to warn you."

"Warn me? About what?"

"The deputy mayor expects there to be trouble today. They are prepared."

"Prepared to do what, exactly?"

"Disperse the crowd. You know."

"I do not. I don't think Shunksville has riot police, Greg. Unless the Steelers get themselves a championship and bid at another ring, I don't see the city springing for any, either."

"Still. They can take names and shit. Michael Ross is really connected."

I thought about Mom's job. She didn't know about the protest, of course. Though, what the fuck did she know about me at all? The fault for that sat on her shoulders, not mine.

"I appreciate the warning, Greg. But haters gonna hate, and birders gotta bird, you know?"

Greg nodded. "Okay. Figured as much." He turned to leave.

"Greg?"

"Yeah?"

"Did you read all those reports?"

He looked at the ground. "Um. Yes. Wasn't supposed to. Was just supposed to 'sort' them into the circular file. Even if they are technically meant to be publicly available. I just put them in the next box over, though." He glanced up, a slow smile spreading over his face.

"Do you really think it's a good idea to put a school here?"

"Of course not. I was here for the fucking whooping crane. Like any building is worth losing a chance at that again."

"Thanks," I said.

"Good luck," he said.

Two more jaunts through the woods and one story time later, Risa and I mounted our bikes to meet the others at city hall. Richard and Louise were picking up Jerry and the posters.

"It's gotta be, what, at least a hundred degrees now?" said Risa.

"The heat index is well above that. There is someone in a full chicken costume. I hope they don't die of heatstroke."

I'd never seen a chicken at the pond before, but a bird is a bird. I had to give whoever donned that costume props for commitment to the cause.

Karen came in full flamingo, her moms in pink to match her. Sure enough Louise and Richard came in raven costumes, though they looked less like birds and more like masquerade guests. Risa wore her "We are not emused" shirt, and I dug out my "Toucan play that game" tank. Both of us had cameras and binos. We sat in the shade of the park across the street as one by one people amassed. Some came in Pittsburgh Penguin gear and some in Philadelphia Eagles. (Okay, fine, all birds are technically in support of the cause.) Still others arrived as peacocks, swans, ducks, and one red fox. Louise and Richard worked the crowd, greeting everyone as they scattered seeds along the ground.

"We'll take over," said Risa. She handed me Richard's seed bag.

"Let's do across the street, by the actual building," I said.

Risa and I laid a careful trail of birdseed from the front door all along the walls until we hit the alley. Deft avian scouts already picked up on the bounty and started to arrive and call their friends. Bolder birds hopped amid the feet of the people milling around the park. A Channel Four truck pulled up down the block. A Channel Eight truck pulled up on the other side of the park.

"There's gotta be at least a hundred people here," I said.

"One person per point on the thermostat," said Risa, wiping her head.

"Look, they have the antenna things on their vans. I think they are going to broadcast live," I said. Ellie King got out of her van with two people, as did Bill Andrews.

We crossed back over to the park. "It's time," said Louise.

"Shit's getting real now," said Risa. "You ready for this?"

"I don't want you to be *owl* by yourself." I grinned.

Across the street and up the stairs into city hall we walked, everyone following Louise like she was the drum major in our parade. The shyer birds who pecked along the building flapped away from the throng of humans suddenly upon them. As soon as we hit the stairs, we ran into a snag. A police officer emerged from the double doors.

"Hey, Frank," said Louise. "We're here for the meeting."

"No can do, Weezy," he said.

"Frank. It's an open meeting. Isn't the whole *point* of this meeting so that the public can weigh in on the school plans?"

"I was told that's a no. It's a closed session."

"Frank," said Richard. "What are they trying to hide? Has a meeting ever been closed?"

"Not that I can remember, no."

"Where's your partner?"

"He's at the other entrance, 'round back."

"Is it just the two of you?" said Louise.

"Yes, ma'am."

"Isn't there another side entrance? On Locust Street?"

Frank shifted. Beads of sweat pearled on his forehead. "Can't say?" He answered like it was a question.

Of course there was an entrance on Locust Street. And on

Main and on Elm. No one went over there, because porta-potties for the perpetual construction site next to city hall sat directly across from the entrance.

"And there's only two of you?" said Louise.

"Yes," said Officer Frank. "But we were told to stand at these two."

"Got it," said Richard. They turned and a small parting in the birder crowd zipped back to let them pass. They led us over to the smelly door, which we found unlocked.

"I wonder if they are as good at planning district mergers as they are at keeping people from voicing their opinion about them," said Risa.

Everyone filed into the building as quietly as a flock can. The halls stood cool and empty. The ornate doors at the end of the hall led to the Shunksville common room. We went in and arranged ourselves in the pew-like wooden benches. The members of city council sat in the front of the room, all of them taken aback. Whispers erupted at their table. The mayor and deputy mayor got up and exited through a back door. They came back a few minutes later.

Bill Andrews's cameraman held the door open for Ellie King and her crew.

Officer Frank came in after them.

"Pardon me, folks?" he said. "This is a closed meeting today. I'm afraid there was an oversight in the fact that all of you went in an unstaffed door. I'm going to have to ask you to leave."

"Where's Jerry?" I said to Risa.

She shrugged.

"No," said a man I didn't know. "It's our right to stay."

"Someone needs to speak for Sarig Pond and Jenkins Wood." That was the hard-core birder dad who almost got scared away by the protestors.

"I'm going to have to ask you to leave," said Officer Frank. He pressed his lips together like he was fighting a smile. That could have been because a chicken stared him down from three feet away.

"No," said another person.

"We'll stay," said yet another.

Though the vents above us blew cool air, the room warmed from the mass of bodies present. I noticed, too, that both Ellie King and Bill Andrews motioned for their crew to scan the room with cameras.

"These meetings are televised on Cablevision Channel Nine," said the deputy mayor into his microphone. "You are welcome to watch at home and comment online at w-w-w-dot—"

"We are hear to comment now!"

"Just start the meeting already. Where are those reports the news keeps talking about?"

"I'm going to ask you again to leave. I don't want to have to get more of my guys down here, okay?"

Heat and tension mingled in the air.

"Fine," said Louise. "We don't want to make trouble." She got up out of her seat and strode down the short aisle like a fucking cassowary. The group had to circumvent the Cablevision cameras, splitting the receding birders into a letter _V_ behind her.

Outside, we found Jerry hanging out with the people who had gathered after we'd gone in. They hadn't tried any other entrances and watched us as Officer Frank escorted us onto Main Street.

"Hey," Jerry said. "Take this." He shoved wooden sticks with pond and wood pictures duct taped to them in our hands. "Now the real fun begins."

"You knew we'd get kicked out?" said Risa.

"Oh yeah," he said.

"That's reassuring," I said.

More birds, actual flying ones, had shown up to. Grackles, sparrows, nuthatches, red-bellied woodpeckers, robins, starlings, crows. They twittered and hopped around the birdseed. Most looked pissed at the invasion of their park, but some calmly realized that our presence correlated with the food.

"What's the word?" Jerry suddenly shouted.

"Bird!"

"What's the word?" he shouted again.

"Bird!" more people answered.

Officer Frank shooed us all over back to the park. A line of counter protestors marched over from the KFC.

Fitting.

"What do we want?" a man yelled.

"Jobs!" his group responded.

"When do want them?"

"Now!"

"What do we want?"

"Education!"

"When do we want it?"

"Now!"

"Birds can fly, fish can swim, but not if you kill them for your gym," called Louise. People laughed but joined in.

Officer Frank held back people from the door. Every once in a while, I'd scatter more birdseed across the sidewalk in front of him. He just kept biting his knuckle as he watched me do it.

"I don't think he sees a lot of action on this detail," said Risa.

"Best day of the summer, I bet," I said.

"Binoculars up!" someone called. A hundred pair of binos pointed toward the building as Ellie King and Bill Andrews exited city hall.

"Oh, this is gold," I heard her say. "Let's see if we can live broadcast this."

"On it," her camerapeople said.

Bill Andrews went straight over to the counterprotestors. Ellie King came over to us.

"Want to go back on the air?" she said to me.

"No thanks. Once was enough."

She nodded. Plenty of other people dressed as waterfowl wanted her attention anyway.

When Risa and I ran out of birdseed, we stood behind Ellie King's camera.

"Thanks, Ted," Ellie King said.

"Who's Ted?" I whispered.

"I think that thing in her ear let's her hear them back at the news studio," said Risa. "She's talking to the anchor on air."

"Got it."

"We were planning on attending the special city council and school board meetings today, but as you can see, we were not allowed in city hall. Protestors both for and against the new combined district's proposed location for the new schools are out in full force here this evening. Here are some residents concerned with the loss of an important ecological habitat."

A few college students gathered near her to talk about the honeybees. Risa and I shook our own pictures on our signs and walked and shouted. Around seven, Ellie King and Bill Andrews left in their news vans and people started to disperse. We walked over to Louise.

"Did that do anything?" I said. "Did they vote on the location?"

"I guess we'll find out tomorrow? I saw two reporters from the *Shunksville Gazette* in there who didn't get kicked out. I think they snuck out the back. We'll have to get the news from them."

"I just hope that . . . ," I said, but then a two-toned call echoed from overhead. My head swiveled around. Risa, Louise, Richard, and Jerry got out their binoculars and peered toward the increasing summer twilight.

"You heard it, too," I said to them.

"Where's that little guy been?" said Jerry.

"Been chasing it all summer," said Risa.

The call came again.

"There. Right there," I said. A shape hopped around a high branch. It flew to another tree. And then.

I followed it with my binoculars. It landed on the ground, finding spare birdseed in the grass. It charged at a tiny sparrow to take the food from it. It opened its beak and sang the unmistakable, melancholy tune.

"That," said Richard, "is a blue jay. A male blue jay."

A call came from another tree. And another. Three jays, two male, one female, scattered the other birds as they tend to do. They claimed the area with the food and no one else ~~would be getting any anytime soon.~~

"But. That's not possible. It's—it's really a blue jay?" I said.

"Seems like it." Louise smiled. "A blue jay with a distinctive Western PA accent. It's probably calling us all jag-offs right this second. We should tell the Shunksville Community College bio class. Bet they'd love that." She looked at Richard. "Come on, Rich. I'm starving. Let's go to Em's Subs before they close."

"I'm in," said Jerry. "Girls?"

Risa shook her head for us both.

"Your loss. See you tomorrow. Good work here, everyone. No matter what happens."

"It's a blue jay," I said.

As if to emphasize the point, the jays called and called to one another in that strange, incredibly un-jay-like song.

"A fucking *blue jay*," I said. I walked over to the mean little fuckers. They didn't fly away. They just moved over, miffed. One looked straight at me.

"Laurel?" said Risa.

"A. Shitty. Ass. Mother. Fucking. Blue. Jay. Bet she had been out looking for the call the day of her accident, so Gran was in a coma for *this*?" It hit me, right there after a probably failed protest in the middle of ever-growing piles of bird shit that the birds had never been Gran. They'd never been anything special. They were just stupid, run-of-the-mill, *awful* blue jays that I'd probably seen all along.

No mystery.

Nothing for the life list.

No winning picture for *Fauna* that would wake up Gran so she'd kick Mom's ass and then Brad's and then get her house back and single-handedly save Sarig Pond and Jenkins Wood.

I couldn't. I just couldn't.

"I have to go," I said to Risa.

"I don't know that I should leave you alone right now," she said.

"Please," I said. "I'll be okay. I just need to . . . go. Please."

"Okay," she said. She frowned and reached for me. I took her hand and squeezed it. But I drew back and shoved my protest sign into the recycle bin. The neat wooden stick snapped when I forced the bin door shut.

I got on my bike and rode home. Mom and Brad sat on the couch with the television on.

"Baby—" Mom started, but I ignored her. I slammed my door and locked it. Then I locked myself into my bathroom and threw my clothes in a heap on the floor. In the shower I let cool water run down over me. I sank to the bottom of the tub.

It was just a blue jay. It was always just a blue jay.

I couldn't bring myself to do anything except try to let the spray erase my utter failure. Eventually I got out because I shouldn't waste water in addition to all the other things I'd done wrong.

I dried off and got under the covers. I pulled the sheet over my head like I did when I was little, trying to hide from the scary world.

The blue jays called from outside.

I knew who they were now.

And they weren't Gran.

The next morning, the traitorous sun rose at the butt crack of dawn. Optimistic beams hit my face no matter which direction I turned. I yanked down my blind, but then the whole thing sprang lose from its mount and clattered to the floor. I sighed and got out of bed. The upside of spending so much time in the shower was that I was clean, though my hair had dried at funny angles since I hadn't bothered to comb it before getting into bed.

I jostled down the stairs, fantasizing about peanut butter toast, when I stopped short on the threshold to the kitchen. There Mom looked up at me from the table.

"Hi," she said, taking a long sip of coffee.

"Um. Hi," I said. I started to back away. Though, lovely odors drifted out of the kitchen that made me rethink my flight plan.

"Laurel, please. Don't go. We need to talk."

"Mom . . ."

"Sit. Have a waffle." Mom got up and went over to the counter where the waffle maker sat. She forked a couple onto a plate and set it down at my place at the table.

My stomach growled.

Stupid, traitorous stomach. It was in league with the sun, surely. The world should stop spinning on its axis, the body should stop needing humany things when stuff was awful. But no, that's never how it worked.

"I bought maple syrup at the farmers' market. This one has a hint of blueberry."

I'm not made of stone. I sat at the table and dug into a flaky, buttery pile of god's gift to breakfast.

Mom poured me a glass of milk from the fridge, sat back down, and took a deep breath. "Laurel, I owe you an apology."

I looked at her, my mouth full. This is not where I thought the conversation would start. Or end.

"I had thought that you were coping with Grandma's accident so well. And you were. You *are*. But I should have been paying more attention. I got caught up . . . I'm sorry."

I swallowed. I shoved more waffle into my face because I wanted to make sure she wasn't about to burst into tears about Brad before I let her off the hook even a little bit.

"I'm sorry about Gran's house. I know it meant a lot to you."

I chewed.

"I'm sorry about things moving so quickly with Brad. I'm just sorry."

I swallowed again.

"I'm sorry, too," I said.

"No. Kid, listen. That's the big thing here. You did not hurt your grandmother. I mean, I grew up with the woman. No one could make her do something she did not want to do. She knew best. Come hell or high water, if she wanted to be looking for a bird on that road, then she was going to be on that road. You could have tried to physically haul her into the trunk and she would have fought you and won. I know it is hard not to wonder 'what if.' I do that all the time. But in this case, it was not you, okay? Please don't blame yourself, honey. I certainly don't. And Gran wouldn't, either. In fact, she'd probably be pissed you were taking responsibility for her actions. God. That woman." Mom gave a small, sad smile.

"Yeah," I said. Gran really could be such a pain sometimes.

"You were on the news again last night," Mom said.

"I tried not to be," I said.

"You were in the background with all the other protestors. I looked at the reports you sent. I don't really understand them. And I still think you have to know that this could affect my job."

"I know," I said.

"But," Mom started, "I also get what all of you are saying. About finding another location for it. It does seem kind of dumb and shortsighted to build on a nature reserve. Surely they could fund a different site. I don't know." Mom shrugged to herself.

"So you aren't mad at me?" I said.

"No, baby. How could I be mad at you? Well, I could maybe about the protests, because you remind me so damn much of your grandmother. I had to bail her out of jail last year when they wanted to tear down the old carriage house on Poplar Road. Some bats lived there or something."

"I didn't know she got *arrested* for that."

"Oh yes. She wanted to tell you all about it, but I forbade it. Last thing I need is for you to get a record because of her."

"Bats eat mosquitos, who carry disease . . ."

Mom put up her hands. "Yeah, yeah, I got it all from her. That thing was a condemned eyesore and the bats could live somewhere else. They fly, don't they? Just pick up and move, bats," she said.

The city had torn down the carriage house. The bats moved to the gazebo at the far end of Jenkins Wood. Now was probably not the best time to bring that up.

"I thought Gran had turned into a bird," I said.

"What?" said Mom.

"Um. The new birdcall we heard. It seemed to multiply after Gran's accident. I thought maybe she'd . . . you know what? It's dumb."

"I don't think it's dumb. Who knows?"

"I followed it. It turns out it's just a blue jay. With a special Western PA accent."

Mom smiled. "Your grandmother loved blue jays," she said. "They were one of her favorites."

I tilted my head in thought. "I don't think she had a favorite. Besides, blue jays are the known jerks of the bird world."

Mom got up and went into the dining room. She slid open a drawer in the china closet. "Look," she said.

I took the picture she held out. It was Gran, my Pap Pap, and a little girl who must have been my mom. Pap held her, arms outstretched, pointed to the sky.

"Look at the back," Mom said.

I turned it over. "To Ava, my little blue jay. Fly, little bird!" I read out loud.

"That's right." Mom gazed at the picture. "She said jays are fierce. They are survivors. She gave me this picture after Pap Pap died."

We sat in silence for a little while.

"I like that," I said. "I never thought of them that way. She never said that to me."

"Well. She wanted you to appreciate as many birds as

humanly possible. Or not bias you or something. She was a little ridiculous with the birds."

"Is Brad out of the picture?" I said suddenly. Mom still appeared to be wearing a diamond on her left hand.

She took a bite of her own waffle and chewed slowly. "No. He's not," she said finally. "I know our relationship has seemed kind of fast. But he's a good one, sweetheart. He really is."

"Do you have to get married, like, tomorrow, though? Can't you wait a while?"

She pushed her food around on her plate. "He and I talked about that. I guess there isn't a big rush. It might be better for you . . . You'll probably be going away next year anyway, honey. You'll be gone and I'll be here alone."

I wanted to tell her that filling up the lonely places in your brain with a rando dude wasn't a good coping mechanism. I only knew this because I'd seen her try so many times before.

Instead, out loud, I said, "Maybe just get to know him a little better, okay?"

Mom nodded. "He will probably be moving in in a month or two, though."

"Mom, really? We were just making progress here," I said.

"Laurel, this is for me. And I think for you. We'll take some time. But I have to balance my needs with yours."

This was a spectacularly bad idea. But she was right. I would be leaving soon. If I wasn't going to before, I sure would be now. Mom was just a lot to take without Gran's help. And at least she wasn't kicking me out for Granocide or something.

"Okay," I said.

Mom watched me. "Really?" she said.

"Sure, Mom." Inwardly I sighed. Maybe she'd never get it. But at least she was acknowledging I might have feelings.

Mom grinned. "I knew you'd come around." She got up and walked to my side of the table and put her arms around me.

I hugged her back, even though I hadn't come around. But it was better for Mom's sake that she believed that.

After I then let Mom talk about Brad for another half an hour, I rode over to the hospital to visit Gran.

"You got arrested over the bats," I said to her. "You should have told me. That would have given me life."

I swear her mouth twitched into a smile for a second.

"We had a protest march and birds participated," I told her. "Oh! Actually, I bet they have the paper in the family lounge. I'll be right back. I'm going to get it." I left Gran and went out into the hallway. Sure enough, a few *Shunksville Gazette*s sat in a neat pile in a corner. I walked back to Gran's room with one.

"Oh, Jerry is on the first page, Gran." I held the paper up. I read the article. "Holy crap, there's another meeting today?" I said. "Gran, get this. 'At least a hundred and fifty angry constituents showed up Wednesday to protest the proposed destruction of a beloved Shunksville park. Despite compelling arguments from city planners, the council was hesitant to vote to move forward with the merger. Representatives from each current district were on hand. The meeting adjourned with a split vote. Deputy Mayor Michael Ross recused himself from the vote, after members of the council suggested he might have conflicts of interest with stakeholders in several key city contracts. The special school board meeting was rescheduled for July fifteenth.' What the actual fuck, Gran?"

Her monitor beeped in reply.

"Gran, I love you, but I gotta go. I think this might be a good thing." I kissed her goodbye.

I was already behind the times when I arrived at the Nature Center.

"Can we get people together again so fast?" said Jerry.

"I think people might already be intending to show up. School board meetings are supposed to be open to the public. It's summer, but you saw what happened last night," said Louise.

"We're going!" sang Karen.

"We are, too," said her Birdscout friend Fred.

Risa came over to me and tugged my arm. We walked over to hide behind Elder Oak. He stood blessedly protestor free.

"Hey," she said.

"Hey." I slid my arms around her waist. "I'm sorry about last night."

"No, don't be. I was just worried."

"Yeah. I was . . . I'm sorry for that. Making you worry. I talked with my mom this morning. Oddly enough, she kinda made me feel better."

"Oh?"

"Maybe Gran *could* be a blue jay." I shrugged. "With a new call."

"The mystery isn't exactly solved, you know. Maybe there's more to it."

"What do you mean?" I said.

"I mean, what bird was that jay imitating in the first place? No one could place it."

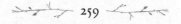

I laughed. "I guess we'll have to keep looking. I might be stuck in a bird quest forever. I understand if you get sick of it."

"Nah," said Risa. "Never. As Brian Michael Warbley says, 'Embrace the mystery around you as much as you can.' I don't mind if you have to go after new calls. I'll wait for you."

I blinked. "What did you say?"

"I'm patient. I can share you with the birds. I'll wait for you."

I smiled. "Thanks," I said.

FIELD JOURNAL ENTRY
JULY 15

Mom had not approved of the idea of me going to another protest. Her colleagues were still texting her about me. And weird stuff showed up daily in the mailbox, or tied to rocks thrown onto the porch. She wasn't happy with me, and neither was Brad. He thought I should leave "the hard stuff" to "the grown-ups" because Mom and I "had enough going on."

But like I was going to listen to Brad.

This time no one dressed as a bird (except Karen). We opted to let a few parents go into the meeting so that everyone didn't get kicked out. Louise and Richard did bring birdseed again.

I looked up to the azure dome above me. Gran's blue jay called and called.

"I hear all of the jays making that sound now that I know who they are," I said.

"Me too," she said. "Funny how that works."

"Yeah."

An hour stretched into two. Risa and I walked around town taking pictures. I got a good one of a purple finch near the park fountain and Risa got a Cooper's hawk hanging out on the awning of the hardware store.

The sun had begun to sink below the horizon when people finally started streaming out of city hall.

"What's the word?" Louise said to Karen's moms. Karen lay asleep in one's arms.

"Well, the proposal isn't dead. Sarig Pond and Jenkins Wood are still the prime site for the merged schools in Shunksville, and Shunksville is still the main town contender. But"—she paused—"there was a lot of debate about the merits of merging at all. There seems to be something—what's the word Richard uses?—*hinky* about the surveys and proposed cost and a lot of things. They've pushed the vote until October. Work for the new schools wouldn't start until next spring. So, we haven't exactly saved the nature reserve just yet. But we have bought some time."

"That's what we needed," said Richard.

"We can plan a lot of bird-ins before then," said Louise.

Risa looked at me. "This is good," she said.

"It is," I said. It wasn't perfect. Gran's house still belonged to the city, which meant that plans could still very well move forward. But this meant it was slower, maybe less likely to happen.

For now, that was enough.

"Well, crew, we'll see you tomorrow at story time," said Karen's mom. "This one needs to go to bed." She nuzzled Karen's head with her chin.

"Night," we said.

"Walk you home?" said Risa.

"Bet we could get some good sunset shots by the river," I said. "*Fauna* entries due in a couple of weeks. I say we get as many as we can."

Risa and I walked our bikes to the little outlook by the river. The mountains rose green and brown above us as the sky darkened all into night.

"What is that?" I said, squinting at the sky. "Is that a contrail from a plane?"

"No. Those are white and look like clouds. That's . . . green?"

"It's bright green. Oh my god, maybe it's some kind of chemical? What if . . ."

"Okay, conspiracy theorist, don't go all whackadoo there. I'm sure there's a reasonable explanation," said Risa.

We watched as the wave of green thickened and seemed to dance across the sky. Pink joined in, cascading across the curve of the sky.

"Holy shit," I said. "I think that's the aurora borealis."

"Seriously? Here?"

"It can travel. I mean . . . I think it's pretty rare, but it can be visible this far south," I said.

"Can we go somewhere with less light?" Risa said.

"I'd say the pond, but there are too many trees. But we can go to Gran's yard. Since no one lives around there . . ."

We hopped on our bikes. Risa had her headlamp and blinkers, so she led. We got to Gran's yard and dropped our bikes on the walkway. It was only a little darker there, but it was enough.

"Wow," said Risa. She got out her camera and started shooting.

The thought crossed my mind that I should, too. But I couldn't. Pink and green and then purple pirouetted and played right there in the Shunksville dusk and I just wanted to drink it in.

"I'm glad I got to see this with you," Risa whispered. She let her camera dangle around her neck. She reached out and took my hand. I turned to her and took her face in my other hand. I kissed her with everything I had.

"Me too," I said.

As the northern lights kept washing across our field of view, I heard it. A sweet, melancholy cry from a blue jay nearby. On Gran's roof, probably. A few moments later, it called from a tree across the alley. Then farther away still.

I'd figured out the mystery song. We'd uncovered the fierce, beautiful survivor of a bird that sang it. Common but still remarkable, like so many things in nature. Gran really had always been like a blue jay, the more I thought about it. Even if she wasn't really embodied in one, I could feel her there, at her house at the edge of the woods and pond, showing me the aurora, just like she said she would.

"Thank you for waiting for me," I whispered.

One more distant jay song faded away and I knew, then, that I had lost a piece of myself. I held Risa close.

Under that same sky, I knew that I had gained something, too.

The hospital had called a few hours after they'd postponed the vote, not long after I'd kissed Risa goodnight. As the aurora continued to scorch the sky with waves of the brightest emerald and kelly and pine, Mom and I sat next to Gran as her heart slowed to nothing. They'd turned the monitors off, so there was no dramatic screeching flat line or alarms or anything. Just calm.

Mom dabbed her eyes with tissues and I held Gran's hand, knowing it would be the last time I would feel the wrinkled palms in mine. They were warmer than I'd remembered from all my recent visits, which was odd for the end of life, wasn't it? Wasn't death cold? It seemed like she was rebelling against convention until the very last second.

So like Gran.

We held her funeral next to Elder Oak, her favorite tree. It was super illegal to bury her there, or even scatter ashes. But her body visited there one last time, before it moved to its own stone angel guard in Grandview. We picked a spot near a massive sycamore that attracted warblers and chickadees and juncos (and thus birders). Nearly fifty people watched as her casket lowered neatly into the ground. Looking into the canopy above, I imagined all of the people who would be stomping on her eternal resting place. Fussing with their camera equipment. Coming to admire the view and the countless migrating species that loved the elevation. Like she and I had done so many times before.

I knew she'd love that.

Afterward I went back to Elder Oak and sat with Risa and Sophie, who'd come back from camp for Gran's memorial.

"Laurel, I have to tell you something," said Sophie.

"Oh?" I said. None of us had talked much the whole day.

"Yeah, I saw a cool bird at the funeral. And I thought it was probably inappropriate, but it *was* your gran and all. And both of you quoted that Warbley guy. 'It's never a bad time to a bird,' you know?"

"Um, yes?"

"So here." She thrust her phone at me. There, on the screen, was a perfectly clear shot of a blue jay peeking out from its nest, looking pretty pissed off so many predators were hanging out near its home. "I liked how blue he was."

"That's a great shot, Soph. Pretty soon you'll be a Warbley devotee."

"No. Never. But . . ." She paused. "I am beginning to see what all of you see in them."

Risa and I laughed. It felt good. It trickled down into the space vacated by all of the horrible feelings I'd had about Gran's accident. Some lingered, and they bubbled up seemingly every few hours. But I decided not to try to squash them down anymore. I found that letting them float to the surface and actually *feeling* them worked a lot better than trying to pretend they didn't exist. Sometimes, stupid feelings felt like Squirrel Fire™ to the eyes, but it still didn't burn as long as it did if you let them fester. Sometimes, you had to wait to will a good day into existence. Or maybe just sit with a day that sucks.

But today, even though Gran was gone, Sophie was on her way to becoming a birder. Because of a jay, no less.

Sophie gave me a hug and left to meet her dad to drive back to camp. I took Risa's hand as we silently took the long route through the woods, and then around the pond for good measure. Bats flapped merrily above us, life tumbling forward without Gran.

"I miss her," I said.

Risa squeezed my hand.

"Will I ever stop missing her?"

"I don't know," she said, "but when you miss her, look at all you have to remember her." She spread her free arm out toward the pond, where a heron was tucking himself into a tree for the night. "When my parents died, my aunt told me that a person's energy never really goes away. It's a law of physics or something. It's still around, somewhere. My money would be on the fact that her energy is hanging out here."

I rested my head on her shoulder.

"Yes," I said. "You're totally right."

A great horned owl called out into the night, where I knew that somewhere, Gran soared right there next to him.

FIELD JOURNAL
SEPT 5
NOTABLE LOCATION: JENKINS WOOD
LIFE LIST ENTRY 3,288: BRIAN MICHAEL
WARBLEY
LIFE LIST ENTRY 3,289: KIRTLAND'S WARBLER

"Is it here yet?" I asked Jerry.

"Oh my god, leave me alone," he said.

Risa and I had been chasing down the latest issue of *Fauna* for days. The October issue would have the winners of the Junior Nature Photographer competition, and Jerry had *Fauna* connections, at least when it came to getting the new issues first. He had a source who brought copies in exchange for Jerry's special suet.

You'd think they'd email you or something if you won, but no. You had to wait for the fucking magazine. Damn it, *Fauna*. Nothing is perfect, I guess.

"I'm just saying, you usually get it way early," I said.

"Laurel," he sighed. "Please go clean something or educate somebody."

I glared at him, but did as I was told. I needed to make the most of my remaining full days at the Nature Center. Monday was the first day of school, and I would have to go back to being trapped in a building for too many hours a day. I wasn't really looking forward to that, since half the town still blamed me for ruining the chances of new jobs and stuff with the school. Sophie would be there, and Risa. But still. Sophie and I had plans to eat ice cream every day until we had to go back as a means to cope.

About an hour later, I heard a shout from inside the Center. "It's here, girls," Jerry called.

I ran inside, where Risa stood, waiting.

"Oh my god," I said.

"Oh my god," she said.

"We should look."

"We totally should."

We both stood, staring at the magazine.

Just then, the Center door banged open.

"Hi, folks," said a tall man with fluffy hair and gold

wire-rimmed glasses. "We got a bird text about a Kirtland's warbler. It's funny, because I was just passing by here on my way to a conference. Have you folks seen it?"

"Seriously?" said Risa.

I looked at the man. He seemed so strangely familiar. Surely I'd have remembered meeting him here? New birders made a mark on me.

"Wait," I said, realization dawning on me. "Are you Brian. Michael. WARBLEY?" Each part of his name came out louder and higher than the next. I couldn't help it. I was losing my shit hard and fast.

He smiled shyly. "Why, yes."

"YOU ARE COMPLETELY MY HERO."

"WHAT WAS THAT ABOUT A WARBLER?" shouted Risa, obviously unable to keep herself together, either.

Jerry rolled his eyes. "Sorry. The kids are just a little star-struck." He strode the few paces across the Center to shake fucking Brian Michael Warbley's hand.

"Always pleased to meet young birders." He grinned. He noticed the magazine in my hand. "Oh, the latest issue of *Fauna*. How you'd get it already?"

"I know people," said Jerry.

Brian Michael Warbley eyed him. "Maybe I should be the one who is starstruck," he said. "It's the photography contest issue. You girls enter?"

Neither Risa nor I could speak.

"Yeah, they entered. They were losing their minds before *you* came in, so now they are just completely gone."

Brian Michael Warbley grinned again. "Well, let's have a look, then." He gently tugged the magazine out of Risa's hand as she stood motionless, her mouth hanging open. He flipped through the pages until he came to the Junior Photography section.

"Any of these yours?" he asked. He pointed to the first two-page spread, and then the second.

"There," I managed to squeak. "That one's mine." I pointed to the lightning tanagers.

"That one's mine," said Risa, pointing to the herons next to it.

"Honorable mentions! That's amazing! I took an honorable mention in this same competition, you know. That's how I got my start!"

"Wait, what?" I said, recovering. "You won first place."

"No, no. People always think that because someone got it wrong in an article and it spread. I keep correcting my Wiki page, but people who think they know better keep changing it back and citing the same wrong sources." He pursed his lips. "But if you go back to issue two hundred forty, you'll see. Honorable mention." He looked at our pictures. "Holy hoatzins! This lighting shot is yours? And this one"—he pointed to Risa's—"how'd you get that angle? You girls are way ahead of where I was when I entered." He shook his head. "You are going to be bigger than me, mark my words."

"I love you, Brian Michael Warbley," I said. "I mean, uh, your work."

"Same. Hard same," said Risa.

Jerry covered his face with his hand.

Brian Michael Warbley put his hand on his chest. "It's an honor to meet such talented photographers. I should get your autograph now while I can."

"Well, you'll have to get your own *Fauna*. That one's mine," said Jerry.

Brian Michael Warbley laughed. "Of course, where . . ." But he stopped. "Did you hear that?" he said, suddenly catlike in his reflexes. "That call?"

High, sharp little bursts echoed against the Nature Center windows. They ended on an up note, like the bird was asking a question.

"Kirtland's warblers, outside, about two o'clock, dollars to ducks they're in a pine if there is one."

All of us gingerly stepped out of the Center, as quickly as we could go without scaring a possible rare bird away.

"There they are," whispered Brian Michael Warbley. "Two o'clock!"

We looked up. Sure enough, there sat several blue-headed warblers, lemon bellies flecked with salt and pepper feathers.

"This has always been the one that got away," he breathed. "These guys are huge in Michigan, but my ex lives there, so the whole state is off limits. I thought I'd never get a decent shot. And here are a whole bunch of them. Anyone know what a group of warblers is called?"

"A confusion," I said. "A confusion of warblers."

"That's right," he said. "Well done."

We snapped pictures while a bird hopped down lower and sat still, an ideal model.

"I think they like the attention," said Risa.

A few minutes later, they flew away.

"Mind if I upload this to Rare Birds? I'm not a PA native, I know. I always defer to my local birders."

"No, do it," I said. When the Birdie Bros realized they not only missed Kirtlands but missed Kirtlands with Brian Michael Warbley, my life would be made complete.

"Thanks," he said, already typing into his app.

"Brian Michael Warbley?" I said.

"Just call me Brian." He looked at our name tags. "And I will call you Laurel and Risa."

"Okay, Brian? Could I get your autograph?"

"Certainly," he said. He signed Risa's *Warbley's Birding Bonanza* and he signed the limited-edition life list Risa had gifted me and that I now had close by at all times. Then Jerry had him sign his bicep for a tattoo.

"Who knew I was so big in PA?" He gave us each a hug. God, he must have a murmuration of birder women flocking to him at all times. "Congrats again, girls. An honorable mention means a lot."

He turned and walked toward the parking lot.

"Brian Michael Warbley," said Risa.

"Brian," I corrected her.

She shook her head, dazed.

A call came from a nearby willow. Not a Kirtland, but a far more common call.

Made it into Fauna, *Gran. Just like you*, I thought at the jay. It called back and flitted away.

"Watch out, Warbley," I said out loud, smacking Risa with my book.

"We're coming for you," said Risa.

"But first you better go help set up for the end-of-summer party tonight," Jerry said. "We got about a hundred of these soda six-pack holders to give out." He turned one over in his hands. "They feed sea turtles instead of strangling them or something. Gotta get the word out for people to buy 'em. Save the world and stuff." He glowered at us. "You know. Your *job*? Congrats and all that, but get a move on."

Jerry would always keep us humble.

Just for a second, before devoting myself to the task of saving sea turtles, I traced my fingers over Brian ~~Michael Warbley~~'s signature. He'd *touched* this. And seeing his name, reminding me that he had been there in the flesh, made me think that Gran had surely put him here in my path, congratulating me in her way, letting me know that I would be okay.

That, every day, I could fly.

ACKNOWLEDGMENTS

Thanks must go first, again, to all of my family, friends, students, and colleagues who continue to support me in my writing and are now subject to incessant birding talk.

Thank you to the Feiwel and Friends team, especially intrepid editor Anna Roberto, who is brilliant and one of my favorite people.

Thank you to Catherine Drayton, who is a great agent, but also a tremendous human being. You are tasked with saving me from myself, and I appreciate that you still do it. Thanks also to Claire Friedman and everyone at Inkwell Management for their continued support.

I owe a lot of specific gratitude to several people for this book. Thanks especially to Jenne Powers, who first took me birding and adjusted my binos so that I no longer saw that black ring. That was life-changing.

Thank you to Gillian Devereux for the urban birding notebook.

Thank you to Melissa Baumgart, Kathryn Benson, and Rebecca Chernoff Udell, without whom Laurel would not be a nature photographer.

Thank you to Morgan Matson, for the title inspiration.

Thank you to the real Birdscouts. You know who you are.

Thank you to Leith Speiden, for the Squirrel Fire™ scene, and for always laughing at my jokes.

Thank you to David Allen Sibley, without whom I would be a shell of a birder.

Thanks to Rachel Maddow who continues to try to save the world.

Thank you to Josh Groban because why the hell not.

Thank you to the Dead Post-Its Society. I love you all.

And thank you to Peter, Katherine, and Charles. You are my flock.

THANK YOU FOR READING THIS FEIWEL AND
FRIENDS BOOK THE FRIENDS WHO MADE

JEAN FEIWEL
PUBLISHER

LIZ SZABLA
ASSOCIATE PUBLISHER

RICH DEAS
SENIOR CREATIVE DIRECTOR

HOLLY WEST
SENIOR EDITOR

ANNA ROBERTO
SENIOR EDITOR

VAL OTAROD
ASSOCIATE EDITOR

KAT BRZOZOWSKI
SENIOR EDITOR

ALEXEI ESIKOFF
SENIOR MANAGING EDITOR

KIM WAYMER
SENIOR PRODUCTION MANAGER

ANNA POON
ASSISTANT EDITOR

EMILY SETTLE
ASSOCIATE EDITOR

ERIN SIU
EDITORIAL ASSISTANT

APRIL WARD
ART DIRECTOR

STARR BAER
SENIOR PRODUCTION EDITOR

FOLLOW US ON FACEBOOK OR VISIT US ONLINE AT
MACKIDS.COM. OUR BOOKS ARE FRIENDS FOR LIFE.